They were meant for each other . . .

Ned stood on the beach and watched the beautiful blond girl in the water. Suddenly she began swimming erratically. *An undertow!* he realized.

He ran to the water's edge. The girl was tiring, maybe even cramping up. There wasn't a moment to lose! Plunging into the ocean, Ned began swimming, pulling with all his might against the cold, resistant water. He had almost reached her when he saw a wave close over her head. She didn't resurface. *No!* he thought, swimming faster.

Ned reached the spot where she'd gone under. Treading water, he stared down into the salty depths. He saw a glimmer of blond hair, sinking, sinking . . . He dove.

His lungs bursting, Ned fought his way back to the surface with one arm; the other was wrapped tightly around the limp body of the girl. She was alive but unconscious.

He carried her out of the water and laid her gently on the sand. Her eyelids flickered and opened. She stared up at him, uncomprehending. "Shh. Don't try to move yet," he told her, brushing a tendril of wet hair from her forehead. "You have to rest."

For a moment, they gazed into each other's eyes. Ned had an unaccountable sensation as he studied the delicate lines of her lovely face. He was certain he'd never met her, but nevertheless there was something strangely familiar about her tentative smile, her beautiful blue-green eyes.

Bantam Books in the Sweet Valley High series
Ask your bookseller for the books you have missed

SWEET VALLEY Saga

THE WAKEFIELD LEGACY

THE UNTOLD STORY

Written by
Kate William

Created by
FRANCINE PASCAL

BANTAM BOOKS
NEW YORK·TORONTO·LONDON·SYDNEY·AUKLAND

RL 6, age 12 and up

THE WAKEFIELD LEGACY

A Bantam Book / June 1992

Sweet Valley High is a registered trademark of Francine Pascal

Conceived by Francine Pascal

Produced by Daniel Weiss Associates, Inc.
33 West 17th Street
New York, NY 10011

Cover art by Bruce Emmett

ISBN 0-553-29794-5

Published simultaneously in the United States and Canada

Bantam Books are published by Bantam Books, a division of Bantam
Doubleday Dell Publishing Group, Inc. Its trademark, consisting of the
words "Bantam Books" and the portrayal of a rooster, is Registered in
U.S. Patent and Trademark Office and in other countries. Marca
Registrada. Bantam Books, 666 Fifth Avenue, New York, New York
10103.

PRINTED IN THE UNITED STATES OF AMERICA

OPM   0 9 8 7 6 5 4 3 2 1

Elizabeth and Jessica Wakefield's Paternal Family Tree

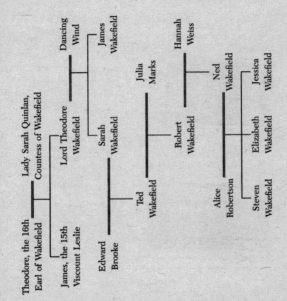

One

1866. Wakefield, England.

Theodore Wakefield pressed his boot heels against Raven's sides, urging the spirited coal-black stallion into a canter. He reined in at the crest of the hill behind Wakefield Manor and turned to wait for his older brother, James, and James's fiancée, Katerina von Alber.

Narrowing his deep-brown eyes against the sun, Theodore gazed at the landscape spread out before him. A sweep of emerald lawn set off the stern gray stone of his family's elegant Georgian house. Below the estate, Theodore glimpsed the village of Wakefield, where mill chimneys contrasted with the lofty spire of the thirteenth-century church and clusters of ancient weavers' cottages. The Calder and Colne rivers sparkled in the distance.

The wind, cool even in summer, whipped the dark, shaggy hair back from Theodore's forehead.

He sat tall in the saddle, his broad shoulders straight. This was his family's land, and he was proud of it.

It will never be mine, though. Theodore's eyes came to rest on the form of his brother who, as the elder son, would one day inherit the manor. James was riding slightly ahead of Katerina, as usual, and even from a distance his uninterested expression was easy to see. At twenty-six, James was ten years older than his fiancée, the daughter of a wealthy German count. The engagement had been arranged by their parents; James and Katerina had only met for the first time when Katerina arrived at Wakefield a month ago, and the wedding was to be held in London in one month.

James had barely made an effort to get to know his fiancée, and Theodore felt sorry for her. He felt sorry for James, too. He knew his father, the Earl of Wakefield, had bullied his brother into the unhappy engagement.

Most people considered James the lucky one, but Theodore felt thankful that he was the second son and not his father's heir. He didn't envy James the role of future lord of the manor. It brought with it too many burdens and limitations. Unlike James, Theodore was free to do whatever he wanted; he would leave for Cambridge soon to study the classics. And he would never be forced into an arranged marriage with a girl he didn't love.

* * *

2

James stayed well ahead of the others as they rode west along the River Colne to Wessenden Moor. Katerina stifled a sigh. After a month, her husband-to-be was still a stranger to her. She had stopped trying to make conversation with him; he seemed happiest with her when she kept her distance. *Thank goodness for Theodore,* she thought. Without him, Katerina would have had no one at Wakefield Manor to talk to.

Theodore kept Raven to a slow pace at Katerina's side. "If you are tired of trotting, you may go ahead with James," she said, choosing her words carefully. Her English was improving daily, but it was not perfect.

"I'm still breaking Raven in. It's good for him to go slow." Theodore bent forward to pat the horse's glossy neck. Then he flashed Katerina a grin. "And besides, I prefer your company."

Katerina flushed with pleasure. "Raven appears as well-mannered as can be. Is he really as wild as you say?"

"He never tolerated a rider until I mounted him for the first time yesterday," Theodore confirmed.

"What is your secret?"

He smiled again. "You'll laugh, but I'll tell you anyway. I talk to him."

Katerina raised her eyebrows. "Talk to him? What do you say?"

He shook his head. "It doesn't seem to matter

3

what I say. For some reason, Raven just responds to my voice. All horses do."

Katerina nodded. She would agree that there was something almost magical about Theodore's deep, kind voice.

They reached Blackstone Edge, where an old Roman road made a broad scar across a lonely stretch of moor. The haunting cry of a curlew sent a shiver up Katerina's spine. She thought of the cozy forests of Germany. *I will never feel at home in this cold, barren place,* she thought with sad conviction. If she loved her fiancé, perhaps . . . but James was as cold to her as the moors.

Still, Katerina could not feel entirely lonely with Theodore at her side. Taking her reins in one gloved hand, she reached up with the other to push a windblown strand of flaxen hair from her eyes. "Tell me," she said to Theodore as they walked their horses along the trail. "Do the ghosts of parted lovers really walk these moors, as I read in the book I found in the manor library?" *Wuthering Heights* had been written, Katerina knew, by someone who lived in a village only a few miles away.

Theodore laughed at her fears. "You shouldn't read romantic novels," he advised. "I have a book for you. It's called *The California and Oregon Trails* and it's about pioneering expeditions in the American West."

As he told her more about the book, his voice grew animated and his brown eyes gleamed. Kater-

4

ina caught her breath. His face, with its lofty forehead and sharp cheekbones, straight nose and cleft chin, might have been carved by a sculptor. He was so handsome, twice as handsome, in Katerina's opinion, as sullen James. "I would like to read it," she said softly.

Theodore winked at her. "But maybe the Indians in it would scare you as much as the ghosts! The moors are much safer than the great plains of America."

Katerina tried to smile with Theodore. How could she tell him that she would rather be anywhere in the world than Wakefield, England, engaged to a man who, from all appearances, despised her?

She felt Theodore's intent, perceptive gaze on her face, and when she glanced at him she saw that his expression had softened with sympathy. "Don't worry," he said. "You'll get used to England. Soon you will love it as much as I do, as if you'd been born here."

"I will never get used to it!" Katerina cried desperately. "You don't know, Theodore. You don't know what it's like to wish each day would last forever, to wish that time would stand still even though you are unhappy, because anything is better than a future with—" Katerina faltered. An uncomfortable silence fell between them, and she realized she had gone too far. She should not have spoken so openly of her misgivings about the arranged marriage. Quickly, she corrected herself. "I mean that the wedding seems so soon. I wish I had more time to become acquainted with James."

Still silent, Theodore nodded. Katerina bit her lip. Overwhelmed by her loneliness, tears sprang to her eyes. To hide them, she dismounted quickly. "You catch up with James," she said with false cheer. "I am going to pick some heather for your mother."

Nodding again, Theodore spurred Raven into a gallop. Katerina watched him go, tears streaming down her cheeks.

A moment later, Theodore caught up with his brother. James had dismounted and allowed his horse to wander off to graze. Having just flushed some grouse, James took aim. But Theodore's thunderous arrival caused James to miss his shot.

James lowered the rifle, cursing. "What do you think you're doing?"

Theodore jumped to the ground, keeping a firm grip on Raven's reins. "What do you think *you're* doing?" he countered angrily. "It's bad enough that Katerina should be bartered like a piece of property by our family and her own, but for you to show her no kindness at all!"

"Don't tell me how to treat my fiancée," James snapped.

"I'll say what I please. At least I have Katerina's interest at heart. You don't care for her at all."

"Perhaps I don't," James said coldly. "Fortunately for you, however, my feelings for her are not your business."

"If you don't love her, why are you marrying her?" Theodore challenged.

James smiled grimly. "Ah, little brother, you're such an idealist. Marriage doesn't have anything to do with love. I may not be happy with Katerina, but I am perfectly happy to marry her."

Theodore was disgusted by his brother's cynicism. "You're lying. Why don't you admit it? You don't want to marry her, but you're afraid to find out what would happen if you stood up for yourself and refused the match," he accused scornfully.

James's expression darkened. "Don't talk of things you know nothing about."

"Oh, I know enough. I know that you want to be earl of the manor, to inherit Father's seat in the House of Lords and play the games of politics and influence. And if you thwart Father's will in this or any other matter, you risk disinheritance. I know all that, but I also know I would never let Father dictate my actions for me, as if I were a servant or a hound."

Speechless with rage, James tore Raven's reins from Theodore's grasp and leaped on the horse. Theodore was too surprised to stop him. But as James whipped a white-eyed Raven into a gallop, Theodore collected his wits. James was heading the horse directly at a low stone wall. Theodore knew

7

the unschooled horse couldn't be trusted to take the wall cleanly.

"Don't jump him!" Theodore shouted after his brother. But the wind seemed to snatch the words from his mouth. Clearly, his brother didn't hear them—or didn't heed them. James didn't alter his course.

In horror, Theodore saw his brother lean into the jump. He saw Raven swerve wildly away from the wall, hurling James against the unforgiving gray stones. And then he heard Katerina's terrified scream.

Two

Theodore helped his mother into the crepe-draped carriage. He could not see Lady Sarah's face behind her black veil, but he knew she was weeping. The carriage rumbled off along the lane, and Theodore turned back to the medieval church and its ancient graveyard. The mourners had departed; only Theodore himself, his father, and Katerina remained.

Hands clasped behind the back of his black frock coat, Theodore walked slowly toward the Wakefield family vault, where the Earl stood, his head bowed with grief. Theodore himself felt numb, as if he were dreaming. *Surely I'll wake from this nightmare soon,* he thought, *and everything will be as it was.* He and James had disagreed about every subject under the sun but somehow had managed to remain friends. James couldn't be gone forever.

But he was. *Dead . . . dead . . .* The word echoed through Theodore's head. Again, he heard himself speaking it to a hysterical Katerina after they had both run to where James's crumpled body had fallen. In his mind he saw his mother rise from her seat on the lawn, her hand at her heart, when he had ridden up bearing the corpse of his brother, her elder son. *Dead . . . dead . . .* Theodore heard again the dull echo of iron and stone as the vault door was shut after the interment. There could be no more sorrowful, final sound in the world.

He lifted a hand to Katerina, who had taken a seat on a bench under a yew tree on the far side of the cemetery. Then he put his hand on his father's shoulder.

The Earl turned. His gray eyes were dry. "My son," he said simply.

Theodore nodded. He was that; his father's only son.

"My son . . . and my heir." The Earl glanced at Katerina, who had begun to stroll among the headstones. "You understand that you have new responsibilities?"

"Well, yes, I suppose . . ." Actually, Theodore had thought of nothing thus far but his loss. Now the tragic irony struck him: with his brother's untimely death, he had become heir to Wakefield Manor.

"The family title and fortune will now be yours,"

the Earl continued, his tone cold and detached, "as well as the manor and the seat in the House of Lords. You will accompany me to London this fall rather than go to Cambridge. And Katerina will be yours as well."

Theodore thought he heard a rustle, as of heavy silk. He glanced over his shoulder, but there was no one there. He looked back at his father. "London? Katerina?" he repeated.

"The wedding will take place as scheduled," the Earl asserted. "Katerina will be your bride."

Theodore stared at his father. Had he heard correctly? Had the Earl just blandly informed him that he was expected to be Katerina's groom in James's place? The Earl gazed calmly back at his son. He had made a statement, not asked a question. It was clear to Theodore that his father expected him to comply.

Shocked and outraged—on his own behalf, on Katerina's behalf, and on behalf of his brother, scarcely cold in the vault—Theodore took a step backward, as if his father's nearness repulsed him as much as his command. "I will do no such thing," he declared. The words spilled out, hot and bitter. "I want nothing to do with a career in politics, or with Katerina. I will not marry her!"

The violence of his son's emotions did not seem to trouble the Earl in the least. "You will grow used to the idea," he predicted. He nodded toward Katerina, now seated on another bench not far away. "She is a beautiful girl, and she is fond of you."

"Fond, yes, as I am of her. But I think of Katerina as a sister—"

The Earl didn't wait to hear his son out. Clearly, in his opinion, the matter was not open for discussion. He strode off, his boot heels striking hard against the slate path, leaving Theodore alone among the graves.

The wind rose late in the day. It was howling by sunset, when Katerina went in search of Theodore, who had been absent at dinner. Her heart was in her throat as she scurried with her candle through the cold, vast halls of the manor. At the entrance to the Hall of Portraits, she paused. She usually avoided this part of the house; the long rows of unsmiling painted faces made her nervous. Taking a deep breath, she stepped inside.

At the far end of the long rectangular room, she glimpsed Theodore's tall, elegant form. He stood in a characteristic pose, with his hands clasped behind his back, staring up at the portraits of his ancestors, generations of Wakefields. The Earl and Lady Sarah's portraits were already on the wall, and James had been sitting for his portrait when he died.

Hearing her approach, Theodore turned. His agonized expression stopped Katerina in her tracks. She had been intending to comfort him in his grief, to see if she might soothe him, as he had so often soothed her during the past month. Now Katerina realized that she must do more if she really wanted to ease his torment. She must confess.

"Theodore, I . . . I heard what your father said to you today. This afternoon, by the crypt." She ducked her head to hide her blush. It wasn't easy to admit that she was guilty of eavesdropping, and to have overheard such a conversation! "And I must tell you," she continued rapidly, not giving him a chance to interrupt, "that I think the Earl is . . . wrong. The suggestion that you and I should marry is preposterous," she said, stumbling slightly over the long word. "So please, don't worry about me. I will return to my parents in Prussia. It is what I want to do."

Katerina spoke with all the assurance she could muster. But in her heart, she longed for something very different. She didn't want to go home to Germany; she wanted Theodore to clasp her in his arms and tell her that he did indeed wish her to be his wife, that the Earl's commands coincided with his own desires.

Theodore began pacing the length of the flagstone-floored hall, Katerina at his side. "My father won't permit you to leave. He has decided our future for us."

"You don't have to act as your brother did," Katerina argued. "You can refuse to obey your father."

"And lose my name and my home," Theodore exclaimed bitterly. "My father would cast me out of Wakefield, and I'm not sure I could bear that. I love this house, this land. I could be happy caring for it . . . caring for you." His voice dropped with resignation. "It is my destiny. My duty."

"No," Katerina disagreed softly. "Your destiny is something you make, not something that is given to you. You can choose, Theodore. You *must* choose."

Not wanting him to see her tears, Katerina gathered her long skirts in her free hand and ran from the hall, her candle flickering as she went.

For hours Theodore roamed the house and grounds, the howl of the rising storm echoing his tumultuous thoughts. For a while, the choice seemed impossible; he stood to lose so much whichever course he took. But finally, after what seemed like an eternity, he made up his mind. He knew he should lose no time in informing his father of his decision.

Theodore found his parents in the south parlor. The Earl stood in front of the fireplace, staring hard into the dancing flames; Lady Sarah sat on a brocade sofa, a piece of needlework lying forgotten on her lap, and a look of quiet sorrow in her eyes.

Theodore hated to hurt his mother further, but he was afraid there was no way to spare her feelings. He stepped forward to stand before his father.

"I have been thinking about our conversation," he announced.

The Earl nodded approvingly. "I knew that once you considered the matter you would see that—"

Theodore cut him off. "I have seen that I cannot allow you to arrange my life for me. I don't want to sit in the House of Lords; I will pursue my own career. And I will not marry Katerina, not one month from now, not ever."

An angry frown darkened his father's brow. "You will marry her or you are no longer my heir—no longer my son."

"George!" Lady Sarah gasped. Her needlework fell to the floor as she rose suddenly.

The Earl's fury seemed to transform him into a giant, but Theodore stood his ground. He remembered Katerina's inspiring words from earlier that evening. *Your destiny is something you make, not something that is given to you.* No, he couldn't back down. He was a man, not his father's puppet.

Suddenly, Theodore recalled another conversation with Katerina, one they had had on the day of James's death. Now he knew not only what he must do, but where he must go. Tossing his head back defiantly, he pulled from his finger the heavy gold ring with the Wakefield crest. He pressed the ring into his mother's hand. "So be it," he told his father. "I am no longer your son, and you are no longer my father. I will leave Wakefield."

"And go where?" the Earl demanded.

"To America!"

"If you walk out that door, you will never enter it again. You will never hear a word from us, or see a penny of the money that would have been yours!" the Earl threatened.

"George, no! Be reasonable!" Lady Sarah begged.

"I don't want your money," Theodore declared. "My freedom is worth far more to me."

His mother took a step toward him, her eyes brimming. "Don't go, Theo," she implored. "Your father doesn't mean—"

"I meant every word I said," the Earl interrupted.

Theodore turned away. "No!" Lady Sarah cried, reaching out for her son. He felt her hand on his sleeve and paused, his heart aching. Before the Earl restrained her from following her son, Lady Sarah managed to slip something into Theodore's coat pocket. As his mother sobbed, Theodore rushed from the room. He did not look back.

Despite the storm and the late hour, Theodore went directly to the stables. Within minutes, Raven was saddled and bridled. Theodore led the horse into the yard and mounted. Spooked by the wind, Raven reared on his hind legs. Theodore grasped the reins firmly with one hand, and with the other reached into his pocket. He felt a cold circle of gold —the ring. *The only thing I will have to remember my home and my family by,* he thought.

16

Just then, he noticed a small, white face at a high open window. It was Katerina, the night wind whipping her pale hair. She raised her hand in a gesture of farewell.

Theodore lifted his hand in return. Then he wheeled Raven around and spurred him into a canter. He was leaving Wakefield Manor forever.

Three

As he jostled elbows with the other travelers crowding onto the steamer, Theodore had never felt so free. By selling Raven and his pocket watch, he had been able to pay for his passage on a steamer to America and had had enough left over to buy an extra suit of clothes and a few other necessities. Now he was wearing or carrying all of his worldly possessions.

In one hand he held a small satchel; with the other, he jingled the few coins in the pocket of his frock coat. Silently, Theodore berated himself for the sentimentality that had kept him from selling the family ring he was wearing once again on the fourth finger of his right hand. It would have brought a nice sum.

I can always sell it when I get to America, Theodore told himself by way of an excuse. That's when he would really need the money, anyway—as he made his way as a stranger in a new country.

As he was pushed toward the railing at the stern of the boat, Theodore marveled at the variety of accents and languages he heard around him. There were English, Irish, German, and Swedish; there were old people and couples with children in tow; there were large families and single men and women. So much variety, and yet they all had one thing in common: All were leaving their homes to seek a new life on the other side of the Atlantic. Through the crush, he glimpsed a lovely young girl in a cream-colored bonnet and a dark blue dress with a high ruffled neck. With her white-blond hair and sky-blue eyes, she was a bright spot in the gray day. She was Norwegian, Theodore guessed, or Swedish. And then he was swept one way by the crowd and she another. *Ah well,* Theodore thought. It was not such a big ship. Their paths were bound to cross at some point during the voyage.

A minute later, the steamer began to move. As if on signal, a fine rain began to fall. The other passengers scurried to shelter inside, leaving Theodore alone on deck. As he watched the coastline of England recede, he had a sudden intuition that he would never again see his mother or the land of his birth.

Still, Theodore knew he had done the right thing in leaving. He was not going to be just another Wakefield face on the wall in the Hall of Portraits;

he was a man determined to live his own life on his own terms. From now on, he would think only of the future and never of the past. As England faded from sight he strode the length of the steamer to the forward railing in order to look ahead across the seemingly endless expanse of gray sea . . . to America.

Air. I must have fresh air, Theodore thought, stumbling toward the door of the men's bunkroom.

All around him, his fellow passengers lay on their bunks, limp with the exhaustion of fighting their seasickness, moaning weakly. A few days into the voyage, just as the passengers had adjusted to the rhythms of life at sea, a storm had struck. For twenty-four hours, the ship had been tossed about like a toy boat; Theodore was sure there wasn't a person on board, with the exception of the sea-soned crew, who wasn't as sick as a dog.

But now Theodore was feeling a bit better. Although giant waves still rocked the ship, making it hard for him to keep his footing, he made his way up to the deck, gratefully sucking the raw, salty air deep into his lungs.

The gale was far from over. The skies were still glowering, and the ship rode waves as high as houses. But Theodore saw that he wasn't the only one eager for fresh air. A number of other passengers had made their way onto the slippery deck. They huddled in clusters, their clothing drenched and their heads ducked against the howling wind. A wave crashed against the side of the boat; Theodore was instantly soaked from head to foot. He saw that the same wave had also splashed a young woman, who now stepped nearer to the main mast, seeking shelter.

She seemed to be alone. Her long skirt and petticoats, heavy with water, dragged as she walked. Strands of long blond hair escaped from beneath the hood of her dark cloak, to be whipped wildly by the wind. It was the girl he'd glimpsed the day he boarded the ship. She looked so small and slender, as if a good gust might blow her right off the deck. . . . *She should not be up here alone,* Theodore thought. *I will offer her my arm.*

He had taken only a few steps in the girl's direction when a large wave slammed against the ship, causing it to list suddenly to one side. Theodore braced himself. Then his eyes widened in horror. The impact had torn a small boy from his mother's grasp and sent him sliding toward the ship's railing. Now a second large wave flung the child overboard!

In an instant, a second figure ripped a life preserver from the ship's rail and leaped into the raging sea after the boy. The young blond woman! Theodore was awestruck by her bravery. But he also knew there was no way that she could rescue the child. Even with the life preserver, her heavy skirts would drag her down. "A life ring!" Theodore shouted to a group of young men standing nearby as he tore off his frock coat. "Throw in a life ring!" Then, without another moment's thought, he too jumped into the churning, deadly sea.

Its icy cold stabbed him like a thousand blades, but Theodore barely felt the pain. Kicking to keep afloat, he fought the raging currents with strong arms. Ahead of him, he saw two bodies being tossed like flotsam by the water. *They're still afloat!* Theodore thought joyfully. *I can reach them!*

But as he stroked toward them the figures slipped beneath the water. A life preserver popped to the surface; the girl had lost her grip on it. Taking a deep breath, Theodore dove down into the icy black sea. His arm struck something solid. The girl! But though she still clasped the little boy in her arms, her body had gone limp. Their bodies pulled Theodore down as he struggled to resurface. He pawed the water with his free arm, his own strength failing fast. Soon his own lungs would burst. . . .

Just in time, Theodore broke the surface of the water. Gasping, he blinked against the salty spray. Something white bobbed on a wave before him. A life ring, with a rope attached!

Without delay, the three were hauled onto the deck. The little boy was quickly revived and restored to the arms of his tearful parents. But the girl lay still, her damp face pale. Theodore bent over her, wondering if he should try to press the water from her chest and breathe fresh air into her lungs. At that moment, her eyes flickered open and she took a shaky breath. A smile of relief warmed Theodore's face. The girl smiled back, weak and uncertain.

"Shh," Theodore said when she tried to speak. "Rest for a moment. Then we will take you below and get you warm and dry."

The puzzlement in the girl's clear blue eyes told Theodore that she didn't understand his words; most likely she didn't speak English. But at the same time, he felt that she understood his intentions. As he supported her with one arm she relaxed against him in a trusting fashion.

At that instant, gazing into the brave, mysterious girl's eyes, Theodore knew that he wanted to spend the rest of his life with her.

The following evening, Theodore called on Alice Larson at the women's bunkroom. He'd polished his boots and dusted his top hat; he wore the new frock coat and trousers he'd purchased before leaving England. Alice too had undergone a transformation since the previous day's adventure. Dressed in a silk gown and an elegant cream-colored bonnet, she smiled shyly up at him, her eyes sparkling and her cheeks rosy.

They had an audience. Theodore grinned at the young women who watched curiously as he took Alice's arm to escort her down the corridor. When he and Alice were relatively alone, Theodore reached into the pocket of his frock coat and withdrew a delicate rose carved from wood. "For you," he said to Alice.

She took the rose, her eyes lighting up with delight. She spoke a few words in Swedish, then added in hesitant English, "Thank you very much, Mr. Wakefield."

"You're very welcome, Miss Larson. A beautiful rose for a beautiful woman."

She might not have understood every word of his compliment, but she blushed prettily. She would blush even more, Theodore knew, if she guessed the flower's true significance! To Alice, it was just a gallant gesture, but to Theodore, the rose was a token of eternal devotion. Unable to present her with one fashioned from gold and jewels, as was the Wakefield family tradition, he had carved one for her from a piece of wood, modeling it after the flower on his signet ring.

As the two strolled toward the massive, noisy dining hall for the steerage-class passengers, Theodore glanced at Alice out of the corner of his eye, his heart pounding. *How can I be so sure?* he wondered, surprised by the intensity of his emotions. But he was sure—she was the one.

He carried their trays of food to the rear deck of the ship, where he'd had a small table set up, complete with linen tablecloth. Alice smiled with pleasure as he pulled out a chair for her. "This is much better than the crowded dining room," she said in halting English.

"Much better," Theodore agreed. "Although your company would make any situation pleasant."

She tipped her head to one side. "My English is not good—I'm sorry."

Theodore expressed himself more simply. "I am glad to be with you." She ducked her head, blushing. "And your English is quite good. You are from Sweden, are you not?"

Alice nodded. "I knew only one or two words of English when I left, but I have tried on this trip to learn a few more every day so I will be ready when we reach America."

"Why did you leave your native country?" Theodore asked, hoping this question would not seem presumptuous to her.

Her blue eyes clouded with sorrow. "Since the death of my parents, I have been living with friends. I am lonely for family. My uncle who lives in America invited me to join him. He and his family are going west to farm on the . . . the . . ."

Theodore supplied the word. "The prairie?"

"Yes." Alice's eyes sparkled. "I have heard that in America, there are fields of grass that go on and on, as far as the eye can see, and that any man can own as much land as he can farm."

"There are great opportunities," Theodore confirmed.

"And you?" Alice asked. "Do you go to join family in America?"

"No. I have no family," said Theodore, unwilling to burden her with the somber details of his recent history. "I go to America to start a new life."

"Will you be a farmer?"

Theodore almost laughed at the thought of himself, an English lord, working the soil like a commoner. But the truth was that he was no longer an English lord; he had a new identity as well as a new life. He would earn his bread by honest labor, like every other man. "I would like to work with animals," he replied. "Perhaps I will be a horse trainer."

"A horse trainer! In the circus?"

This suggestion also made Theodore smile. "Perhaps."

After their meal, the two walked along the moonlit decks, enjoying the peaceful calm of the sea, the clear starry sky, and each other. They talked and talked of their hopes for the future, Theodore pausing patiently to explain unfamiliar words to Alice. At last, reluctantly, he escorted her back to the women's bunkroom.

He took her hand as she moved to step through the door. "I would very much like to call on you again," he told her, a serious, hopeful note in his voice.

She squeezed his hand gently. "Yes, I like that. I

like you to call on me again. Good night, Mr. Wake-field."

"Good night, Miss Larson." His hat in his hand, Theodore watched her disappear into the dimly lit bunkroom. When she was gone, he whispered the sweet name again. "Good night, Miss Larson . . . Alice Larson. . . ."

Theodore strolled down the corridor to the men's bunkroom, a dreamy smile on his lips. At the start of the passage, Theodore had felt so alone. Now thoughts of the brave and beautiful Swedish girl who'd captured his heart filled each moment of his day. Theodore had never felt this way about a girl. More than ever, Theodore was glad he had struck out on his own. He was a free man. And he knew what his next independent step would be: He would ask Alice Larson to be his wife.

Theodore sat on the edge of his hard cot, his head in his hands. *A week . . . can it be only a week that I've been trapped here?* Theodore wondered as he stared with dull eyes at the bare walls of the hospital.

Upon his arrival at the Castle Garden immigration station in New York, a health examiner had quarantined Theodore on the suspicion that he might be carrying typhus. Theodore had not come down with the dreaded, highly contagious disease, but he was still not free to leave the Ward's Island hospital. And with every monotonous day that passed he grew more desperate. What were the chances that he would be able to find Alice now?

Alice . . . Alice . . . It pained Theodore immeasurably even to think the beautiful name. Bored and depressed, he replayed the events of the transatlantic journey one more time in his mind. The great storm—the rescue—the gratitude that had flooded his heart when Alice's eyes opened as she lay on the deck of the ship. He'd fallen in love with her at that very moment. A bond had been formed between them, a bond Theodore had believed only death could sever.

Death . . . or quarantine, he thought dismally. Theodore hoped with all his heart that Alice would still be waiting for him when he was finally released. He was certain that fate had brought them together. He had saved Alice's life so that their destinies might be joined. Leaving England a lonely exile without a home or family, he had arrived in America with the woman who would be his wife. But no sooner had they set foot on American soil than they were parted. Sentenced to quarantine, Theodore had not been able to join Alice according to their arrangement. He had been herded with other unfortunates onto a boat to Ward's Island. Just as the boat was about to leave the dock, he had caught a glimpse of Alice as she stepped into what must have been her family's carriage. The slump of her slender shoulders told Theodore that she was discouraged after a long day and evening of waiting for him. Had she given up? Did she think he had deserted her? Worst of all—what if she and her relatives had already left New York?

Independence day! After weeks of quarantine, Theodore was being released!

The ferry shuttling him from Ward's Island pulled up at the dock on Manhattan. Despite the fact that he was weak from his period of confinement, he sprinted all the way to the immigration station. He wouldn't let himself entertain the possibility that bad news—no news—might be waiting for him there. He forced his legs to move faster, hoping against hope.

Castle Garden swarmed with people, just as it had when Theodore and Alice's ship had arrived. Theodore dodged a group of immigrants, then hurdled over a toddler clutching a bedraggled doll. He fought his way to the immigration office.

"A message," he panted breathlessly. "I must know if a message was left here for me. From Miss Alice Larson, for Theodore Wakefield."

The young man walked over to a wall of cubbyholes stuffed with papers and packages. When he returned, his hands were empty.

"No note? No word?" Theodore asked desperately.

"Nothing."

Utterly dejected, Theodore stepped away from the office and allowed himself to be absorbed by the bustling crowd. As he stood among the mass of newly arrived immigrants, he almost doubted for a moment that a beautiful blond Swedish girl named Alice Larson had ever stepped off the boat here.

He had no way of tracking her down, no way of knowing exactly where her family might have been staying in the city or where they were planning to settle out west. Nonetheless, Theodore knew he must look for her. He walked north up Broadway, peering at each face he passed, glancing in every window, at the occupants of every carriage-for-hire. He kept walking as dusk settled and the lamplighters commenced their evening work; he walked far into the night, up one avenue and down another, searching and hoping.

Theodore's hope had died by the time the first pale pink light of dawn began to brighten the eastern horizon. He was footsore, hungry, bone-tired . . . and still alone. His despair was complete.

He found himself in front of the train station. *Why not?* he thought. New York held nothing for him. But at the ticket counter, he faltered. He realized that he had given no thought to exactly where he would go or what he would do in the New World. Now Theodore thought of the vast continent stretching north, south, and west from the spot where he stood at that moment. He could go absolutely anywhere! But the country that once had captured Theodore's imagination now seemed to him empty. Without Alice at his side to share the adventures of the New World, his life here would be meaningless.

Theodore's chin sank to his chest. He fought back the tears of defeat and the desire to give up, to return home to England. No, he decided at last. He couldn't go back. Because no matter how vast this country was, Alice was there, somewhere, somewhere in the wild, lonely West.

Theodore checked the list of fares. He had just enough money to get himself to Cleveland, Ohio. That wasn't very far west, but it was a start. "One ticket to Cleveland," he requested, laying the money on the counter, his hand shaking slightly. It was all the money he had in the world. Theodore twisted the ring on his finger; he thought of the rose he had carved for Alice. "Somehow I will find her," he vowed, oblivious to the ticket seller's curious stare. "If I die searching, someday I will find her."

Four

"You are getting much too big to drink from a bottle," the pretty half-Indian girl lectured. "You are more trouble than you're worth!"

Theo laughed at the sight of Dancing Wind shaking her finger at the long-legged colt. He watched the foal nuzzle Dancing Wind's hand and then trot off to join the other horses tethered near the makeshift stables that had been quickly erected by the circus members that afternoon.

"I didn't think Raven would survive when Redwing died," Theo remarked. Redwing, Theo's favorite stunt mare, had died that spring after foaling. "Your nursing has pulled him through. You have a magic touch."

Dancing Wind was pleased by Theo's praise, but she felt he gave her too much credit. She shook her head, and the glossy black hair that fell in a shimmering river to her waist swung gently. "You're the one who's able to work magic with animals just by speaking to them. You're the Magnificent Theo W.!"

His eyes crinkling, Theo laughed heartily. "What's so funny?" Dancing Wind asked. "Isn't that your name?"

"It's my name now," Theo conceded. "The name I took when I joined the circus as a horse trainer eight years ago. But I was born another person." He winked at her. "Once I was just plain Theodore Wakefield."

Dancing Wind shook her head again. She didn't believe him. Surely tall, handsome Theo W., with his twinkling brown eyes, his iron-strong arms, and his ability to talk to animals, had always been magnificent!

"What about you?" Theo asked as they walked among the circus horses. He adjusted Arctic Prince's tether post so that the snow-white stallion could reach the best grass. "You weren't born 'the Dancing Wind of the flying trapeze,' were you?"

"Of course not!" She giggled. "My adoptive family, the Flying Montecatinis, gave me that identity four years ago. Before that I was just plain Dancing Wind."

"That's not so plain. It's a beautiful name."

"My mother, Owl Feather, chose it," said Dancing Wind. "She was an Awaswan Indian from California. My father met her when he went west during the gold rush. I think it was hard for her to leave her tribe, but she loved him."

"Did he strike it rich?"

Dancing Wind smiled. "He found a nugget or two, nothing more. He always said that my mother was his biggest treasure." Her smile faded and sorrow shadowed her face.

Theo put a hand on her slender shoulder. "I'm sorry."

Dancing Wind sighed and bent to pluck a wildflower from the waving grass. "I never really knew her," she told Theo. "She died of smallpox when I was a little child. My father did his best to raise me on his own."

Dancing Wind paused. She had been with the Bellamy Brothers Circus for three months, since the Flying Montecatinis had left Tommy's Big Tent Circus because of a disagreement with the management over their billing. No one at this circus knew the full story of how the half-Indian girl had come to be adopted by the Flying Montecatinis, a family of trapeze artists from southern Italy. While Dancing Wind was tireless and without fear when it came to circus stunts and physical labor, it was not so easy for her to share her thoughts and feelings. She was naturally reserved, and as a result of her unusual life, somewhat solitary.

But although she did not know him well, Dancing Wind liked Theo W. He impressed her as strong, kind, honest, and trustworthy. She contin-

34

ued her unusual tale. "My father and I had always moved from place to place, living in rough mining camps and cowboy towns. Four years ago, when I was twelve, he was shot and killed during a saloon brawl. Tommy's Big Tent Circus was passing through town, and when Mama Montecatini heard my sad story and saw how much I resembled her own daughter, Isabella, she immediately insisted that I come to live and work with them. Ever since then, the Flying Montecatinis have treated me like a member of their family."

Theo gave her shoulder another sympathetic squeeze. "You've suffered more than your share of losses in your short life."

Dancing Wind smiled bravely. "But for everything and everyone I have lost, I have gained something else to cherish. I am not alone. The circus is my family now."

The horses settled, Theo and Dancing Wind crossed the train tracks to a hillside path. They hiked up and found themselves on the top of a wooded bluff. Below them, like a river of gold in the last light of the summer day, the great Mississippi River flowed in a broad curve. They sat down side by side on a large flat rock. Dancing Wind tucked her slim legs up under her long cotton skirt and clasped her knees with her arms.

Staring ahead at the red ball that was the sinking sun, Theo said, "The circus is my only family, too."

Dancing Wind had often wondered why such a

handsome man did not have a wife and children. "Did you, too, lose your parents when you were young?"

Theo frowned slightly. "I did lose my parents, but not to death, the way that you did." He looked at Dancing Wind, a strange, questioning expression in his clear brown eyes. She felt that he was debating something; she hoped he would find her worthy of his confidence. "I left my home in England half a lifetime ago," Theo explained, "when I wasn't much older than you are now. I don't know if my parents are still living or not. We did not part on good terms."

Dancing Wind nodded but said nothing. "I came to America to start a new life," Theo continued. "And during the ocean crossing I thought that I would also be starting a new family here. There was a Swedish girl on the boat . . . Alice." A pained note crept into Theo's voice. "We had an understanding. But we were parted on our arrival. I never saw her again."

He stopped. Dancing Wind sensed that even after all these years he was overcome with emotion at the memory. "Do you . . . do you still think of her?"

"Not a day passes that I don't think of her. For years, I searched for her. I traveled the country as a railroad porter, and at every stop I inquired after her."

"But you never found her," Dancing Wind concluded.

"No, I never found her."

Clearly, Theo felt that life had lost all meaning when he lost Alice. He had never married; Dancing Wind guessed he had never even loved another woman.

But like her, he was not entirely alone. "You are happy with the circus, though, aren't you?" Dancing Wind asked hopefully.

"I am happy," Theo assured her. His eyes crinkled. "Who wouldn't envy the life we lead?"

It was exciting, Dancing Wind agreed. They lived in a brightly painted circus train and traveled constantly; she didn't have to go to school; and their fellow circus members were wonderful, talented, interesting people.

The sun was gone. Around them, the forest had grown dim and shadowy. Theo rose to his feet and extended a hand to Dancing Wind. "Come. We still have chores to do before we rest."

Somewhat reluctantly, Dancing Wind followed Theo back down the path. True, she still had to mend a torn seam in her costume, and she needed to get a good night's sleep before the next busy day of practicing and performing. But she would rather have sat close by Theo's side in the moonlight, talking all night long.

* * *

37

A month later, the circus camped in Blackberry Hollow, Iowa, not far from the Minnesota state line. Whenever the circus train pulled up at a tiny, seemingly deserted rural town, within an hour a hundred people would emerge from the cornfields, the houses, the stores. As soon as the school bell rang, the children came running to squeal over the baby elephant, the snakes, and the glittery costumes. Families brought their dinners in baskets or pails and picnicked on the grass, all wanting to be first into the big tent for the evening's show.

That night, Dancing Wind hummed cheerfully to herself as she finished applying her makeup in the curtained-off section of boxcar that served as her and sixteen-year-old Isabella Montecatini's dressing room and bedroom. She pirouetted in front of the mirror, admiring her reflection. Her creamy-gold complexion glowed with health; her dark eyes, which tilted up slightly at the corners, were sparkling as if she had a secret. She knew that her slender, gently curving figure was the envy of Isabella, who had to struggle against a tendency to grow plump.

"Why the happy song?" Isabella inquired.

Dancing Wind slipped into her sequined outfit. "Why not?"

"Because you're usually so quiet and serious. You always tell *me* to stop singing and chattering!"

"Then I must have learned to sing and chatter from you, my adopted sister," Dancing Wind teased. But she had to admit, Isabella was right about her mood. The last time Dancing Wind had felt this happy was when she was a tiny girl. She remembered her mother telling her Awaswan folk stories, her voice a soft, magical singsong. Dancing Wind knew the tune she was humming right now was one she had learned from her mother.

Dancing Wind pinned on a gossamer cape stitched with multicolored feathers. Chalking their hands as they went, she and Isabella hurried together to the big tent. It was packed with townspeople of all ages, clapping and laughing as Max and Sam, the clowns, performed a skit involving a large bucket of water and a clever elephant named Ruby. While the crowd focused on the clowns' antics, the Flying Montecatinis quickly mounted the ladders to their perches high above the dirt floor of the tent. Poised for her first leap, Dancing Wind looked down and caught the eye of Theo below. He was standing where he always stood to watch her routine, at the edge of the ring opposite her perch. And as always, his silent encouragement gave her wings.

When Max, Sam, and Ruby had taken their bows and the applause began to fade, four clowns positioned themselves below with a safety net, and Angelo Montecatini gave Dancing Wind the signal wave. Gripping the bar of the trapeze tightly, she dove calmly into the open air.

Swing, swing, swing—she arched her body

through the air, pumping her long, slender legs, her toes pointed. She soared higher and higher and then let go. After releasing the bar, Dancing Wind tucked into a ball and tumbled through the air, counting the beats in her head as the audience gasped. *One, two*—she stretched out her arms and felt Angelo's strong hands grasp her wrists. Now she heard a collective sigh of relief, followed by wild cheers.

A few minutes later, the Flying Montecatinis were bowing to the delirious crowd. Dancing Wind tossed back her glossy dark hair and searched for Theo's face. When she found it, the pride she saw there made her glow with triumph. Since that night on the river bluff, she and Theo had had many more talks. They were closer friends than ever. In fact, Dancing Wind had started to care for him as more than a friend; she was falling in love.

She wanted to ask someone if this was what love was like—wanting to be with someone during every waking moment, and dreaming of him each night. But she was afraid to confide in anyone, even Isabella. She knew Isabella would only tease her. And she would gossip, too; soon everyone in the circus, Theo included, would have heard about Dancing Wind's naive questions.

The last act ended, and the crowd departed. The evening wasn't over yet for the circus members, however; they had to clean the tent and grounds and tend to the animals. Brooms in hand, Dancing

Wind and Isabella swept fresh sawdust over the dirt in the ring. Eager to finish her tasks so she could look for Theo in the stables, Dancing Wind worked quickly. But Isabella leaned idly on the handle of her broom, her black eyes focused on the other end of the tent, where Henrik the lion tamer was helping Sam and Max feed the elephants.

"Don't you think Henrik is the most handsome man in the troupe?" Isabella asked dreamily.

Dancing Wind glanced at Henrik. His biceps rippled as he lifted a bale of hay, tossing it to Ruby. "He's a nice man. But I think the Magnificent Theo W. is more handsome," she ventured.

"Theo W.?" Isabella scoffed. "Why, Henrik could wrestle him to the ground in a minute. Look at Henrik's muscles and his shiny blond hair!"

Dancing Wind stuck her tongue out at Isabella and finished her sweeping. "I'm done with my half," she announced. Before Isabella could beg her help with the rest of the chore, Dancing Wind dashed off.

She found Theo with the horses. He greeted her with a warm smile. "You're just in time to feed our little friend."

He had prepared a mash for Raven, whom they had recently weaned from the bottle. Dancing Wind held the bucket while Raven ate greedily. "If he keeps eating like this, soon he'll be as big as his sire, Arctic Prince," she predicted.

41

"He'll be a fine horse," Theo said with satisfaction. "He has as much spirit as his namesake."

"His namesake?"

"The horse I sold to pay for my passage to America was also named Raven."

Raven finished his meal. Kicking up his heels, he cantered off. Dancing Wind watched the horse go. *A Raven in the Old World, a Raven in the New,* she thought. A long-lost love whom Theo had never forgotten. Did he live completely in the past?

She didn't realize she'd spoken her question out loud until Theo started. "Do you really think I live in the past?" he asked.

Dancing Wind's eyes widened. "I didn't mean—"

Theo shook his head. "No, you're right. I *have* been living in the past, for many years. But I've begun to realize that I may have been denying myself much happiness."

He stepped closer to her. Dancing Wind turned to him. She could see his face clearly in the light of the full, white summer moon. As Theo studied her face, raised expectantly to his, she knew that his thoughts had shifted. He was no longer thinking of the past, but only of the present moment. He was thinking of *her.*

Theo put his hands on her shoulders, pulling her toward him. "Dancing Wind," he said, his voice husky.

She leaned forward, her eyelids dropping shyly.

Her dreams were coming true. Theo was going to kiss her!

Before their lips could meet, Isabella's voice pierced the night. "Dancing Wind!" she called. "Come to bed!"

Theo stepped back from the near-embrace, his grip on Dancing Wind's shoulders loosening. "It's late," he said, once again friendly and calm. "You'd best go in."

"Good night, Theo," she whispered.

As she hurried across the pasture toward the circus train, Dancing Wind was both disappointed and encouraged. They had come so close to sharing their first kiss! It had been many years since Theo lost his heart's desire, and she sensed he was at last ready to love again. He felt something for her, of that Dancing Wind was certain.

Five

The circus had been in Prairie Lakes for three days; after the second show that evening, they would break camp and move on. That afternoon, as the usual crowds of curious townspeople milled about the grounds, Dancing Wind wandered with them. It had been more than a week since the night in Blackberry Hollow when Theo had almost kissed her, and he hadn't *once* tried to kiss her again!

A sudden inspiration struck Dancing Wind—she knew whom she could go to for advice about her relationship with Theo. Laura the Lovely was the circus's bare-back rider and one of Theo's good friends. Laura must know all about love, Dancing Wind thought; it was no secret that she and Angelo Montecatini were going to be married soon.

Laura was in the tent that served as a stable, grooming her golden mare, Morning Star. Dancing

44

Wind glided over to her silently so as not to catch the attention of Theo, who sat not many yards away mending Arctic Prince's bridle.

Laura gave Dancing Wind a knowing smile. "Are you looking for your special friend?"

"Actually, I want to talk to you." Dancing Wind's cheeks flamed. "I—"

At that moment, Bucky the Clown started yelling at someone who'd tried to sneak into the horse tent. One of the many young boys from town who were always hanging around, Dancing Wind presumed. Then, as Dancing Wind watched in surprise, a small blond girl scampered by with Bucky in hot pursuit.

Laughing, Laura dashed after the pair. Sweeping the little girl up in her arms, she faced Bucky. "It's all right with me if she hangs around," Laura declared, kissing the child on the cheek. "Is it all right with you, Theo?"

Resting her arms on Morning Star's broad back, Dancing Wind watched Theo. She saw him glance up and nod amiably. Laura set the child on her feet. Immediately, the little girl marched boldly up to Arctic Prince. "My name's Jessamyn Johnson," she announced to the horse. "What's yours?"

Theo stepped over to her side and squatted so he was at eye level with her. "This is Arctic Prince, the star of the circus," he told Jessamyn. "Have you ever ridden a horse this big?"

45

"I've ridden one twice as big!" Jessamyn boasted. "But never one as pretty. Can I ride him?"

"First we have to put his bridle on." Theo explained the procedure in a patient, friendly tone, his eyes never leaving the little girl's face.

Laura the Lovely held the child up so that, with Theo's assistance, Jessamyn could slip the bridle over Arctic Prince's ears. "Well done!" Theo commended her.

Jessamyn clapped her hands, clearly pleased with herself. Dancing Wind smiled. "You have an accent," the little girl said to Theo. "Are you from another country?"

Theo stroked his chin. "I guess I do still have a bit of an accent. Yes, I'm from England."

"My mother has an accent, too," Jessamyn said. "She came from Sweden. But that was before I was born. *I'm* American."

Theo's expression became intent. "Sweden? Is your mother—is your family coming to the show tonight?"

Jessamyn nodded. "We're going to eat a picnic dinner and then watch the second show. I wish we could see both performances!" she added wistfully.

"Well, this is better than watching." Laura lifted Jessamyn onto Arctic Prince's back. "You get to ride on a circus horse of your very own!"

Laura led Arctic Prince to the field outside the tent, keeping a careful eye on Jessamyn. Theo watched them until they disappeared from sight.

When Dancing Wind approached him, she was surprised to see that he appeared to be in the grip of a very powerful emotion. He blinked at her, as if for a moment he didn't recognize her. Dancing Wind laughed. "You look startled, as if you'd seen a ghost!"

"I feel as if I have," Theo confessed. "That child —Jessamyn. Dancing Wind, I think she may be my Alice's daughter!"

My Alice's daughter. What could he mean? "She can't be," Dancing Wind breathed, a worried frown shadowing her face.

"She's the very image of Alice," said Theo. "And she said her mother is Swedish."

"But many Swedes have settled in this region. What are the chances—"

Theo dismissed this consideration with a wave of his hand. "Dancing Wind, tonight I may see my true love for the first time in many years!"

All color drained from Dancing Wind's face. Theo was too caught up in his own excitement to notice. "If it is the same woman, I'm sure she will be happy to see her old friend," Dancing Wind predicted cautiously.

"We were more than friends," Theo said. "Our lives were one. Now the hand of fate has brought us together again, as it did on the ship many years ago. It has brought her back to me."

"As you said, many years have passed," Dancing Wind reminded Theo. "She's probably a married woman, with a family and a home. If you are correct, you just met her child!"

But Dancing Wind's desperate words made little impression on Theo. "Time will not have changed her," he predicted. "She will still be my Alice—young and beautiful. And the feelings we once shared . . . such feelings never die."

"But what can you do about these feelings?" Dancing Wind bit her lip, willing herself not to cry. "What can you do if she's married to another man?"

Theo shook his head. "I don't know," he admitted. "But I must go to her after the performance tonight. We'll talk. And if our hearts tell us to . . ."

His words trailed off. *To what?* Dancing Wind wondered. *To leave your present lives and the people who depend on you in order to pursue a foolish, romantic dream of yesterday?* She took a step backward, then another. Theo's eyes were distant and dreamy; he was no longer aware of her. He didn't even notice when she turned and ran from the tent, her own eyes blurring with tears.

Dancing Wind had never been so distracted before a performance. The possibility that Theo might have found his long-lost love had shattered her usual cheerful tranquility. As she got ready for her act her heart ached with pain and jealousy. Over and over she replayed the scene of Theo telling her his plan to seek out Alice. He had talked to Dancing Wind without seeing her. *Did he ever really have feelings for me?* Dancing Wind wondered as she and the other Flying Montecatinis mounted the ladders to the high trapeze.

She knew she must concentrate on her act right now, but her mind was racing with jumbled thoughts. She could see Theo standing off to the side far below, in the spot where he always stood during her act. More than ever, she wanted to shine in his eyes.

How can he not love me? Dancing Wind asked herself, wiping a tear from the corner of her eye. She was young and strong and brave—his companion in adventure, his friend. How could he prefer an old married farm woman he hadn't seen in years?

The signal came, and Dancing Wind flew from her perch like a bird. Despite her preoccupation, she knew her routine well, and she and Angelo executed their first stunt flawlessly. The crowd roared. Then it was Isabella's turn to tumble through the air into the grasp of her father, Guillermo.

For a few moments, while Guillermo and then Angelo were performing solo stunts, Dancing Wind and Isabella crouched together on a perch, catching their breath. Again, Dancing Wind sought out Theo. If she could only catch his eye—if he would give her just one smile . . .

But Theo wasn't looking up at her. He was gazing out at the crowd, searching for someone who might be seated there. He was looking for Alice.

Bitter tears choked Dancing Wind. Every evening for the past several months Theo had watched her performance, every evening until this one, until Alice had entered his thoughts again. Now, as he turned his back on her, Dancing Wind felt her heart breaking. She had to do something, something to make Theo really *see* her again.

"I'm going to try the triple roll," Dancing Wind whispered suddenly to Isabella.

Isabella stared at her. "You mustn't. It's too difficult. You're not ready!"

Dancing Wind shrugged off Isabella's words. Isabella was much too cautious. She never liked to try anything new. "I can do it. Just watch!"

An instant later, Dancing Wind sprang from the perch, her arms extended. Angelo, swinging by his knees from a bar, caught her hands. He swung her, higher and higher and higher. Soon he would toss her to Guillermo.

The moment came. Angelo released Dancing Wind and she tucked into a tumble as she sailed through the air, hugging her knees. One rotation, two . . . she went for the extra roll.

Still in a tuck, Dancing Wind heard Guillermo catch his breath. He wasn't prepared for her triple roll. Quickly, she unfolded her body, stretching her arms toward him. But he was already swinging back, away from her. Though he extended his body to its fullest length, holding on to the trapeze with his feet and ankles rather than his knees, he could not quite grasp her. Their fingertips brushed, and then Guillermo was gone. Dancing Wind fell through empty space.

She had been in a trancelike state, focusing only on the triple roll and on Theo. But as soon as she felt Guillermo's hands slip away from her, Dancing Wind snapped out of her trance. Instantaneously, she was aware of her danger. She was plummeting downward with dizzying speed!

As she fell Dancing Wind heard the frightened screams of the audience. Squeezing her eyes shut, she willed her body to go limp so it would bounce harmlessly on the safety net.

Dancing Wind's body hit the net. But she didn't bounce. Instead, there was a ripping sound. The net had given way! Her fall only partially broken, Dancing Wind plunged toward the ground. She opened her mouth to cry out Theo's name, but before she could, her body made contact with the hard earth floor of the circus tent. Pain exploded through her bones, and the world went black.

Six

Theo was only half aware of the Flying Montecatinis' trapeze act. Every few seconds, he quickly scanned the blur of faces in the audience. Jessamyn had said her family would buy tickets for the second show that night, but what if they'd decided to attend the earlier one? What if Alice was in the tent at that very moment?

Theo's eyes came to rest on a blond woman, and his heart jumped to his throat. No, it wasn't her, he realized, half disappointed and half relieved.

At that instant, the woman he was watching put her hand to her mouth, her eyes widening with terror. There was a burst of horrified exclamations from the crowd.

Theo whirled on his heel in time to see someone falling. Dancing Wind!

"No!" Theo dashed forward. The net hadn't

saved her; he could see her fragile body crumpled on the ground. "No!" he cried again. *Please let her be alive. Please don't let her die,* he prayed.

Others were hurrying to Dancing Wind's side, but Theo shoved them out of the way. As he approached he heard her weak voice. Her eyes were closed; she was only half conscious and she was calling his name. "Theo," she murmured. "Theo."

"I'm here." Theo knelt beside Dancing Wind, cradling her head in his arms. "I'm here. You're safe now."

As Theo spoke these words he was overwhelmed by a strange sense of *déjà vu.* For a brief instant, he wasn't in a circus tent in Minnesota. It was 1866 and he was on the deck of a boat to America. He'd just saved a young Swedish girl from drowning. It was Alice who was lying in his arms.

No, not Alice. Theo felt a tear glide down his cheek. *Dancing Wind. It's Dancing Wind.*

For the first time, Theo realized how blind he had been. How could he not have noticed how much he cared for Dancing Wind? As he held her in his arms, not knowing whether she would live or die, Theo knew that he'd never forgive himself if he lost her now. Dancing Wind had given him so much in the past few months; she'd taught him to laugh and share again. She'd taught him to look ahead to the future, encouraged him to forget the past. And he'd given her nothing in return. *How could I not have seen?* he asked himself. *We are so much alike. Dancing Wind is alone, without family; we are both exiles, far from our roots. Destiny brought us together and now it might separate us.*

In his moment of clarity, Theo recognized something else. Even if Jessamyn's mother did turn out to be his long-lost Alice, things would not be the same between them. Dancing Wind had been right. He could not ask Alice to leave her husband and children. What kind of life could he offer her in exchange? They had fallen in love half a lifetime ago. They would be strangers to each other now.

Two clowns pushed their way to Theo's side with a makeshift stretcher. Tenderly, Theo eased Dancing Wind's body onto it. She moaned, her hand fluttering to her right hip. It was oddly twisted; broken, Theo surmised grimly.

As he and Max carried Dancing Wind from the tent on the stretcher, Theo heard the ringmaster assuring the distressed crowd that Dancing Wind was all right. Outside, another crowd of people pressed forward to see what was happening—the people who were waiting for the night's second show. Theo saw a blond head, a delicate profile. Beside her were two blond children. Could it be . . . ?

He would never know. He couldn't look now, not when Dancing Wind needed him more than ever. Not now, when the future could finally hold something more for him. As he gazed at Dancing Wind's pale face, he knew what he had to do. He would not leave Dancing Wind's side, that night or ever.

When the train scraped over a rough piece of track, the rocking motion jolted Dancing Wind awake. She opened her eyes slowly. She felt as if she had plunged into a deep lake of pain and was now swimming laboriously to the surface.

She lay on her bed in the circus car, her face turned toward the window. Dawn glimmered in the east. Her whole body ached, but a sharper throbbing seemed to center on her right hip. She tried to move her hand to touch the injury but couldn't. Someone was holding the hand tightly. With an effort, Dancing Wind turned her head on the pillow. She looked right into the warm, worried eyes of Theo.

He was sitting at Dancing Wind's side, clasping her small hand in both of his own. Now he lifted the hand to his lips, kissing it gratefully. "I thought you might never open your eyes again," he said, his voice hoarse with emotion.

She stared at him in wonder. "I . . . I fell, and then . . . I don't remember."

"You broke your hip," Theo told her. "We brought you here—you were unconscious—and before the circus packed up, Dr. Good from Prairie Lakes set your hip."

"How long before I am better?" she asked. "When will I be able to perform again?"

Theo squeezed her hand. "The break was very bad. Dr. Good said the bones will never fully mend."

Dancing Wind closed her eyes and turned her head away from Theo. *The bones will never fully mend.* A tear pushed its way between her lashes and rolled down her cheek. She would never again be the Dancing Wind of the flying trapeze—she would be a cripple. What chance did she have now of winning Theo's heart? During the long, agonizing night, as she had drifted in and out of consciousness, Dancing Wind had thought she heard a beloved voice telling her he loved her. Of course it had been only a dream. . . .

Because he loved another. Suddenly, Dancing Wind remembered the incidents that had led up to her fall from the trapeze. "Alice," she whispered. "Did you find her?"

Theo reached out and gently turned Dancing Wind's face back toward him. "I didn't look for her," he replied. "I didn't have to go searching for love because it had been with me all the time. You are the only woman I want, Dancing Wind."

Now Dancing Wind was sure she was dreaming. But when Theo bent to kiss her, it felt very real.

As the morning sun burst above the horizon, Dancing Wind's pain and heartbreak dissolved in the warmth and comfort of pure joy. Theo rested his head on her shoulder, and she wrapped her slender arms around his neck. Peace settled over them. *I will get well*, Dancing Wind thought, stroking Theo's hair. The doctor's prognosis didn't matter. How could she fail to heal and flourish with Theo's love to see her through?

Dancing Wind left the train quietly, before daybreak. Isabella slept soundly, a peaceful smile on her face. *She is dreaming of Henrik*, Dancing Wind thought, a smile momentarily touching her own face.

Leaning heavily on her wooden crutch, she eased herself down the steps to the ground. The trampled grass alongside the tracks was white with frost. *It is time*, Dancing Wind thought. Autumn had come. That very day, the circus would pack up and leave its latest stop in Cottonwood Creek, Nebraska, to head south for the winter.

With her crutch, Dancing Wind could move quickly, almost gracefully; without it, her limp was extreme. Now she swung lightly across the sparkling field to where the horses were tethered. Nickering with recognition, Raven trotted toward her. The colt no longer needed special feeding, but he was still Dancing Wind's favorite. As she reached out to touch him, a strange envy filled Dancing Wind's heart. His legs were so long and straight, his stride so easy and clean. Her hip had healed as much as it ever would; the injury had left her partially crippled, with one leg shorter than the other, and in almost constant pain. She would never again float over the ground like Raven, never again sail through the air with the Flying Montccatinis.

With the rising sun, the circus came to life. Dancing Wind looked back at the camp, where the others were cooking a quick breakfast before loading the animals into the boxcars. The scene was so familiar, and yet for some reason this morning Dancing Wind felt removed from it. *I do not belong anymore,* she thought. Everyone was kind, but she knew they kept her on only out of charity. There was really no little chore she did that someone else couldn't do just as well. No, she couldn't stay with them any longer.

As for Theo, Dancing Wind loved him deeply. But she didn't want to burden him, either. Many a night Dancing Wind had lain awake thinking about the way in which their love had come about. A feeling of guilt had taken firm root in her heart. If she hadn't fallen from the trapeze, Theo would have gone after Alice; he would never have declared his love for her. *Did I know it would happen that way?* Dancing Wind wondered now as she led Raven back toward the camp. *Did I want it to happen that way?* The events of that fateful night were a blur in her memory; it was impossible to recall exactly what she had thought and felt at the time. One thing was certain, though: she had been trying to capture Theo's attention when she tried the difficult stunt. Dancing Wind couldn't help feeling that she had trapped Theo somehow. Now she must set him free.

In the bustle of preparation for departure, Theo did not observe Dancing Wind quietly packing her belongings into a compact bundle. At last, the animals were all loaded and the train whistle blew. About to hop on board, Theo saw Dancing Wind standing by the tracks, the bundle at her feet.

"Come." He put a hand under her elbow. "I'll help you up."

Dancing Wind shook her head. She felt torn in two, but she knew she had made the right decision. "I'm not going," she said calmly.

"What?" Theo was taken by surprise. "The train will leave without us. We must hurry!"

"I'm staying behind. I have decided. I will find my way to California. My mother's tribe, the Awaswans, will take me in. I'll be of more use there."

Still gripping her arm, Theo stared for a long moment into her earnest face. Then he let go of her and jumped on board the train.

Swallowing her tears, Dancing Wind turned away. She heard a metallic screech as the train began to move. Suddenly a sack landed by her feet, followed by Theo! As the train chugged forward he fell to one knee before her, her hands held tightly in his own. "The night of your accident, I vowed that I would never leave you. Don't you remember? Dancing Wind, I want you to be my wife. Say you will marry me."

"I cannot marry you," she said, her voice quavering with emotion. "I release you from your vow. You deserve a woman who is strong and whole."

"Dancing Wind." Theo rose to his feet and put his arms around her. "No person I have ever known, man or woman, is as strong and whole as you. You are the best part of my life. Think of the years we will have together!" Lifting her from the ground, he whirled her in a dizzy circle. Her black hair flying out behind her, Dancing Wind couldn't help laughing. "We will spend the winter in Cottonwood Creek, and then travel together to California in the spring," Theo promised. "Say yes. Say that you'll marry me."

In Theo's arms, she felt as light as a feather. With Theo's help, she could still fly. "Yes," said Dancing Wind. "Yes, yes, yes!"

Seven

1888. Cottonwood Creek, Nebraska.

Dancing Wind left her crutch on the porch of the small red-shuttered farmhouse and walked barefoot across the yard. The pleasurable tickle of the new spring grass between her toes almost made her forget that she limped.

Arriving at the chicken coop, she reached into the pocket of her apron for handfuls of dried corn and grain, which she scattered for the hungry, squawking fowl. After feeding the birds, she strolled on to the edge of the yard.

Resting her arms along the top of the split-rail fence, Dancing Wind gazed out on the land. *Our land,* she thought with a rush of pride. She and Theo hadn't journeyed to California after all; Theo had been afraid that further travel would seriously strain her health. Instead, they had homesteaded right here in Cottonwood Creek, in the same town

61

where they'd left the circus to get married. Now, after four years of hard work, they owned a small but prosperous farm.

Dancing Wind lifted a hand to shade her eyes from the sun. In the distance, she spied Theo repairing the windmill that pumped their water. Watching her husband work brought a rush of affection and gratitude to her heart. Their life together was rich and full. They had faced many challenges over the years: plagues of grasshoppers that had devoured crops; summer droughts that had withered plants; sudden winter blizzards that had battered their home and killed stray cattle. But they had come through it all, and now their love for each other was stronger than ever. Dancing Wind was content. Only one thing was missing from her life with Theo: a child.

And Theo loved children; he was a favorite with their neighbors' three boys, especially Lars, the Petersons' youngest. He frequently entertained them with tricks and games he'd learned in his years with the circus. Still, he swore to Dancing Wind that he did not mind that they didn't have a baby of their own. Time and again he told her, "You are all I want. And your health is so fragile as it is. It's better this way."

Now Dancing Wind smiled. She couldn't wait until his work was over and she could tell her husband the wonderful news!

* * *

It was evening, and the two sat on the porch swing watching the setting sun turn the green wheat fields to gold. Theo's arm was around his wife's shoulders. Dancing Wind held the small leather-bound book she used as a journal. She carried it in her apron, never knowing when she might be able to steal a moment from her busy days to jot a few lines. She had started keeping the journal soon after she and Theo settled in Cottonwood Creek, to record the events of their married life, her childhood memories, and the Awaswan folk tales she'd learned many years ago from her mother. Dancing Wind had never cared much for school and book learning, so she was surprised that writing in her journal should bring her such joy. Somehow, writing filled a space in her life, the space that had been created when she lost the ability to run and jump. It had made her feel whole again.

Now Theo tapped the cover of the book. "What will you write about today?"

She glanced at him, her expression a mixture of mischief and solemnity. "I think I will write about what it would be like to have a child, a little boy like Hans. Or maybe a little girl!"

Bending, Theo kissed her hair. "We don't need children. I like the life we have, just the two of us."

Dancing Wind knew he said this only to make her feel better. Usually she went along with him, grateful for his selfless patience. But that day she had a different response. "Well, I'm sorry you feel that way, since soon you will be a father," she said, looking down at her hands demurely.

"What?" Theo had been rocking the swing gently with his feet; now his boots froze to the floor, jolting the swing to a stop. "Do you mean to say—"

Dancing Wind nodded, her eyes crinkling. "Yes. I'm expecting."

"Expecting!" Theo stared at her, and she studied his face anxiously. Was he pleased? "But it's dangerous. Your health—"

Dancing Wind waved her hand. "Despite my bad hip, I'm stronger than most women. I'm not afraid. Oh, just think, Theo! A child, a Wakefield to carry on your family name in the New World. A son or daughter to help us with the farm."

Tenderly, Theo took her face in his hands. His eyes were warm with concern, but also with intense joy. "I thought I was as happy as a man could be. But now I see I'm only beginning to learn the meaning of true happiness. You are teaching it to me."

As their lips met in a kiss Dancing Wind had a feeling that she would never be more content than she was at that moment.

The pains began on the day of their fourth wedding anniversary, not long after Theo had left for the fields. It was autumn and the crops had been harvested; Theo would spend the morning plowing the soil to prepare it for winter.

For a moment, Dancing Wind was frightened and wanted to run after him. But then she remembered the story her mother had told her when she was a little girl about her own birth. Owl Feather had begun feeling her pains while Dancing Wind's father, Jake, was out hunting. Their cabin had been in the woods of California, completely isolated. No one lived nearby to help; Owl Feather had been on her own. Jake had returned to the cabin to find his wife resting in bed, a new baby cradled in her arms.

My mother was brave, and I can be brave, too, Dancing Wind vowed, even as her face contorted with pain.

She lay down in the bedroom she shared with Theo, clutching the quilt as hard as she could to keep from crying out. Breathing deeply, she willed herself to be calm. Try as she might, however, she could not banish the anxious whispers that filled her mind. It had been a difficult pregnancy, and Dancing Wind was afraid—afraid that something was wrong with her, afraid that something was wrong with the baby.

A few hours later, the contractions were coming regularly. One was especially hard; Dancing Wind moaned. At the sound, Theo, who had just entered the house, rushed into the bedroom. His eyes grew wide as he saw his wife's condition. Kneeling at her side, he gently blotted the sweat from her forehead with his handkerchief. "Will you be all right while I run for Felicity?"

With an effort, Dancing Wind smiled and nodded. Felicity Peterson, their neighbor, was an experienced midwife; Dancing Wind would feel much better with her friend to help her through this ordeal.

Night fell, and Dancing Wind's labor continued. Despite her pain and exhaustion, she could hear Felicity and Theo's hushed conversation, see the looks they exchanged. She could tell that something was wrong.

"I've been here for hours and nothing has happened," Felicity said to Theo in a low voice. "I'm afraid the baby may be in the breech position—it is certainly in distress. I need Dr. Baker's help with this delivery."

"I'll go for him." Theo was already halfway to the door, shoving his arms into the sleeves of his overcoat.

As the door opened and then slammed shut, Dancing Wind heard the wind howling outside. "Felicity," she whispered. "Am I dying? Is the baby dying?"

Felicity took Dancing Wind's hand. "Shh. Save your strength. The baby will be fine and so will you." She forced a smile. "The baby knows it's cold outside. It would rather stay inside you, where it's warm!"

To please Felicity, Dancing Wind tried to smile, too. Then she summoned all her strength. She would just keep trying. She had to, for her baby's sake . . . and for Theo's.

Theo lashed the horse with his whip, urging it to a gallop. He felt as if he'd been gone for hours, although he saw by his pocket watch that it had taken less than an hour to drive the buggy to Dr. Baker's house and back. Thank God he had found the doctor at home!

Theo tied the horse in the yard. He and Dr. Baker hurried into the house. His heart in his throat, Theo ran to his wife's side. Dancing Wind was being very brave, but he could see at a glance that she had weakened. She tried to lift a hand to touch his face, but could raise it only a few inches before it dropped back to the bed. Bending his head so Dancing Wind wouldn't see his tears, Theo cursed himself. She should never have become pregnant; she was not strong enough. Why hadn't he taken better care of her?

"Have something to eat," Dr. Baker advised Theo. "And get some rest. It may be a long night."

Reluctantly, Theo left the bedroom. In the kitchen, he cut himself a piece of cornbread and bit into it. It tasted as dry as dust. Suddenly a cry of agony pierced the night; Theo had never heard such a sound. Pushing back his chair, he ran to the bedroom in time to hear another kind of cry: the cry of a newborn baby.

Felicity was already busy cleaning the infant and bundling it into a warm, dry cloth. She flashed Theo a tired, triumphant smile. "It's a boy. You have a son."

"A son!" Theo's heart contracted with relief and happiness. "How is my wife?" he asked the doctor. "Will she be . . . ?"

The doctor, still bending over Dancing Wind, shook his head. "It's too soon to say. There is another baby on the way. She's having twins!"

Twins! Stunned, Theo sank into the rocking chair next to the bed. They were having not just one baby, but two! Of course, Theo welcomed them both. But at that moment, his only thoughts were for the safety of his wife.

Dancing Wind continued her exertions far into the night. Finally, the second child was born—a girl. Both babies were healthy; it seemed like a miracle to Theo. But the long and difficult labor had taken its toll on Dancing Wind. She lay still and pale beneath the quilt, her breathing rapid and shallow and her eyes closed.

Felicity's husband, Lars, came for her and offered to drive Dr. Baker home as well. At the door, Theo took the doctor's hand. "Thank you."

Dr. Baker gripped Theo's hand tightly. "She is very weak," he warned. "Very weak. Come for me again if she begins to fail."

To fail . . . Theo couldn't bear to entertain the thought.

Felicity had laid the swaddled babies in the crib Theo had built in anticipation of the birth. Now Theo lifted them gently. He placed the tiny boy in the crook of Dancing Wind's right arm, the girl in her left. Dancing Wind opened her eyes. As weak as she was, she was able to cuddle the babies to her. "They're so small," she whispered.

"They're perfect," Theo said. When Dancing Wind tried to speak again, he put a finger to her lips. "Shh. Just rest."

Dancing Wind looked down at her babies, then up at Theo. Her expression was full of love for them and for her husband. But there was something else in the brown depths of her eyes, and when Theo recognized it a lump came to his throat. Dancing Wind didn't need to speak to tell him that she knew she was going to die.

Theo bowed his head to the bed, his eyes flooding with tears. As much as he wanted the children, he wanted Dancing Wind more. How could he live without her?

"Names," Dancing Wind whispered. "We must name them."

Theo raised his head. "Choose Awaswan names, for your mother's people. Beautiful names like your own."

"No. They are Wakefields." Dancing Wind

smiled faintly. "They are your heirs. Call them James and Sarah."

As Dancing Wind spoke the names of Theo's brother and mother, long lost to him, she closed her eyes. A look of peace settled over her smooth golden face.

"No!" Theo exclaimed, just as he had done on the night when Dancing Wind fell from the high trapeze. "No!"

He'd been powerless to prevent her from falling then, and he was powerless to prevent her from dying now. Dancing Wind was gone.

To Theo, it was as if night had fallen forever; he felt that day would never come again to his heart. Tears streaming down his face, he bent forward, embracing his wife and children. "Goodbye, Dancing Wind."

Eight

1905. Vista, California.

"Will you be back for tea?" Theodore Wakefield asked, looking up from the cherry seedling he was planting.

His sixteen-year-old daughter laughed merrily. Sometimes her father was so quaint! After all his years in America, he still spoke with an English accent. And Sarah certainly didn't know anyone else in Vista, her Napa Valley hometown, who made a ritual of tea and cake every afternoon at four!

As the lady of the house, it was Sarah's role to pour the tea. "Of course I'll be back." She tapped his shoulders lightly with her leather riding crop. "Without me to serve, you and James would sit helplessly with empty cups and plates."

Theodore chuckled. "The older you get, the sassier you get."

Sarah planted a kiss on her father's graying head.

"And the sassier I get, the more you love me," she teased.

Theodore smiled benevolently at his only daughter. Sarah knew he couldn't deny that she was the apple of his eye, just as he couldn't help spoiling her. He often told her that the shape of her eyes made her resemble her mother, Dancing Wind, and that her dark blond hair was the same shade as that of her grandmother and namesake, Lady Sarah. So every time he looked at his daughter, Theodore caught a glimpse of two other beloved women, long since lost to him.

"Ta-ta!" Sarah untied Plummy's reins from the fence and, bunching her blue skirt in one hand, swung herself up into the sidesaddle. Bending, she adjusted the strap that secured the leather rucksack containing her lunch and books. Then she gave Plummy a nudge with her boot heel.

They cantered across the field toward a fence. Rather than stopping to unlatch the gate, Sarah set Plummy up for the jump. He cleared it neatly. Settling back into the saddle, Sarah glanced back over her shoulder. Her father had risen to his feet, and she could see him shaking his head. He always forbade her to jump that fence; then he would turn around and jump it himself on his favorite horse, Raven. Laughing, Sarah tossed her father a wave. He might lecture her, but she knew he admired her spirit. He would think something was wrong with her if she suddenly became meek and stopped insisting on getting her own way. Ever since she was a child, Sarah had been strong-willed and single-minded. It was a quality that had gotten her into many difficult situations. Luckily, however, her twin brother, James, was of a more serious and responsible nature, and he was always there when Sarah needed a rescue. It was James who had helped her back on her pony after she was thrown from the saddle, who had pulled her from the frozen duck pond the winter she fell through the ice, who had talked her into coming home when she'd run away—all the way to the far end of the orchard! —at the age of seven because her father wouldn't let her keep a litter of stray kittens.

It was a beautiful northern-California summer day. As she urged Plummy up the rise of a small hill, Sarah was glad that after her mother's death, when she and her twin brother James were still tiny babies, her father had sold his farm in Nebraska and moved west. She had never seen the prairie but she knew it was as flat as a tabletop. How could it compare to the green, rolling hills of the Napa Valley, lush with woods and meadows, orchards and vineyards?

Sarah kept Plummy to a path that skirted her father's property. In the distance, she spied a small group of hired pickers harvesting the fruit from the peach and apricot trees. The farm was prospering, and every year her father was able to expand his orchards, planting more young trees. Often the two

73

of them rode out together. Riding the fences, Sarah's father would reminisce about his birthplace in Yorkshire, also a land of rolling hills.

Sarah slowed Plummy to a walk. Reaching up, she unclasped the gold pin that held her hair in a knot. She shook her head, and the long, dark-blond hair cascaded down her back, glinting with gold highlights in the sun. Her grip on the reins loosened as she lapsed into daydreams. Sarah liked to think about her father's romantic past: the tragic, untimely death of his older brother; his renunciation of an arranged marriage, a title, and the family inheritance; the journey to America and the lost fiancée; his years of wandering and life in the circus; the farm in Nebraska and his love for the mother she and James had never known; his trek west with his two babies. It was better than a novel! Sometimes it didn't seem fair to Sarah. Now her father was an ordinary, middle-aged man who worked hard to build a good life for his two children. All the exciting things had happened before she was born!

When they reached the far boundary of the orchard, Sarah jumped down from Plummy's back. Knotting the reins so he wouldn't trip himself, she let the horse wander off to graze, then settled herself in the shade of a gnarled cherry tree. There was a ladder leaning against the trunk—left behind by one of the pickers, she surmised as she unfastened the top button of her fitted white shirtwaist in order to cool her neck.

She pulled a few books out of her rucksack, then lay back, using the bag as a pillow. Which to read? She was well into both the autobiography of women's rights activist Elizabeth Cady Stanton and a gothic novel called *Wuthering Heights*. The latter was part of her father's collection; in recent years, he had stocked his library shelves with British books of all sorts. Putting both volumes aside, Sarah opened a fabric-covered journal in which she was writing a fanciful story. Sarah had read Dancing Wind's diary, one of her father's prized possessions, and she couldn't help feeling that her own life was ordinary compared to the adventures of her deceased mother. So Sarah used her own journal for fiction. Life was much more interesting, Sarah was convinced, when you spiced it up!

In the story Sarah was currently writing, the heroine, liberally modeled after herself, had run away from home to escape the persecutions of a cruel stepmother; thank goodness her father had never remarried in real life! The heroine was about to meet the hero, the man who would rescue her from all her perils. Sarah was momentarily stumped, however, as to what the hero should look like. Would he be tall and dark like her own father, or golden-haired like a Norse god? Were his eyes black and flashing or blue and kind? Should he be as gentle as a brother or a more mysterious and intimidating figure?

Sarah dipped her pen in the small jar of ink she'd brought with her and scratched a few lines. *Her cloak soaked with rain and her raven-black curls tumbling down her back, Serena hastened toward the abandoned mansion. Then, in a flash of lightning, she glimpsed a tall and forbidding shape under the old oak tree. . . .*

A cherry fell in Sarah's lap. She picked it up idly. Removing the stem, she popped the cherry in her mouth and prepared to resume writing. At that moment, another cherry dropped, and then another. Soon it was an absolute shower. What was going on in the tree above her? Startled, Sarah jumped to her feet and looked up—right into the laughing brown eyes of Edward Brooke.

Edward, a young man Sarah knew slightly from school, was sitting on a branch of the tree, a burlap sack bulging with fruit slung over his shoulder.

"Edward!" Sarah exclaimed, relieved that it was just him and not the more menacing figure of her imagination. "What are you doing up there?"

Edward pushed a shock of dark brown hair back from his forehead. "I'm picking cherries, as one of your father's employees. What are *you* doing down there?"

Hurriedly, Sarah shut her journal, even though the ink was not quite dry and would probably smudge. "I was writing in my diary. About what a

76

good harvest we're having this year," she added untruthfully.

Edward grinned. "Your expression was very . . . entranced. I wouldn't have thought that topic would be so absorbing!"

Sarah blushed. "Never mind what I was writing about. Just come down from there and help me eat this lunch."

Edward climbed down the ladder, and in a few moments he and Sarah were seated face to face on the grass, her modest picnic spread out before them: bread and butter, pickled vegetables, and cheese. "I'm glad you're here, because there's twice as much food as I could eat by myself. My father packed this for me," Sarah explained. "He says in England they call it a ploughman's lunch."

"A ploughman's lunch for the lady of the manor," Edward remarked, his eyes twinkling.

Sarah blushed again. She suspected that Edward was poking fun at the fact that her father had named his estate Manor Farm after Wakefield Manor, the home of his youth. It did sound a bit pretentious. "Yes, I'm roughing it today," she said airily. "I left the china and silver at home!"

Edward tossed his head back in a hearty laugh. "Well, china or no, I appreciate your hospitality, Miss Wakefield."

"Miss Wakefield!" Sarah handed Edward a piece of bread and a chunk of cheese. "You really don't need to be so formal."

"Well, your father *is* my employer," Edward reminded her.

"I don't see what difference that makes. You were my schoolmate, so of course you should call me Sarah."

"I'd be glad to, Sarah."

The serious note in Edward's deep voice sent a thrill chasing up Sarah's spine. No one had ever spoken her name in quite that way. Determined not to blush again, she said quickly, "Why are you picking fruit for my father, anyway?"

"He pays a good wage. And since I've finished with school, it's time for me to make my own way in the world."

"Of course," Sarah responded, although making one's own way in the world wasn't something she thought about often; she knew she would always have her father to take care of her. "But doesn't your father run the livery stable in town? Why don't you work for him?"

"Oh, I do." Edward gestured with his bread-and-cheese sandwich. "Picking fruit is only seasonal employment, a little extra money in the bank. My father gets me the rest of the time. But I'm planning to branch off on my own soon." He leaned forward, his elbows on his denim-clad knees, his eyes intense. "There's no future in the livery business, Sarah. Soon the horse and buggy will go the way of the covered wagon. We've entered the century of the motorcar!"

Sarah nodded eagerly. She had been green with envy when the LeMaitres, who cultivated a prosperous vineyard nearby, became the first family in Vista to own an automobile. "My brother and I talk ourselves blue in the face trying to convince our father to buy a Ford or one of the Model E Watsons. But he's so old-fashioned! He has the same opinion about electric lights in the house." She imitated her father's English accent. "'Motorcars break down and electricity fails, but you can always count on horses and candles!'"

Edward laughed. "But you're a modern woman, I see." He indicated the Stanton book, *Eighty Years and More.*

Sarah nodded. "Elizabeth Cady Stanton didn't live to see the day, but it will come. You'll see—this will be the century of the motorcar *and* of the woman voter!"

She was pleased that Edward didn't ridicule her radical views. "Women should have the vote," he agreed. "They work and make decisions all the time. They should be allowed a voice in government as well as in the home."

To Sarah's surprise, Edward suddenly took her hand. What was he going to say to her now? As she held her breath Edward turned her hand slightly so he could read the time on the gold-faced watch tied with a green velvet ribbon to her slender wrist. He was only checking the time, Sarah realized with some disappointment. But she didn't think it was just her imagination that he held her hand for a moment longer than was necessary.

"I must return to work." He rose to his feet.

"Oh." Reluctantly, Sarah stood as well and gathered her things together. Then she found she didn't know what to say. In theory, she considered herself a modern woman, but in practice, she felt it would be too forward to come right out and say to Edward that she hoped to see him again very soon.

Fortunately, Edward's thoughts appeared to be running parallel to her own. "The pickers work until sunset," he said nonchalantly. "Do you ever ride out at that hour?"

Sarah looked up at him. He was taller than she remembered, and underneath his work shirt she could see that his broad shoulders were taut with muscles. "I think I might ride out at sunset tomorrow evening," she replied. "And this corner of the farm is my favorite destination."

Edward smiled. "I'll keep that in mind." He strode over to where Plummy was grazing and led the horse to Sarah, then offered her a leg up. "Good afternoon, Miss Wakefield."

"The same to you!"

As Edward hoisted the sack of fruit to one shoulder and gripped the ladder under his other arm, Sarah gave him a goodbye salute with her riding crop. As Plummy trotted off Sarah looked at her watch, remembering Edward's touch. She'd reach the house with some time to spare before tea, and she decided to use it to write a little more of her story. All at once, she knew just how she wanted her hero to look. He would be tall and broad-shouldered, with dark hair and twinkling brown eyes, and the most captivating smile. . . .

On Sunday afternoon, a little more than a week after her first meeting with Edward, Sarah waited impatiently for his knock on the door. Promptly at four, she heard a firm rap. Smoothing her hands down the corseted waist of her white muslin gown, she hurried to the front door and swung it open eagerly. "Hello!"

She had never seen Edward look so handsome. In a crisply pressed suit and jaunty bow tie, he looked quite distinguished. *A man, not a boy,* Sarah thought, her cheeks pink with pleasure. And he was the first man she had invited home to meet her father and brother, although of course James would remember Edward from school.

After a week of "accidental" meetings in the orchard, Sarah and Edward had agreed that it was time he presented himself formally to her father as a suitor. *Won't they be surprised!* Sarah thought as she took Edward's hand to lead him to the parlor, where she had laid out the things for tea. No sooner had Edward taken a seat than Mr. Wake-field and James, in the middle of a debate about whether to diversify the farm by raising cattle and sheep, entered the room. Edward stood up again quickly.

"Father, James," Sarah began, "I've invited my new friend, Edward Brooke, to join us for tea. You both know Edward."

Did her father hesitate an instant before extending his hand to take Edward's? Sarah couldn't be sure. "Of course," Theodore affirmed. "Edward."

He didn't say "nice to see you" or "welcome to my home," Sarah noted. Her twin was more enthusiastic. "Edward, hello!" James shook Edward's hand vigorously. "It's good to see you."

The three men sat, and Sarah poured out cups of tea. Then she passed the tray of tiny sandwiches and delicate cakes; she had spent quite a bit of time making sure the tray looked perfect.

After each man had filled his plate, there was a moment's awkward silence. Sarah looked expectantly at her father. Surely now he would ask the sort of questions a father always asked a prospective suitor for his daughter.

But Theodore drank his tea, appearing almost to hurry through the usually leisurely afternoon ritual. It was James who initiated a conversation with Edward. "Do you think there are enough work opportunities to keep you in Vista now that you're out of school?"

The two young men chatted excitedly. Sarah made a few interjections of her own, attempting to draw her father into the discussion. But while he listened politely, Theodore maintained an aloof manner. As soon as he'd drained his cup and finished off the last crumb of his cake, he rose to his feet. "There's no day of rest for the farmer," he said affably. "I have some work to attend to, if you'll be so good as to excuse me."

Sarah swallowed her disappointment. "Of course, Father."

For Edward's sake, she kept up a cheerful demeanor. But as soon as they'd made plans to meet the next day at sunset and said goodbye at the front gate, her smile collapsed into a puzzled frown. Why had her father been so cool to Edward? How could he have been anything other than impressed by Edward's impeccable manners and pleasant nature?

Not one to keep quiet for long when something was on her mind, Sarah hurried to her father's study. Theodore was seated at his heavy wooden desk, using a magnifying glass to study a ledger filled with rows of tiny, neatly printed figures.

"Father," Sarah said without preamble, "don't you like Edward?"

Theodore closed the ledger and removed his glasses. "Sarah, sit down."

Obediently, she took a chair at his side. Theodore rested an affectionate hand on his daughter's shoulder. "I do like Edward, my dear. I hired him, after all. And in our working relationship, I have found him efficient, amiable, and conscientious."

"He is all those things," Sarah agreed eagerly.

"But as a prospective suitor for you . . ." Theodore paused, clearly considering how best to broach the subject. "Sarah, you know how much you mean to me." His voice shook with emotion. "In you, I cherish both the memory of my beloved Dancing Wind, your mother, and my own mother, whom you are named for."

"I know, Father," Sarah said, her eyes misting.

"I want the best for you, and for James. I hope to see him attend college. And you—I hope to see you settled in a happy and suitable marriage with a man who is capable of supporting you in the manner you deserve."

"Women go to college, too, you know!" Sarah reminded him.

Theodore smiled. "Yes, I know. And you are smart enough to go, if you want. And perhaps it will be there that you will meet the man who is your match. I've just remembered," he added. "We have been invited to dine with the LeMaitres. Mrs. LeMaitre told me that George especially looks forward to seeing you."

Sarah's lips tightened. She found George LeMaitre and his brothers unbearably pompous. Just because they were rich, and because their father let them drive his car around town, they thought they were royalty. "Of course I'd be happy to dine with them," she lied.

The answer satisfied Theodore. "Good." He kissed his daughter's cheek. "I knew we would understand each other, my dear."

"We always do." Sarah returned her father's kiss. "I'll leave you to your work."

Sarah went to the kitchen and began washing the tea things. *You knew we would understand each other. Yes,* Sarah thought, *I understand you, Father. Only too well.* He hadn't said it in so many words, but clearly he didn't consider Edward an appropriate match for her. He wanted her to marry someone rich and horrible, like George LeMaitre!

What an old-fashioned, utterly English idea, Sarah thought as she spread a light cloth over the leftover sandwiches, which would be their supper later. *To practically forbid me to continue seeing Edward just because he doesn't have any money!* Sarah knew her father meant well. He did love her and want the best for her. But she also knew her father was wrong. After all his years in his great adopted home, he hadn't learned America's most important lesson: that people should be judged not by their name or fortune, but by what they do and who they are.

Sarah sighed. But she was not downcast for long. Her father could be very stubborn—no one knew that better than the daughter who took after him!

And Sarah was determined to have her own way,

as usual. A smile curved her lips as she considered the challenge that faced her. She would keep peace with her father, but she would also keep seeing Edward . . . in secret. Sarah thought of the romantic stories she had made up and written in her journal. Maybe her own life wasn't so ordinary after all!

Nine

The November day was raw, and Edward's bare knuckles were red from the cold and from gripping the handlebars of his bicycle, trying to keep it from wobbling, which wasn't easy to do with Sarah perched precariously in front of him. "This is a case where your father would be right." Edward pedaled steadily along the dirt road that led to the gate of Manor Farm. The cold, damp air made his breath come in white puffs. "A horse would be safer!"

Sarah giggled. Just then, a gust of wind snatched the scarf from her hair. Instinctively, she reached for it. Thrown off balance, she, Edward, and the bicycle tumbled to the ground.

Unhurt, Sarah nevertheless was unable to rise because she was now giggling helplessly. Grinning, Edward disentangled himself from the bicycle. "No one can say I don't see a lady home from school in style!"

Sarah's laughter dissolved into a sigh of pleasure as Edward embraced her, his mouth meeting hers in a deep, warm kiss. For a moment, she gave herself over to the joyful feeling of being close to him. Then she pushed him away playfully. "We shouldn't be kissing!"

School had been dismissed early that day and wouldn't resume again until an epidemic of influenza, an infectious and occasionally fatal respiratory disease, had passed. Edward gave her another quick kiss. "I'll take my chances."

"We already are," Sarah reminded him.

For months now, she and Edward had been meeting secretly, usually in town in the afternoon when Sarah got out of school. Edward would steal a few minutes away from his new job as a ticket seller at the Vista train station; they would just have time for a quick embrace among the trees along the train tracks. The best days were when Sarah's father went away for business purposes: to buy seed and supplies, and to negotiate the sale of his produce. Then Edward would come out to the farm and the two would wander for hours hand in hand through the orchard, talking of their plans for the future. With each clandestine meeting, their love for each other grew stronger, but there was always an undercurrent of unease, because each time they were risking discovery by Sarah's father—and his extreme displeasure.

Now they stood up and dusted themselves off. "Promise you'll take care of yourself," said Edward, tenderly brushing a loose tendril of hair back from Sarah's cheek.

She smiled, her cheeks glowing pink from the cold. "I'm as healthy as a horse. I won't get sick."

Edward remounted the bicycle, pointing it back toward town. "See you soon, then!"

Sarah waved after him, then ran to retrieve the renegade scarf. Shaking it out, she tied it quickly around her hair and ears. The rising wind seemed to be growing colder by the minute; an early winter storm was definitely on the way. Ahead of her, Sarah spotted her twin brother. James had walked straight home from school, while she had stopped first at the Vista train station to meet Edward. "James, wait for me!" she called.

James turned and stood, his cap pulled tight over his ears and his shoulders hunched to protect his neck from the wind. "Where's Ed?" he asked.

"Oh, he dropped me off a little farther back."

Sarah halted for a moment to draw off her new leather gloves. "Put those back on!" James lectured. "You mustn't catch cold with influenza going around."

"I'm just taking care of this." Sarah pulled a ring from her finger and held it up for a moment for James to see. Then she put it in the pocket of her coat. Together, the two walked briskly toward the farm.

It was a slender, plain gold ring—all Edward could afford—but it meant the world to Sarah. He had given it to her for her seventeenth birthday a few weeks earlier as a token of his steadfast love. Of course, Sarah could not wear it publicly. Her father would be angry if he knew she had continued to see Edward, and furious if he knew they were talking about marriage!

James, however, knew about both Edward and the significance of the ring. He was Sarah's staunch ally; on many occasions he had covered for his twin sister when she met Edward after school. Sarah knew that James genuinely liked Edward; he didn't share their father's snobbishness. Like Sarah, James felt that while their father was right about most things, he was wrong about this.

"You can't hide the ring—and Edward—forever, you know," James said through a sneeze. "When are you going to tell Father?"

"Edward wants to tell him now, but I think we should wait. It will be soon enough when I graduate from school in the spring." Sarah stopped again.

"Now what?" asked James.

She put a hand to her forehead. It was throbbing. "I have a headache. We fell off the bicycle back there. Maybe it jolted me more than I thought."

James looked concerned for his sister, but as

usual he didn't pass up an opportunity to tease her. "You may be coming down with influenza. You'd better not sneak out tonight to meet Ed!"

"Our friendship isn't like that!" Sarah defended herself hotly. "We only meet by daylight, and you know it."

At that moment, James was struck by a whole bout of sneezes. Now it was Sarah's turn to worry. "We'd better get to bed," she advised, taking her brother's arm. "I think we both may be coming down with it."

They hurried homeward, the wind fairly pushing them up the drive. Just as they reached the house the icy rain began. "Not a moment too soon!" Sarah exclaimed as they slammed the door behind them. Shedding their coats, they hurried to the kitchen stove to warm their hands. Outside, the wind howled, eerie and relentless. But soon a new sound met the twins' ears.

Sarah looked at James. "Is that . . . ?"

"Hail," he confirmed.

They rushed to the window. The rain had indeed turned to hail; pebble-sized chunks rattled against the house.

There were rapid footsteps in the hall. Their father burst into the kitchen, his arms loaded with canvas sheets. "The seedlings!" he exclaimed.

James and Sarah needed no further explanation. The peach and cherry seedlings had to be covered or else hundreds of dollars' worth of baby trees would be destroyed by the hail. Both twins reached for their coats. "No, you stay here," her father instructed Sarah. "We can do it."

While her father and brother braved the storm, Sarah slowly mounted the stairs to her bedroom under the eaves on the second floor. By the time she reached the top, she was feeling weak-kneed and light-headed.

From her bedroom window, Sarah looked out on the sea of white. Putting a hand to her forehead, she suddenly realized she was burning with fever. Another wave of dizziness washed over her. In the act of unbuttoning her blouse, she fell back on her bed in a faint.

For Sarah, the next three days passed in a haze. One minute she burned with fever, and the next she shook with chills that the heaviest blankets couldn't dispel. She ached from head to toe, and felt too weak even to lift her head from the pillow. Throughout the course of the illness, she was aware of one thing: the constant, reassuring presence of her father. Sarah knew that James was stricken as well, and that their father had abandoned the work of the farm temporarily to nurse them. He kept Sarah bundled in clean, dry nightgowns and blankets; when her fever was hottest, he held cool cloths to her forehead; when her throat was raw from coughing, he helped her sip soothing herbal teas; at night, he sat by her bed and read to her until she drifted peacefully to sleep.

Soon, with warmth and bed rest, Sarah felt much better. On the fourth morning, she sat up in bed and stretched her arms over her head, basking in the sun streaming through her bedroom window. She swung her feet over the side of the bed and took a few experimental steps. She was weak from not eating, but otherwise her energy had returned; the illness had passed as quickly as it had come. It felt so good to breathe easily, to stretch, to walk!

Wondering how she could get a message to Edward, who must be very worried about her health, Sarah padded over to the window to look out on the bright fall morning. To her surprise, she saw a man on horseback leaving the yard. She would know that unruly thatch of red hair anywhere—it belonged to Dr. Daly, a close family friend of the Wakefields and Vista's only medical practitioner.

Quickly, Sarah slipped on some woolen stockings under her nightgown. Wrapping a blanket around her, she hurried down the hall as fast as her shaky legs would carry her. The door to her brother's bedroom was ajar. Since he had fallen ill at the same moment as she had, Sarah assumed James would be in much the same state that she was that morning: sitting up in bed, suddenly feeling hungry and alert. Instead, she found her twin still bedridden, still coughing, his face pale and slick with sweat.

Theodore, sitting at his son's side, looked up as Sarah entered the room. Immediately, she read the anxiety in his expression. "I saw Dr. Daly. How is James?"

"Come, back to bed with you," her father said.

In a minute, he had Sarah tucked under her blankets once more. "But I feel fine!" she protested.

"It won't hurt you to spend one more morning resting," her father insisted. "Dr. Daly would concur. If you overexert yourself, you could suffer a relapse."

Reluctantly, Sarah accepted the wisdom of this advice and leaned back against her pillows. "But James. Is he still ill?"

"Yes." Theodore's brow furrowed with lines of worry. "In the last day or so, his condition has grown worse rather than better. This morning I sent for the doctor. It seems—it seems James's influenza is complicated by a serious case of pneumonia."

"Pneumonia!" Sarah exclaimed. Then she remembered: the storm. James had already been exhibiting influenza symptoms when he exposed himself to the damp cold while helping their father save the peach and cherry seedlings. "What did Dr. Daly say we should do for him?"

"Nothing but what I've been doing thus far." Theodore's smile looked forced. "Both of my chil-

94

dren have always been as sturdy and stubborn as mules. Our Jim will be back on his feet in a flash."

"We'll see to it," Sarah agreed. Of course James would recover! How could he not, with his devoted father and sister both taking care of him?

But as the days passed James continued to weaken. Theodore and Sarah tended his needs round the clock, but the infection had taken an unbreakable hold. His inflamed lungs were filled with fluid, and he coughed painfully, incessantly.

On Saturday night, three days after her own recovery, Sarah sat on the edge of her bed with her journal open on her lap. The last entry detailed the joy of a rendezvous with Edward. Sarah laid her hand on a new, blank page. Even with her door shut, she could hear James coughing. Would he never stop? Sarah put her hands to her ears, pressing hard, feeling that soon she would have to start screaming to obliterate the sound that haunted her even in her sleep. Angrily, she tossed the journal aside. She could not write in it. What was there to record but that her beloved twin brother was dying?

Taking a deep breath, Sarah smoothed the crumpled skirt of her burgundy wool dress and stepped into the hall. Her father had been with James for hours; she should relieve his watch, urge him to eat something, to rest, before he became ill himself. As she reached James's door, though, a new sound met Sarah's ears: the sound of dry, quiet sobs.

Theodore sat at the side of his semiconscious son. He mumbled something . . . was it a prayer? And did she hear him speak the name of her mother, Dancing Wind?

Sarah tiptoed away, her heart aching with pity. *Poor Father*, she thought as she prepared a meal for him in the kitchen. Seventeen years ago he had watched his wife die, and now this. How much could one man bear, even a man as strong as Theodore Wakefield?

On Sunday morning, Sarah opened her eyes slowly. Blinking, she realized the sun had woken her. For the first time in days, she had actually slept through the night. How could that have happened? Suddenly, she realized that the house rested in peaceful silence. James wasn't coughing! He was better!

Sarah ran to her brother's room. James was alone; Theodore, too, must finally be getting some sleep. For a moment, Sarah's heart jumped into her throat. James lay so quiet, so still. But his eyes were open, and as she entered he turned his head. The effort stole his breath, and for a moment he could not speak. Kneeling at his side, Sarah took his thin hand and squeezed it. Then she touched his forehead, which was strangely dry and cold. "What can I do for you?" she asked gently.

James stared into his sister's face with an intensity that made her shiver. It was almost as if he was memorizing her features, as if . . . as if . . . "Tell me a story," he whispered.

Sarah told him the story that had been their favorite as children—a story their father often recited about how, after years of loneliness, he had fallen in love with a beautiful half-Indian circus girl, the Dancing Wind of the flying trapeze. Sarah's words seemed to act as a lullaby; slowly, James's eyes closed. A feeling of terrible certainty stole into Sarah's heart. The moment had come—she should run for her father. But before she could rise, Theodore himself entered the room. In a glance, he grasped the significance of his son's pale, peaceful countenance and his daughter's brimming eyes. Quickly, he crossed to the other side of the bed. Bending, he pressed a goodbye kiss on James's forehead.

James's raspy breathing slowed. Now he sighed, one final time, deep and long. And then there was nothing.

"No!" Sarah cried. Clasping her brother's limp form to her, she buried her face in the blanket. She felt as if someone were reaching inside her own body to tear away half her heart. Her twin was gone.

While his daughter shook with sobs, Theodore sat as if carved from stone, silent with immeasurable sorrow.

* * *

The door shut behind them with a click of awful finality. Slowly, Sarah removed the hooded black wool cloak in which she'd bundled herself for the cold buggy ride home from the cemetery.

The house seemed unbearably quiet and empty without James's lively presence. The only sound was the clock on the mantel. *Gone, gone, gone,* it seemed to say with its relentless, monotonous ticking.

Theodore shuffled to the cold fireplace. Sarah watched him, her eyes bright with compassionate tears. She was grief-stricken, but her father was devastated. His broad back was bent like that of an old man; he had lost his only son. With the iron poker, Theodore stirred the dead embers. "If I hadn't dragged the boy out into the storm when he was already weak with fever . . ." he said hoarsely. "Just as I should never have let my brother, James, mount Raven all those years ago."

"Father, no!" Sarah ran to his side and gripped his coat sleeve. "You mustn't torture yourself. It wasn't your fault, then or now."

Theodore turned to her, his eyes still shadowed with doubt and agony. "No one loved James more than you," Sarah continued softly. "No one could have cared for him better than you did."

Her father put a hand on each side of her earnest face. Then he embraced her with a surprising fierceness. "I thank God that you were spared, my dear child. You are all the family I have left in the world."

Resting her cheek on her father's chest, Sarah thought guiltily of Edward. Edward had come to the funeral, but had stayed out of sight on the edges of the gathering. More than ever, Sarah dreaded the prospect of disappointing her father. Would she have the courage to tell him about Edward when the time came? What would she do if she had to choose between the two men she loved?

Ten

1906. Vista, California.

Sarah strolled up the drive to Manor Farm, swinging her schoolbooks by their strap. Around her, the April world was fresh and new and green. The orchards were a sea of fragrant blossoms; the voices of nesting birds blended into a beautiful symphony.

It was impossible not to take part in the pleasure of spring, and for the first time since her brother's death the previous autumn, Sarah felt happy. Of course she wished that James were with her, looking forward to their high-school graduation in just a few months and planning to stand as best man in her wedding to Edward. But Sarah knew that her twin would always be by her side in spirit.

With a sigh, Sarah twisted Edward's ring from her finger and put it in her pocket. The only thing she couldn't love about spring was that each day of the season brought her closer to the inevitable confrontation with her father.

Sarah stepped through the side door of the house and was surprised to see her father seated at the kitchen table. "Hello!" she called cheerfully. "I thought you would be out in the orchard on an afternoon like this. What keeps you—"

She stopped. There was something lying on the table in front of her father. A book. It was her journal.

The blood drained from Sarah's face. Her journal, entrusted with all her most private thoughts! Her journal, which used to be filled with fairy tales, but where she now wrote mostly of her ever-growing love for Edward. And her father had found it. Found it, yes. But had he read it? Would he stoop to such an invasion? Theodore's face was blank; it was impossible to tell.

"That book is mine. I must have left it lying about." Sarah was surprised at how calm her voice sounded. She took a step toward the table. "Here, I'll take it."

Theodore placed his hand over the small book. "I know your penchant for flights of fancy." He spoke through clenched teeth, clearly fighting for self-control. Sarah's palms grew damp. "Tell me that what you've recorded here is fiction."

"You read it!" she gasped. The blood rushed back into her face, flooding her cheeks with angry color. "How could you violate my privacy in that way?"

Her father slammed his fist on the table. "How could *you* flagrantly disregard my wishes?" he roared. "And lie to me—lie to my face—for these many months?"

"I wouldn't have had to lie if you hadn't been unreasonable," Sarah defended herself. Her heart pounded and her throat grew tight with frightened tears. In all her life, her father had never raised his voice to her.

"There is no excuse." Theodore's voice fell but it was still ice-cold. "However you have been behaving behind my back with this young man, your lying is a far worse betrayal of the trust we've always shared."

"Don't you think I wanted you to be able to trust me?" Sarah cried. "Do you think I wanted to deceive you?" The tears spilled over, flowing down her cheeks.

Theodore stood. "Sarah." He crossed the room and stood before her, resting his hands heavily on her shoulders. She looked up at him, apprehensive. "I understand that you are very young. It's natural for you to have strong feelings. But in this case, your feelings are misguided."

"No." Sarah shook her head firmly. Her feelings for Edward were real, no matter what her father said. Their love was the kind that came only once in a lifetime.

"Yes," Theodore insisted. "Your feelings are misguided, and you are making a mistake. But I am ready to forgive you . . . if you inform Edward immediately that you will no longer see him."

"No," Sarah repeated stubbornly.

"My child." Theodore's expression softened a little, and his voice became almost pleading. "It is for *your* sake that I request this. It is *your* future I seek to protect. You are the last of the Wakefield line, Sarah, and you are worthy of—you deserve—a better match."

Her eyes flashing, Sarah pushed her father's hands from her shoulders. "Edward is a good man, worth far more than the spoiled LeMaitre boys and others like them!"

"He has nothing to offer you," Theodore argued, "whereas George LeMaitre could give you—"

"I don't love George LeMaitre," Sarah declared. "I love Edward Brooke."

"You will love the man I choose for you!"

Sarah stared at her father. Had he gone mad? "How can you say such a thing?" she asked him. "You, of all people? Don't you remember, Father? Don't you remember when you were young? You refused an arranged marriage with a woman you didn't love. If you hadn't, you would never have met my mother! You left your family and gave up your home just to have the freedom to determine your own destiny. How can you deny me the same freedom?"

Her words hit home. Sarah could see that her father recognized the tragic irony of the situation. For a moment, he was silent. A desperate, defeated expression dimmed his gaze. Sarah held her breath, hoping. She thought of all the times she had gone against her father's wishes when she was younger, how determined she'd always been to have her own way. And he had indulged her, proud of her high spirit. *We can make peace*, Sarah thought.

But her father's moment of indecision passed. His manner hardened again. "You will cease all communication with Edward Brooke or you will cease living under this roof," he informed Sarah. Turning on his heel, he strode from the room.

In utter dismay, Sarah watched him go. Her father was not going to relent. In his old age, he had become as stubborn and heartless as his own father, the Earl of Wakefield.

The hours passed. Sarah lay on her bed, staring at the ceiling as the last light faded from the sky. In a strange way, she felt relieved. After all these months of deception, her father knew about Edward. She no longer had to hide the truth from him.

Instead she was faced with the choice she'd dreaded for so long. Either she remained her father's daughter and stopped seeing Edward, or she disobeyed her father and . . . and what? Theodore's harsh words echoed in her brain. *You will cease to live under this roof.*

It was late when Sarah finally heard her father's slow, heavy footsteps retreating down the hall to his bedroom. She waited one more hour. Then, when she was sure her father must be asleep, she got to her feet. Quietly, she filled a small bag with a few items of underclothing, a clean shirtwaist, and what little jewelry and money she possessed. Carrying her shoes and coat, she slipped, ghostlike, down the stairs.

In the kitchen, she laced up her boots, shouldered the bag, and eased open the door. The cool, clear April night was bright with stars. Taking a deep breath, she stepped out into it.

The moon sharply illuminated Sarah's figure as she hurried across the yard toward the driveway. With each step, however, she felt her feet grow heavier. She put a hand to her heart; it was racing like a locomotive. Back in her bedroom, she had thought she'd made up her mind. She would run away to Edward. She loved him, truly and deeply; there was nothing else to do. But now, another truth held her in the yard. She didn't really want to leave her home. Though she knew her father was being incredibly unjust, she still loved him.

Pivoting slightly, Sarah looked back over her shoulder at the moonlit house. She caught her breath. There was a pale face at her father's bedroom window. He had seen her! He was going to try to stop her! She should have known. Of course he would never let his only child walk away from him like this. He had come to his senses; he was willing to talk things over in a reasonable fashion. *When he lifts the sash and calls to me, I will go back*, Sarah thought, already imagining their tearful reunion, the affectionate apologies on both sides.

But the window remained tightly closed. After a long moment, the face moved away, leaving nothing but darkness and silence.

Eleven

After an hour of shivering in the chilly April night, Sarah decided to risk waking Edward's parents by throwing pebbles against Edward's bedroom window. A minute later Edward's puzzled and sleepy face appeared, and he threw up the sash. He was obviously surprised to see Sarah standing below.

"Sarah! What—"

"Shh!" She motioned for him to come downstairs.

In a few minutes the front door of the Brookes' house opened and Edward emerged. He shut the door noiselessly and turned to Sarah. A look of concern appeared on his face when he saw her shivering body and forlorn expression. He put his hands on Sarah's shoulders. "Tell me," he said gently. "Tell me what's happened."

Quickly, Sarah related the events that had led up

to her decision to run away: her father discovering and reading her journal, the argument and his ultimatum, her long hours of self-examination. "And so I decided . . . I thought that . . ." Sarah stuttered to a stop. Her cheeks grew pink. Suddenly, she recognized how truly bold her action had been. She had left her father's house and come to offer herself to Edward. What if he wasn't ready? What if . . . what if he didn't want her?

Edward slid his hands from Sarah's shoulders and around her back, folding her close to his broad chest. "You love me that much?" His deep voice shook with emotion.

Lifting her face to his, she nodded. "I do. I do love you that much."

"And I love you, with all my heart." Bending his head, Edward kissed her.

For a long moment, they stood as if melded into one form. Then Edward pulled back slightly. He cleared his throat and smiled at her almost shyly. "Well, you took me by surprise, but I think I can handle it." Taking her hands in his, he got down on one knee. "It looks like we shouldn't waste any more time, Miss Wakefield. Will you do me the honor of becoming my wife?"

Sarah beamed. There was nothing in the world she wanted more. "Yes, Mr. Brooke," she replied with equal formality.

"Hurrah!" Edward declared, jumping to his feet. Grasping her slim waist with his strong hands, he lifted her high in the air. Then he set her on her feet once more and grew practical. "We can't really turn to my parents, either. We've kept them in the dark as well, and they wouldn't approve of a hasty marriage. I say we hop the next train to San Francisco and find a justice of the peace there."

Sarah nodded her consent.

Edward checked his pocket watch. "The first train from Vista to San Francisco doesn't leave until six this morning, but another train heading to San Francisco will pass through the station in about thirty minutes. It doesn't usually stop, but I can try flagging it down. Are you ready?"

Sarah hoisted her bag. "I'm ready!"

After the ten-minute walk to the station, Edward used his keys to open the stationhouse. There he left a note for the stationmaster explaining his sudden departure and enough money for the two one-way tickets he took. Sarah felt a bit like a hobo when Edward succeeded in getting the speeding locomotive, brakes screaming, to stop just long enough for them to clamber on board. They handed over their tickets and collapsed into seats by a window. Suddenly, Sarah was ravenous.

Edward must have read her mind, for he rummaged in his coat pocket and produced a couple of pieces of candy. He grinned ruefully. "Well, this isn't much of a wedding-day breakfast, but it will have to do until we get to San Francisco."

Our wedding-day breakfast. Sarah's eyes misted

with sudden emotion. As distraught as she was over the rupture with her father, this was still the happiest day of her life.

Edward clasped her hands in his. "Sarah, we didn't have much time back there to talk about all of this. Are you sure this is what you want to do? We can always take a train back to Vista."

"No," Sarah said firmly. "This is what I want. I want to be with you."

"I promise to take good care of you," Edward said. "Of course, I would have preferred to have your father's approval, but you'll see." He squeezed her hands. "When he sees how happy we are together, everything will be all right again. Someday you and your father will make peace, Sarah."

"Shh, Edward. Let's just think about how wonderful our life together is going to be."

Edward leaned over and kissed her gently. "We'll always remember this day," he predicted.

"April eighteenth, 1906," Sarah agreed, feeling a sudden thrill. "Our wedding day."

"Let's find a hotel and book a room," Edward suggested as they disembarked from the train in San Francisco. It was around four o'clock in the morning; the sky was still dark, and there were scarcely any people around. "It's too early to find a justice of the peace. We can ride the cable car, and when we see a place we like, hop off."

A little while later, they were seated on the cable

110

car and were headed up an impossibly steep street. As they rattled down the other side of the hill, they got a breathtaking view in the pale predawn light of the sparkling bay and dramatic headlands beyond.

"That's where I want to stay," Sarah exclaimed suddenly, pointing at a quaint three-story hotel.

"Your wish is my command."

Edward asked the driver to stop and then helped Sarah out onto the sidewalk. Together they entered the hotel's lavishly decorated lobby. Sarah's heart pounded and she felt sure her cheeks were stained a guilty red. What would the desk attendant think of an unmarried girl checking into a hotel at dawn with a young man?

But perhaps I already look like a newlywed, Sarah thought, drawing off her gloves. Twisting the ring on her finger, she watched nervously as Edward signed the register *Mr. and Mrs. Edward Brooke.*

Together, she and Edward climbed the wide, carpeted stairs to their room on the third floor. Sarah was about to step through the door when Edward grasped her arm. "Wait." He grinned. "We have to do this properly!" Stooping, he swept Sarah up in his arms. Squealing with laughter, she clasped her arms around his neck. With great ceremony, Edward carried her over the threshold.

"What a lovely room," Sarah said, her eyes taking in every delightful detail. There was a view of the water from the brocade-curtained windows; the

shiny wood floors were scattered with soft rugs;
fresh flowers stood in a vase on the chest of drawers; and on the big four-poster bed, there was a
colorful quilt.

Edward sat down on the edge of the bed. Duck-
ing her head to hide her shyness, Sarah busied herself placing the few personal things she'd brought
with her in one of the drawers. She had to bite her
lip to keep from giggling. Being alone with Edward
like this made her feel incredibly nervous and
giddy. *Soon we will be husband and wife,* she
thought, darting a glance at his handsome profile.
Tonight will be our wedding night!

"The lavatory is down the hall on the right," Edward said, "if you'd like to freshen up. It'll probably
be eight or nine o'clock before any justices of the
peace open their offices."

Sarah stepped up to Edward and held out her
hands to him with a smile. "I can hardly wait."

At that moment, a strange feeling washed over
her. She felt her stomach drop slightly. Looking at
Edward in alarm, she saw that he, too, wore an
uncertain expression. Then she felt the vibrations
through the soles of her boots. The floor was shaking. *It must be an earthquake!* she thought.

Sarah gasped. "It's only a tremor," Edward assured her, pulling her onto the bed beside him.
"There's nothing to fear."

Sarah held her breath, hoping he was right.
Growing up in Vista, both she and Edward had

experienced minor quakes. "Of course," she said, her voice unnaturally high. "It will pass."

But it didn't pass. Instead, the rolling and rumbling increased in intensity. As the horrible shaking went on and on and on, Sarah realized that this was an earthquake of a magnitude she could never have imagined. "My God," Edward exclaimed hoarsely. "The earth must be ripping in two!"

Picture frames were swinging wildly; as Sarah watched in horror the plaster wall behind them began to crumble. The couple embraced fearfully, Sarah hiding her eyes against Edward's chest.

Suddenly, the entire room tipped. The heavy wooden bed, along with the rest of the furniture, slid and crashed to the front end of the room, throwing Edward and Sarah with it. It was like plunging off a cliff. Over the roar of destruction, Sarah heard herself scream. She held on to Edward with all her might. The hotel was collapsing!

As suddenly as it had begun, the quaking stopped. Edward's arms were still tightly wrapped around Sarah, and her face was pressed into his chest. *Am I alive?* she wondered, dazed. Everything was black. "Edward?" She coughed as the dust entered her mouth. "Are you all right?"

When Edward also began coughing, Sarah could have wept with relief. He was alive! They had survived.

But the hotel had fallen into ruins around them.

113

Gingerly, Sarah and Edward got to their hands and knees and felt the space around them. It was tiny. As the dust settled they were able to see their surroundings dimly. The ceiling had fallen in on all but the small corner of the room where they were huddled. Sarah shuddered as she realized how close they had come to being killed. But though they were still alive, they were far from safe. "We've been buried," she whispered. "Buried alive."

Edward took her in his arms again. She knew he couldn't deny that their situation appeared dire. "We'll find a way out," he said without conviction.

"There's no way out. Edward, this cramped, airless space will be our tomb." Sarah began to cry quietly. "I wanted only one thing, to become your wife. And now . . ."

Edward smoothed a hand over her hair. "I love you as much as if you were my wife."

"But I'm not."

"Then let's marry right now! We don't need a justice of the peace in order to vow our eternal love for each other." Gazing deep into Sarah's eyes, Edward said, "Sarah Wakefield, I promise to love and cherish you always, until death do us part."

Overcome with emotion, for a few seconds Sarah could not speak. Then she managed to swallow her tears. "I promise to love and cherish you, Edward Brooke," she whispered. "Until death do us part."

"Here, I'll make it official." Edward fumbled in

his pocket and pulled out a small piece of paper. In the murky light, Sarah could see that it was the receipt the desk clerk had written up for them when they checked into the hotel. Now Edward turned it over. With a pencil, also from his pocket, he wrote a few quick words.

He handed the paper to Sarah, and she read aloud what he had written. " 'On this day, we were married.' " Edward had signed and dated the statement; now she did the same.

"My wife," Edward said.

"My husband."

Their lips met in the most tender, meaningful kiss they had ever shared. Edward pulled Sarah closer, crushing her body against his own. As the kiss deepened, all the passion they'd been harboring during the months of their courtship rushed over them like a powerful wave. "Shall we stop?" Edward murmured in her hair.

"No," Sarah breathed. She wanted to be swept away; she wanted to go as far as their love would take her.

Sarah lay still in Edward's arms. For some reason, she was strangely calm, even though she felt herself growing groggy from lack of oxygen and weak with hunger and thirst. She was facing death, but she was not alone. The long life she and Edward had hoped to share had been stolen from them, but at least they had had this moment. In

God's eyes they were married, and now their union was complete. *Edward and I will be together eternally,* Sarah thought with peaceful certainty.

She felt herself slipping into what she knew might be her final sleep. Suddenly, she was jolted awake by the scraping sound of shifting boards. She clutched Edward. "Is this it?" she cried. "Is the rest of the building collapsing?"

Squeezing her eyes shut, Sarah waited for her body to be crushed. Instead, there was a sudden flash of torchlight. Rough hands grasped her arms; urgent voices inquired if she was all right. They had been unearthed by rescuers!

The men, their faces streaked black with dirt and sweat, dragged Edward and Sarah free from the rubble, then hustled them across the street to the relative safety of a small park at some distance from the crumbling buildings. Sarah and Edward blinked at each other, still in a state of shock, and then stared back at the ruins of their hotel. Sarah hugged herself to keep from shaking. *I'm alive,* she thought in disbelief. *I'm alive!*

Edward put his arm around Sarah's trembling shoulders. "It's a miracle."

"It's a nightmare," she said.

Both were right. By great fortune, they had escaped with their lives, but while they had been trapped, the world had changed horribly. Stately buildings now lay in ruins; screaming people ran in the streets, dodging recklessly careening vehicles;

116

fires raged; alarm bells clanged; smoke and dust choked the air.

"I must go help the men who rescued us," Edward announced. "Who knows how many people are still buried alive, as we were?"

"No!" Sarah clutched his sleeve. "Please don't leave me."

Edward brushed her cheek with the back of his hand. "I must. I'll be back with you as soon as I can. Wait here."

Helplessly, Sarah watched as Edward ran back to the ruins of their hotel to join the rescue effort. Of course he had to go, she realized. He could not stand by and do nothing when the cries of the injured and imprisoned could still be heard. But selfishly, she wished he could stay with her. She was still trembling from her brush with death; she needed the support of his strong arms.

Her eyes followed the form of her husband as he conferred with the other men on how best to proceed. Suddenly, above the other sounds of the devastated city, the wail of a child pierced the air. It was coming from the ruined hotel! Her heart in her throat, Sarah watched as a man—her Edward!—climbed a pile of rubble, seeking the source of the cry, then disappeared through a window opening. *How can he possibly hope to find a tiny baby in all that wreckage?* Sarah wondered. She clenched her hands in tight fists, her fingernails digging into her palms. She counted the seconds in her head; they seemed to drag on like hours.

But in truth, only a minute passed before Edward reappeared on a high ledge, the child in his arms. "He did it!" Sarah shouted, pride and relief flooding her, making her knees go weak. She saw Edward wave in her direction even as he acknowledged the triumphant cheers of the other rescuers, and she lifted a hand to blow him a kiss.

Edward turned to find an easier means of descent. At that instant, the ground beneath Sarah's feet began to rumble. *No. Not again!* she thought in horror. But the quaking had resumed. It was an aftershock!

The rolling earth threw Sarah to her knees, and it hurled Edward and the child from the ledge. Heedless of her own safety, Sarah scrambled to her feet and ran across the street toward the ruined hotel, her mouth wide in an agonized scream. "Edward!"

He lay on his back on the hard, buckled stone of the sidewalk, the baby clutched to his chest. The baby was crying; miraculously, it was alive and unhurt! But Edward himself was motionless, his eyes wide and staring.

Sarah fell to the ground and clasped his head in her arms. "Speak to me," she begged. "Oh, Edward, please, please . . ."

One of the rescuers reached past her and put his hand on Edward's throat to check the pulse. Sarah heard the man's voice, but tried to push it away from her. "Dead," the man said to the others standing by.

"No!" Sarah cried. "No. He can't be. He's my husband. We were just married. Don't take him away from me!"

Holding the baby, Sarah sobbed hysterically as the men lifted Edward's limp body onto a stretcher and carried it to a wagon that was serving as a makeshift ambulance. She stared after the wagon, barely noticing when the child's mother, crying with joy and relief, snatched the baby away from her.

The wagon rumbled away along the ruined road, disappearing into the whirl of smoke and flames. Now empty, Sarah's arms fell limply to her sides. "My husband. Don't take him away from me." She whispered the words over and over as she stood, devastated and alone, in what felt like the end of the world.

Twelve

Two days after the earthquake, Sarah walked slowly up the drive to Manor Farm. She felt about a hundred years old. Had it been only forty-eight hours since her world had turned upside down?

Hours after Edward's death, she had collected her wits enough to find the hospital to which his body had been carried, and then she had gotten a message to his parents. Stunned by their sudden and unexpected loss, Mr. and Mrs. Brooke had hurried to the ravaged city to bring their son's body home for burial. They had brought Sarah back with them on the train, and despite their shock and distress, they were sympathetic when she told them the story of her and Edward's elopement. Of course, it wasn't the real story, the whole story; Sarah had said that her father disapproved of her

120

friendship with Edward simply because he felt she was too young for a suitor.

And no one need ever know that we weren't actually married by a justice of the peace, Sarah thought as she unlatched the gate. If only for the briefest, most poignant of moments, in spirit she and Edward truly *had* been husband and wife. By now, news of her elopement and Edward's death would have reached Manor Farm; in the small town of Vista, word traveled fast. *Will Father be angry?* Sarah wondered listlessly. *Will he order me off his land?* She really couldn't predict how he would receive her. She wasn't sure if he would forgive her for her past actions, and now Sarah realized that she didn't even care. All she wanted to do was climb the creaky stairs to her bedroom, lay her head on her old familiar feather pillow, and fall asleep forever.

Her father was in the yard, hammering a new board into place on the front steps. He had his back to the drive and did not notice Sarah's presence immediately. As she stood for a moment, watching him work, Sarah was overcome by a wave of emotion. Suddenly, she felt seventeen again instead of a hundred, frightened from her recent brush with death, bewildered at the chain of events that had brought her complete love and then utter loss in the course of an hour. She felt like a little girl, and she longed for nothing more than for her father to fold her in his arms and tell her everything would be fine, as he had countless times in the past when she was hurt or sad.

At that moment, he turned. Tears streaming down her face, Sarah hesitated. She couldn't take another step, not knowing whether or not he would accept her.

She didn't need to. Her father went to her. Striding across the yard, his own eyes damp, he embraced his weeping daughter. "When I heard that you were seen boarding the train to San Francisco, and then the earthquake hit and we learned of the destruction in the city, I thought . . . I feared . . ." His voice cracked.

"I'm here, Father," Sarah sobbed. "And I'm sorry. I'm sorry I ran away. If I hadn't, Edward would still be alive."

"Shh." Theodore stroked her hair. "You mustn't blame yourself. There was nothing you could do."

They stood together for a long moment, Theodore rocking Sarah in his arms as if she were a child. Sarah recalled that she'd comforted her father when he felt responsible for James's death; now it was his turn to ease her pain. "Can you . . . can you forgive me for running off to get married?"

"Of course, my dear. We must put the past behind us. I am still your father and you are still my daughter—my only child."

"You are all I have." Sarah closed her eyes against the memory of Edward's plain pine coffin being carried off the train at the Vista station.

"And I will always be here for you," Theodore told her. "You are home, Sarah, and you are safe here. Come inside."

Together, they walked up the stairs into the house. *I am home,* Sarah thought with a rush of gratitude. *And I'll never have to leave again.*

Sarah sat up abruptly in bed, her eyes wide with fright and her nightgown damp with sweat despite the cool June breeze wafting through the open bedroom window. For a long moment she sat, hugging herself and panting breathlessly. Gradually, her body relaxed. She grew sure of her surroundings; she was safe in bed in the room she'd slept in since childhood, with the comforting sun streaming in upon her. *I'm not in San Francisco. There is no earthquake. The earthquake is in the past,* Sarah told herself, falling weakly back against the pillows.

How many more mornings will begin this way? she wondered as she tried to summon the strength to rise and dress herself. It was tempting to lie in bed all morning. After all, school was out—she had graduated the previous week—and her father, worried about her health, would already have performed her household chores. But if she stayed in bed, she risked falling asleep and reentering the recurrent nightmare that had haunted her since her return to Manor Farm.

Sarah squeezed her eyes shut, hoping to force the dream images from her mind. Shuddering, she climbed out of bed. She dressed listlessly and then made her way to the staircase. Halfway down she had to pause, gripping the banister, to fight off a wave of nausea and dizziness. It was to be expected, she thought; lately, she had been sleeping little and eating even less.

She found her father waiting for her in the kitchen. He had cooked a big breakfast, hoping, she knew, to tempt her appetite. Instead, the odor of fried eggs and ham made her stomach turn. But she smiled wanly, lifting her face to his so he could press a good-morning kiss on her cheek.

Theodore put a hand under Sarah's chin, turning her face so he could study it. "You slept poorly again," he guessed, his brow creased with concern.

"I tossed and turned a bit," Sarah admitted, her tone as light as she could manage. "But I do feel better." She took a seat at the table.

Her father placed a plate of steaming eggs and ham and crusty homemade bread in front of her. Sarah tore off a bit of bread and dipped it experimentally in the egg yolk. She wanted to force down a few bites, just to please her father. But the instant the food touched her lips, she knew she could not swallow it. Dropping the bread, she jumped up from the table and ran to the side door.

A minute later she returned, her face pale. Her father had not tasted his breakfast, either, and now he peered at her anxiously. "You're sick," he pronounced. "It's time to take you to Dr. Daly."

Despite Sarah's feeble protests, her father soon had her settled in the buggy, a light blanket tucked over her skirt. A short drive brought them to Dr. Daly's office, on the first floor of his little frame house in town.

"It's nothing, really," she told Dr. Daly as he closed the door to the examining room behind them. "I've been having nightmares and not sleeping well, and as a result I don't have much of an appetite."

"Your father may be overreacting," Dr. Daly agreed. "I know that since James's death he's felt particularly protective of you. But there may be something amiss, and it's always better to be safe than sorry."

In a matter-of-fact manner he proceeded to ask Sarah a number of questions, a few of which were so personal they made her blush. Then he examined her briefly. Finally, he sat back, looking at her with an odd expression. "My dear, I hope this will be happy as well as surprising news."

Sarah sat forward on her own chair, her heart beating fast from a sudden intuition. "Is there . . . am I . . . ?"

"You are expecting." Dr. Daly smiled kindly. "You have suffered a terrible loss, my dear. But now—what a comfort it will be to have a child to remember your late husband by!"

Sarah was frozen in her seat. She gulped,

momentarily unable to speak. *My late husband.* "Yes," she whispered. "What a comfort."

"Come see me again soon," the doctor instructed as he ushered her back into the parlor that served as his waiting room, "and we can talk about what to expect over the next months. In the meantime, make sure you get some nourishment. Your appetite will soon be back to normal, I promise."

Theodore had risen to his feet, and now Dr. Daly tactfully left them alone. Sarah's hands clenched into tight fists. *What am I going to tell him?* she wondered. As they walked out to the buggy Sarah realized she had to tell him the truth.

"Well?" Theodore helped his daughter into the buggy. "What is the doctor's diagnosis?"

Sarah waited until the horse was trotting briskly down the street. Then she took a deep breath and blurted out, "The doctor says that I am expecting a child."

Theodore's thick eyebrows shot up. Sarah watched him apprehensively. To her surprise, a smile gradually spread across his craggy face. "A child. A grandchild! Another Wakefield. Of course, it will be named Brooke after its father, but it will be a Wakefield all the same, eh, Sarah? I hope your marriage license was not lost in the earthquake. We'll need it when we register the baby's birth."

Sarah bit her lip. *He doesn't need to know. No one needs to know. It will be better that way. I will say the license was lost.* But even as these thoughts tempted her Sarah knew she couldn't lie to her father this time. She couldn't live with such a lie for the rest of her life. She was an adult; she must take responsibility for her own actions.

Sarah took another deep breath. "Its name will not be Brooke," she said quietly. "Edward and I . . . he gave me the ring I wear long before we went to San Francisco. We wrote our vows on a scrap of paper, but there was no legal marriage."

"No marriage?" They had passed the town limits and were on the drive leading to Manor Farm. Now Theodore reined in the horse and whipped his head around to stare at his daughter. "No marriage?"

Sarah shook her head, trying her best to appear calm and unafraid. "No *legal* marriage. The earthquake came before we could visit the justice of the peace."

"But in the meantime you were carrying on as husband and wife," Theodore roared.

"We were not carrying on! We behaved with propriety at all times—"

"You were sneaking around behind my back." Theodore's eyes flashed with fury. "Does the entire town know about your behavior?"

Sarah's cheeks flushed hot with anger. "Father, there was nothing to know. Nothing happened between us until we went to San Francisco. We may not have been married on paper, but we were married in spirit."

"In spirit," her father scoffed. "The words are meaningless. The child you carry has no father, no name."

"Edward is its father," Sarah cried, "and I will name it whatever I want. What does it matter what it's named?"

"It is not entitled to the name of Brooke and neither will it possess that of Wakefield," Theodore declared coldly.

He snapped the whip, urging the horse into a canter. His final words echoed in Sarah's head as they drove the rest of the way home in ominous silence.

Theodore did not speak to Sarah for two days. Then, as she took a pie from the oven early one evening, he came in from the yard. "Leave that," he commanded. "Go upstairs and pack your bags."

Sarah set the pie on the windowsill. "Pack my bags?"

"You heard me. Pack everything you will need for the next seven months."

Seven months . . . until the baby is born, Sarah calculated. Bewildered, she hurried upstairs. At random, she threw garments, shoes, books, and jewelry into two large satchels. Then she tied on a wide-brimmed hat trimmed with blue ribbons and presented herself before her father in the kitchen. "The horse is hitched up," he told her. "Let's go."

The sun was setting as they neared town. Not far

from the train station, the buggy came to a stop. Theodore bent to retrieve a package, which he placed on Sarah's lap. "There is enough food there for dinner and breakfast, and money to provide for all your needs. And here is a train ticket to Mendocino."

"Mendocino?" Sarah's face grew pale.

Her father nodded curtly. "When you arrive there, you will go to Mrs. Clark's boardinghouse two blocks north of the station. She is expecting a young widow by the name of Sarah Brooke. Mrs. Clark will give you the keys to the house I've rented for you. There is a physician in town, Dr. Schmidt, and he will attend you when your time comes. If you need more money, you may telegraph me and I will send it."

"You're sending me away." Sarah's voice was small and choked with tears.

"I've requested Dr. Daly's silence and cooperation in this matter," her father continued, ignoring her. "I will tell our acquaintances that you have gone away for your health, to cure the nerves that were shattered by the earthquake. No one will know of the illegitimate birth."

Theodore helped Sarah from the buggy but did not move to hug or kiss her. Sarah stood silently, a bag in each hand. Her father's speech left no room for questions or protests.

A few minutes later, she was seated once again on a train. But this time she was heading north up the coast to the isolated town of Mendocino . . . and she was alone.

Sarah knew it would be easy to crumble, to let her shoulders sag, to collapse into tears of self-pity. In the past few months she had undergone a lifetime's worth of tragedy. And her troubles weren't over yet! But her father wasn't the only one who could be strong. *I won't give in,* Sarah promised herself, lifting her chin. *I won't cry. I might not know what the future holds, but I'll be ready for it. After all, I'm a Wakefield, too!*

Thirteen

1907. Mendocino, California.

"That's enough breakfast for you, Teddy," Sarah told her baby. Then she lifted little Edward above her head, laughing at his attempt at a smile. "What a big boy you're getting to be!"

Holding Teddy against her shoulder, Sarah paced the parlor of the small rented house on the cliffs where she had been living for more than seven months. She patted Teddy's back lightly until he emitted a tiny burp. Then she returned to her seat in the rocking chair by the back window.

The front of the house looked out on the main street of the quaint little coastal town. In back, a small yard quickly gave way to a steep, rocky cliff. Sarah had spent many an afternoon during the course of her pregnancy strolling along the cliffs, a heavy wool shawl wrapped around her, contemplating her situation to the sound of the crashing

131

waves below. She had made few acquaintances in town, thinking it best that she keep to herself. Dr. Schmidt, the sweet elderly man who had delivered Sarah's healthy baby boy after an uneventful labor, could not have been kinder.

Remembering Dr. Schmidt's beaming face as he had placed the newborn in her eager arms, Sarah sighed. He had looked as proud as a grandfather. *My own father should have been with me,* Sarah thought.

"But he will arrive soon," Sarah whispered to the baby, who had fallen asleep in her arms. "And when he sees you, he will love you as much as I do. He will take us home and we will be a family, the three of us."

Her father's last words to her at the Vista train station had been a promise to come for her after the birth of the baby. Accordingly, Sarah wrote to him with the news as soon as Edward was born on New Year's Day, 1907. She and her father had had no other communication while she'd been away, so Sarah was free to imagine—to hope—that he had undergone a change of heart. She was certain her father would not be able to remain cold and stony when he held Teddy in his arms, especially when he saw how much the baby looked like him.

It was a beautiful winter morning, windy and fresh, with dramatic white clouds skidding across a cornflower-blue sky. Sarah bundled herself into a wool cloak, wrapped Teddy in a soft, thick blanket, and stepped out the back door into the yard. The air was bracing, and she took deep breaths of it, enjoying how light and strong she felt after so many months of being heavy and slow.

After walking along the cliffs for twenty minutes, both her cheeks and little Edward's were rosy, and Sarah turned to head back. As they neared the house Sarah saw a tall figure in a dark overcoat and striped muffler standing in the yard, his hands clasped behind his back and his gaze turned out to sea. Her heart, which had been pumping vigorously, seemed to stop beating for an instant. She knew that broad stern back, the sweep of dark hair dusted with gray. . . .

Her eyes bright with a painful mixture of anxiety and hope, Sarah approached her father. Theodore's own eyes grew soft as they rested on his daughter, but he did not smile. His hands remained clasped behind his back as he bent forward to kiss her forehead. He did not move to touch the baby, and Sarah, who'd been about to offer the child for her father's inspection, held Teddy close.

"You look well," her father observed.

"I feel well," she replied. "I had an easy time, and Teddy is perfectly healthy, thank goodness."

"Teddy." The beginnings of a pleased smile touched the corners of Theodore's mouth.

"Yes, Teddy. I've named him Edward Wakefield."

Sarah feared her father would be disappointed

133

that Teddy was short for Edward rather than for Theodore. She was right. Instead of smiling, Theodore gave the baby a quick, cool appraisal, then turned away, avoiding her eyes. "I've come to take you home, Sarah."

Sarah's heart flooded with gratitude. Because her father was a proud man, he was going to maintain his pose of distance and disapproval. *But really,* she thought, *he loves us. He wants us back!* "I'm so glad! It will only take me a minute to pack our things—"

"You don't understand." Theodore paused to clear his throat. "I've come to take *you* home. You alone."

Sarah was confused. "But the baby . . ."

"The baby must be left behind. He can be put up for adoption. We will find another home for him."

Sarah stared at her father in shock and disbelief. His tone was as calm as if he were discussing whether he'd prefer cherry or peach pie for Sunday dinner. She clutched the swaddled infant closer to her. "Never!" she cried.

"Sarah, you know the story I told in town," her father reminded her. "You went away for your health. You simply cannot return to Vista with a child."

"Then I will not return at all," she declared.

"If that's the way you wish it." Theodore's jaw tightened. "You will not return to Manor Farm now, or ever. I will see that you are cared for, however, as long as you take up residence far from Vista."

She was being banished! The incredible realization hit Sarah like a spray of icy ocean water. Unwittingly, she echoed the defiant words Theodore had spoken to his own father many decades earlier. "If you won't recognize your own daughter and grandchild, I don't want your money," Sarah declared, tossing her hair back.

Theodore was startled. For a long moment, he stared back at his willful daughter. They were so much alike. Too much alike, perhaps. There was no way he could bring himself to give in and accept her and her child, just as there was no way she could give up her baby.

Theodore turned away from Sarah. Sarah couldn't tell whether there were tears in his eyes, and as her father strode off, disappearing around the house without a backward glance, she realized that she would never know. Standing alone on the cliffs, Sarah succumbed to tears herself. She would never again see her father or the home where she had been raised.

She pressed her face against little Teddy's plump, downy cheek. It wouldn't be easy, she knew, but somehow she would make a home for her son, even though she was only eighteen, alone in the world with a child and no husband.

But how will Teddy feel, she thought suddenly,

when he grows up and realizes he has no father, that his parents were never even married? Sarah had been so busy worrying about her own situation that she hadn't stopped to consider what the consequences of illegitimacy would be for her son. The other children would find out, and their parents would forbid them to play with him. Teddy would be ashamed—of her, and of himself.

As Sarah gazed deep into her baby's eyes, she realized what she must do. She must make a sacrifice, very different from the one her father had proposed, but in its own way no less difficult.

Teddy would never know he was illegitimate. She would raise him to believe that she was his aunt, that his real parents were dead, killed in an accident. "I'm not your mother," Sarah whispered to the baby, practicing the painful words. "I'm your aunt."

She sobbed. As if in sympathy, Teddy scrunched up his face and began to cry. Hushing him, Sarah walked toward the house. It would be hard, but there was no alternative.

"I'll provide for you and protect you," Sarah told the baby, lifting her chin and silently commanding herself to be strong. "And you will never know that I am your real mother."

Fourteen

1924. Chicago.

Seventeen-year-old Ted Wakefield burst through
the side door into the first-floor apartment of the
white frame house in the Lincoln Park section of
town. He found his aunt sitting at the kitchen table
with her stockinged feet up on a chair; she'd kicked
off her high heels and tossed aside her brimless
summer hat.

Ted dropped the bag holding his schoolbooks
and tennis racket on the table and straddled a chair
facing her. "Another long day at the office, huh,
Aunt Sarah?"

For a number of years, his aunt had worked as a
clerk-typist for the Chicago district attorney. The
D.A. was busier than ever since the onset of Prohibition. "The usual," Sarah said, unpinning the thick
coil of dark blond hair from the nape of her neck
and shaking it loose. "I was just thinking how

happy I am that the days of corsets are past!" She patted the loosely belted waist of her cotton dress. "If you ask me, the new fashions have done as much to improve women's status as getting the vote did a few years ago."

Ted laughed. "Here." He handed her some envelopes. "I ran into the postman on my way in."

Sarah flipped through the mail. "Nothing but bills," she observed with a sigh.

A pang of guilt stabbed Ted's heart. His aunt never complained, but he knew it wasn't easy for her to make ends meet. In the aftermath of the Great War, the country was prospering and she had a secure job; the two of them lived comfortably. But despite her frugality, Ted knew she was never able to put much aside in the bank account she'd started so he could go to college. *She's done so much for me,* Ted thought. Not that she ever drew attention to the sacrifices she'd made. But he knew the whole story: his parents, James and Edwina Wakefield, had been killed in a train crash in California shortly after his birth, and his young aunt, only in her late teens and herself recently orphaned by the death of her own father, had decided to raise her beloved older brother's child as her own.

Someday I'll pay her back, Ted thought. *I'll have money and I'll give her everything she's ever wanted.* He couldn't keep the news to himself a moment longer. "Guess what, Aunt Sarah? I've gotten another job!"

"Another job? What about the paper route?"

"I'm keeping the route," he replied, "but that's just nickel-and-dime stuff—it'll never pay for college. I found something else that starts next week, right after I graduate. I'm going to be a waiter at a jazz club, the Black Cat Café. They say the tips are swell!"

"I bet they are." Sarah frowned slightly. "I don't know, Teddy. Perhaps you shouldn't work at a place like that. My boss was telling me just today that he might have some overtime work for me. With a few extra dollars a week—"

"I won't allow you to work overtime just to make things easier for me," Ted declared. "You work long hours as it is."

"But Ted, those jazz clubs . . ."

Ted knew what she was thinking. She'd never been to one, but obviously she'd heard they were only a step up from the speakeasies spawned by Prohibition. "Everything at the Black Cat is on the up-and-up," he assured her. "And all the best musicians play there. Think of the swell folks I'll meet!"

Sarah smiled despite herself. "Swell folks? Gangsters and bootleggers are more like it."

Ted took her hand in his. "I promise you I won't get in any trouble." To his surprise, tears sprang suddenly to his aunt's eyes. "But if it upsets you that much, Aunt Sarah, I won't take the job."

She shook her head, wiping away the tears with a rueful laugh. "Oh, it's not that, Teddy. I was just thinking how much you resemble your gr—I mean your father, James. Now that you're grown, you're his very image." She'd told him before that he was built like his father, tall and broad-shouldered, and that he'd inherited his father's mischievous brown eyes and unruly dark hair. "And that's what I have to keep in mind," Sarah continued. "You're grown up now. I respect your decisions, and what's more, I trust your good sense. I just hope you don't turn into a complete lounge lizard and forget all about your college plans!"

His aunt's tone was teasing, but he knew she was set on his becoming the first Wakefield to earn a college degree and go on to a prestigious career, maybe even as a lawyer like her boss. "That won't happen," Ted vowed.

"Get on with you, then," she commanded, her eyes twinkling. "Open those books before I change my mind!"

It was a hot summer Saturday night at the Black Cat Café. Balancing a tray of soft drinks and near-beer in each hand, Ted deftly wove his way among the closely packed tables. The air of the club was cloudy with cigarette smoke and pulsing with the cool, smooth sounds of a jazz quartet. Ted delivered the drinks and pocketed the generous tip casually handed to him by a man in a cream-colored suit and diamond cuff links. Heading back to the bar, Ted scanned the crowd. In their clinging silk gowns, feather boas, sequined turbans, and glittering beads, the women were as bright as tropical birds. The whole scene was like a moving picture, but with sound and color. Ted absolutely loved it. And he was actually getting paid to hang out here!

He delivered another round of soft drinks, turning a blind eye as the patrons spiked the drinks with liquor from their hip flasks. His aunt wouldn't approve, but Ted knew there probably wasn't a nightclub in Chicago where this sort of activity didn't go on, and the clientele at the Black Cat was classier and more discreet than most.

Suddenly, a reverent hush fell over the audience. Ted stood quietly, too, the empty tray held behind his back, his eyes half closed. Emmet "Slim" Stark, one of the greatest jazz saxophonists of the age, was playing a solo.

The deep, plaintive notes of the saxophone resounded through the small room. As the solo concluded with a long, drawn-out wail, the crowd roared with appreciation. Ted clapped and whistled. In just a few weeks, he had learned a lot about jazz—enough to know he was hearing the very best at that moment.

A few minutes later, the musicians put down their instruments and stepped off the small stage for a break. Ted rushed over to their table with a tray loaded with glasses. "Compliments of the house," he said, smiling at Slim Stark. Resting the tray on the table, he put out his hand. "That was a great set, sir."

Stark's coffee-colored face, gleaming from exertion, cracked into a smile. "Thanks for the compliment and the refreshments," he said, his voice as deep and melodious as that of his sax. He struck a match on the tabletop and lit a cigarette. "I hope you're a music critic as well as a waiter."

The other band members chuckled; Ted laughed as well. "No, I'm just an ordinary fan." Ted started to pull up a chair. He talked to the musicians who played at the Black Cat every chance he got, and he was dying to ask a virtuoso like Stark a few questions about his technique. But just then, a customer at an adjacent table raised his hand and snapped his fingers for service. Ted couldn't neglect his job.

By the time he returned to Stark's table, the band was back onstage and the table was empty except for a young woman whom Ted hadn't noticed previously. She had glossy black hair smoothed back into a knot adorned with feathers; her red sequined dress was slit at the side, exposing slim, crossed ankles and gold-buckled high heels.

"Can I get you something?" Ted offered.

"I'm not sure," the girl said. "Why don't you sit down while I think about it?"

Ted took a chair. "How do you like the music?"

She smiled. "It's swell. My dad's the bee's knees, don't you think?"

"Your dad?"

She nodded toward the stage, then held out one slender hand. "Tina Stark. Pleased to meet you."

Ted pumped her hand. "Ted Wakefield. Pleased to meet *you*!"

Tina's eyes crinkled in a laugh. "I thought you would be. Stick around and I'll make sure you get a chance to talk to him all you want after the show. Care to dance?"

His head spinning, Ted took Tina's hand and led her to an open space on the floor. They did the Charleston, Ted spinning Tina, then dipping her low. Tina kicked up her foot, laughing breathlessly. "You can really cut a rug, Ted Wakefield!"

"That's why they hired me," he joked.

Now they danced side by side, crossing and uncrossing their hands over their knees. "I'll have to make sure my dad books at the Black Cat more often," Tina said. "The waiters at the other clubs aren't nearly as much fun!"

As usual, Ted worked late that night, but the hours flew by like minutes. Whenever he was caught up on his drink orders, he talked to Tina. He told her about high school, where he'd been an editor and reporter for the student newspaper, and of his plans to attend college. In turn, he discovered that Tina was training to be a jazz singer. "Music is in my bones," she said. "I eat it, sleep it, breathe it. When *I* finish school next year, I want to travel and perform with my father."

"Gosh, are you lucky. I'd give anything to be inside the jazz scene the way you are."

"But you are inside it! You work at the spiffiest club in town. And you know how to talk to people."

Ted supposed Tina had a point. One thing was for sure: he'd been bitten by the music bug. "Ever since I first came to the Black Cat, jazz fills my head constantly, even when I'm not on the job," he confessed. "Maybe that's because jazz isn't just music—it's a way of life. It's free and daring and forward-reaching. It's the soul of the twentieth century."

Tina sat forward, her elbows on the table and her eyes sparkling with admiration. "You talk like a poet. Have you ever thought about writing about all this?"

"I'm no F. Scott Fitzgerald," Ted said modestly. "I just wrote for my high-school paper. I'm not a real reporter."

"You could be a real reporter if you submitted something to a real newspaper," Tina reasoned. "How about the *Chicago Post*?"

Ted laughed at the thought. "Like I told your father, I'm a fan, not a music critic."

"You wouldn't actually have to critique the music. That type of article is for the people in the business. You could write for the rest of the world. Write about the music the way you talk about it."

Tina gave Ted's hand a friendly, encouraging squeeze. "Don't sell yourself short. You could be great."

As Ted gazed into Tina's earnest eyes he felt his soul fill with sudden inspiration. She was right. He shouldn't sell himself short. He had never considered himself anything more than a mediocre journalist during his days on the school paper, but maybe that was because he hadn't found his true subject. "I'll try it!" he exclaimed.

Ted phoned Tina even before sharing the news with his aunt. "Hello, Ted!" she said, sounding pleased but not surprised to hear his voice.

The two had become good friends. They saw each other every night; when Ted was working at the Black Cat, Tina often spent the evening there, and when he was free, he sometimes accompanied her to other clubs to hear her father play. Wherever they went together, they were escorted to the best table in the house. Tina seemed to take pleasure in introducing Ted to the many famous musicians she knew through her father. She told Ted that in his company, she felt as if she were experiencing the jazz scene, so familiar to her, for the first time.

"What's up?" she asked him now.

"Can you meet me in front of the Art Institute in half an hour?"

"I was just about to start dinner—"

"Forget about cooking," Ted declared. "I have something to show you, and after I do, I'm going to take you out for the best dinner in town!"

"Something to show me? What is it?"

Ted grinned. He had her guessing now! "Show up at the museum in half an hour and you'll find out," he teased. "See you then."

It was dusk when Tina stepped out of the cab in front of the massive Art Institute. Ted was waiting for her by one of the lion statues that flanked the broad cement steps. He had his hands in the pockets of his pinstriped trousers; some papers were tucked under his arm.

"OK, I'm here," Tina greeted him. "What do you have to show me?"

With a flourish, Ted handed her a typeset sheet. He held his breath as she scanned it quickly. "'Backstage at the Black Cat,'" Tina read aloud. "'By Ted Wakefield, guest columnist.'" She looked up at him, her eyes wide. "Ted Wakefield, guest columnist? Is this what I think it is?"

He nodded, grinning. "My first newspaper article! And this is only the beginning. The editor at the *Post* liked this piece so much he's considering signing me to write a weekly jazz column!"

"A weekly column," Tina breathed. "Ted, that's wonderful!"

It was a dream come true, Ted had to agree. He was going to be a published writer! "To top it all off, I'll be getting paid, and paid well," he told

Tina. "I won't need to wait tables and deliver papers anymore."

"Then you'll definitely make it to college," said Tina. "Nothing stands in your way now!"

"You're not kidding," Ted agreed.

Fifteen

Ted strolled down the sidewalk, his hat tipped back on his head and his loosely knotted necktie flipped over one shoulder. It was a steamy, breathless late August evening, but he felt cool and light in the new, baggy summer-weight suit he'd bought just that day. It was a bit of a splurge, but he'd rationalized that he needed some new duds for the job. A newspaper columnist, especially one who covered the jazz scene, needed to make a stylish appearance. And besides, he'd be able to impress the girls with his fancy clothes when he went to college in a few weeks.

Ted knew he looked conspicuous, grinning from ear to ear. But for him, life couldn't be better. His guest column had turned into an almost weekly column and was a big success. *Yep, I'm making a name for myself,* Ted thought with satisfaction, lifting the oversized bouquet of roses he was taking to Tina and sniffing their sweet, expensive scent.

Ted allowed his eyes to be pleasantly dazzled by the neon lights of a motion-picture marquee. Having quit his paper route and table-waiting job, he was as free as a bird. On a typical day, he slept until noon and then spent the summer night wandering from one jazz club to another, usually with Tina and his other new musician friends. It wasn't going to be easy to give up such a swell routine and return to the books.

Ted approached the Uptown Lounge, where Emmet Stark and his band were booked for a few nights, straightening his hat and tightening his tie. He gave his name to the burly bouncer at the door, then made his way to the front table where Tina was sitting. There was a roll of drums and the scream of a trumpet as the band finished up a number. Ted contributed to the riot of applause. Then he blinked in surprise as Stark stepped to the front of the stage and held out a hand to his daughter. "For the next number," the sax player rumbled into the microphone, "we're going to get some help from a very special guest."

Tina grasped the microphone her father handed her. Smoke swirled around her slim, sparkling, swaying form as the band began playing. After a few beats, Tina's voice, rich and velvety, melted into the quartet's soft, sensuous sound.

It was a torchy tune, and Ted was spellbound.

He'd never heard Tina sing before. She was wonderful! All around him, faces wore the same rapt expression. *This music is transforming,* Ted thought, wondering if he could possibly describe the voice—the faces—the magic of this moment on paper for his next column.

Tina finished, her voice lingering long on one last, delicious note. The crowd at the lounge leaped to their feet, applauding and whistling furiously. Tina returned the microphone to her father and left the stage. "That was fabulous, Tina!" Ted exclaimed when she was back at their table. "You're better than Bessie Smith."

Tina's eyes sparkled with pleasure. "You really think so?"

"Of course," Ted declared. "I wouldn't say it if it weren't true."

"I'm going to miss you when you start college," Tina said. "I won't have anybody around to flatter me."

As Ted tapped his feet to the sound of Slim Stark and the band, he took in Tina's words. Suddenly, the idea of college grew fuzzier and fainter in Ted's mind, retreating into the distance until it was just a tiny, dim dot. He knew that his aunt hoped he would study law and become a famous attorney. But Ted could hardly imagine anything more boring, especially compared with the excitement of his current life. He made up his mind. He wouldn't go to college, even though he'd been accepted at

Rosse College, one of the most prestigious schools in the Midwest. Why bother? Why just study life when he could live it?

On Saturday, Ted strolled into the kitchen in baggy trousers and with his shirttails untucked. Lifting his arms over his head, he stretched and yawned. "What's for breakfast?" he asked his aunt.

She looked up from her newspaper and laughed. "Breakfast? I just ate my lunch! You must have had another late night."

Ted poured himself a cup of coffee. "I guess we're just running by different clocks these days."

"I know," she said. "I feel as if I never see you anymore."

There was no blame in her voice, only regret. Still, Ted felt guilty. It occurred to him that his aunt might be lonely. They used to eat breakfast and dinner together, and often in the evenings they would listen to the radio and talk. Since Ted had started writing for the *Post*, however, their paths rarely crossed. Sarah was already at work when Ted woke up, and in bed by the time he got home from the clubs.

"But now that you're up, you have to open this letter before another minute passes," Sarah said, animated again. "The postman brought it this morning. It's from Rosse College!"

Ted didn't comment. Finally, his complete lack

of enthusiasm registered on Sarah. "Ted, aren't you excited about starting college?"

"I'm just not sure I want to go to Ohio," Ted said, wishing he didn't have to have this conversation with his aunt. "I like Chicago."

"I know Rosse is a small town. But it's only half an hour by car from Cleveland, so it can't be totally provincial," Sarah pointed out. "And the journalism department is very strong, so you—"

"I know all that," Ted said abruptly. "It's not just Rosse. I don't want to go to college, period."

"Not go? But Ted! We've planned this for so long. And with the money I've saved and what you've earned, you can go in style. Nothing stands in your way now."

"I'm not worried about money. I can make as much as I need writing for the *Post*."

Sarah looked down into her half-empty cup. "I think it's grand that you've done so well with the *Post* this summer. You're a good writer. But just think how much you could grow by attending college. It would be a whole new world."

"I like the world I'm living in just fine," Ted said stubbornly.

"You'll never know what you're missing by limiting your options this way," she argued. "You may never have another chance like this!"

Ted tossed his coffee into the sink with an angry gesture. "They're my options," he snapped, "and

I'll do what I want with them. I wish you wouldn't try to tell me what to do. You're not my mother!"

Even as he spoke, Ted regretted his selfish, childish words. They were so unfair. The fact was that his aunt had been both mother and father to him. She'd worked for him, cooked and cleaned and sewed for him, taught him how to read and write his ABC's, and how to throw a baseball. She'd dedicated her life to ensuring his well-being. *But maybe that's partly why we're fighting like this*, he thought.

Sarah's usually rosy cheeks had gone pale. "I'm sorry, Aunt Sarah," Ted said gruffly. "But you can't live my life for me. And I can't live yours for you."

When she didn't reply, he took the letter from Rosse and turned away. He didn't want to see her cry.

It was late when Ted parted with his friends outside the Black Cat Café. He hopped into a taxi and sped uptown. In front of the house in Lincoln Park, Ted tipped the driver generously, then climbed out of the car. Trudging up the steps, he saw that a light was on in the living room. *Aunt Sarah must be up*, he thought, surprised and somewhat annoyed.

He'd been avoiding his aunt for days, ever since their confrontation over the college issue. Ted was standing firm in his decision not to go to Rosse. Still, that night he felt somehow jittery and unsure of himself, thinking about the fact that the very next day, classes started there. What would it be like to walk across the wide green lawns with flocks of other freshmen; to listen, pen in hand, to the lectures of wise, distinguished professors?

Easing the front door open, Ted shook those thoughts from his head. He'd have to tiptoe past the living room. He didn't want another lecture from his aunt about how he'd be making a mistake by not going to college.

But when he caught a glimpse of his aunt, something about her attitude made him pause. She was sitting on the living-room sofa, as motionless as marble. There was something in her limp hand—a letter, Ted guessed.

He stepped into the room. "Aunt Sarah, are you all right? Have you received bad news?"

She jumped, startled at his sudden appearance. "Bad news?" Ted was struck by how pale she was. "Yes, yes, I guess it is." Her fingers tightened on the sheet of paper and her voice cracked. "It's a letter, a letter from a solicitor in Vista, California." Ted knew that Vista was the town where his aunt and his father had grown up. "My father, your grandfather, has died. He left all of his money to us in his will. There's a sizable amount."

Ted wrinkled his brow. "What do you mean? My grandfather died years ago. Didn't he?"

Sarah shook her head.

"Then why did you tell me that he did?" Ted

walked over to his aunt and stood staring down at her. "Why?"

To his surprise, he saw that her hands were shaking. In fact, her whole body was trembling. "My father and I were . . . estranged," she began. The words were flat and toneless. "When I was a girl, about your age, there was a young man—Edward Brooke. We were in love. But my father forbade me to see him. Edward was poor, a working-class man. He wasn't good enough for me, in my father's eyes. So we eloped to San Francisco. But before we could be married, the great earthquake struck. Edward was killed. I went home to Vista, and my father and I reconciled."

Ted was astounded by this story. He'd had no idea his aunt had had such a tragic, romantic adventure in the days before she adopted him. But he still didn't understand. "If he took you back . . ."

"He took me back for a while. But then I found out—I found out I was pregnant."

Ted gasped. "Pregnant?"

"When he discovered I was going to have a child, my father didn't want me in his house. He didn't want anyone to know of this family shame. I had to leave, so I picked a place where I thought I could find work. Chicago was booming. So I came east with my baby."

The incredible words sank slowly into Ted's numb brain. "Your *baby*?"

For the first time, Sarah lifted her eyes to his. They were misty with tears. "My baby. You."

"No," Ted whispered.

"I couldn't tell you the truth. Don't you see that?"

"But my father and mother—James and Edwina—"

"James wasn't my older brother. He was my twin," Sarah said. "He never married or had children—he died of influenza at seventeen. There was no Edwina." She took a deep, uneven breath. "Ted, I am your mother and Edward Brooke, my Edward, was your father."

Ted continued to stare at her, paralyzed. She reached for a brown envelope on the coffee table. "The solicitor sent these with the letter and bank draft." She handed him a heavy, elaborately engraved gold ring and a small, worn leather-bound book. "The ring was my father's. That's the Wakefield family crest. And the journal belonged to your maternal grandmother, Dancing Wind."

Ted clutched the ring and book, his head swimming. It was too much for him to absorb all at once. His aunt was really his mother and his real father was her forbidden love, who'd died in the San Francisco earthquake; his parents had never married, which meant he was illegitimate; all these years his grandfather had been living alone in California and Ted had never known him.

"Say something," Sarah begged him, her voice hoarse.

Ted's mouth suddenly tasted bitter with hurt and betrayal. He'd always been grateful to her for what she'd given him, but now he could see only what she'd withheld from him: his grandfather and the truth. "You lied to me. All my life, you've been lying to me!"

"I had to. It was best for you. Can't you see that—"

"I don't want to hear it!" Ted shouted. "I don't want to hear any more lies. And to think you've been trying to tell me how to run my life when you couldn't even run your own!"

He didn't give Sarah a chance to explain herself further. He didn't give himself a chance to reflect on how difficult her position had been. Instead, he stormed from the room.

In his bedroom, he stood with his hands pressed against his skull and his eyes squeezed shut. *Aunt Sarah's not who I thought she was . . . and neither am I. Here I've been, carrying on as if I owned the world, when in reality I'm nobody. I have to get out of this house. I have to think!*

Ted opened his eyes. A thought struck him. Why not get out of town altogether? If he left that night, he could make it to Rosse College by the start of classes the next day.

Quickly, he pulled a suitcase from his closet. In

a few minutes, he'd stuffed it with clothes and personal belongings and all the cash he had on hand.

Grabbing his jacket, Ted tore down the hallway and out the front door. "Ted!" his aunt—his mother —cried. "Ted, wait!" Ted didn't heed her.

Half an hour later, he found himself at the train station buying a one-way ticket to Rosse, Ohio. With his world turned upside down, there was only one thing Ted was sure of: He could no longer stay in Chicago. He wanted to start a new life. In another town, maybe he could discover who Ted Wakefield really was.

Sixteen

1925. Rosse, Ohio.

"Swallow that fish!" Harry Watson shouted, hoisting his foaming mug of near-beer.

Ted's arm was slung casually around Harry's shoulders. "Watch out," he warned jovially. "Arnie's in the hot seat now, but it'll be your turn soon."

As Ted had predicted, Harry was the next new pledge to be initiated. Lifting his goldfish with a dramatic flourish, Harry tossed back his head, popped the fish like an aspirin, and chased it with a gulp from his mug. Ted and the other Gamma Delta Iotas cheered.

Seizing Harry's hand, Ted pumped it vigorously. "Congratulations! Now we're brothers as well as roommates."

"This is swell," Harry agreed. "There'll be no stopping us now, ol' chum!"

The initiation completed, Harry and the other new fraternity members were taught the secret Gamma Delta Iota handshake and presented with traditional gold-and-blue striped neckties embroidered with the Gamma Delt crest. Then it was time to prepare for the party—the Gamma Delts had invited dates for dinner and dancing.

As the autumn sun set in a blaze of purple and orange, Ted took charge of the grills set up in the courtyard of the fraternity house. The music had already started, and through the open French doors he could see a bunch of kids working up an appetite by dancing a vigorous Charleston. The band was hot—Ted himself had scouted it out at a new local jazz club, the Back Room, and booked it for that night's party.

Tapping his foot, Ted ladled out cups of hot cider from a simmering kettle. From across the yard, he caught Harry's eye and wiggled his brows suggestively. His arm firmly around the slender waist of his new girl, a pretty coed named Stella, Harry sent Ted a broad wink in return. Ted laughed. Harry really was a card! They'd had a lot of fun together since they had met the previous summer on a road trip to the U.S. lawn-tennis championships in Forest Hills, New York. Harry's father, Taylor Watson, was a big name in the automobile business, but Harry himself was just a regular fellow—not a snob at all. He was always up for an adventure, always ready to fire up his sporty Watson coupe and help

Ted chase down the latest jazz sounds in nearby Cleveland or Akron.

Ted had struck a healthy balance at Rosse. He was still writing to put himself through school; he had a byline with a Cleveland paper now, as well as with his hometown *Chicago Post*. But he was also enjoying his coursework, learning more about both jazz and writing by taking music and journalism classes. He exchanged letters with Tina and knew her singing career had taken off. He and his mother had reconciled during his Christmas break the previous year. Ted had insisted that she keep all of the money her father had left them; after all she'd done for him, he wanted her to be financially secure for life. And things were going well for him. He was confident he'd always be able to earn a decent living.

"Hey, Teddy," Stella purred as she sashayed up with Harry. "Tell me I look like a million dollars. This unappreciative stiff"—she elbowed Harry, who doubled over in mock pain—"hasn't paid me one stingy compliment all night."

Ted looked Stella up and down. She wore a deep-green beaded flapper dress that set off her big emerald eyes, and a feather-and-jewel band circled her short auburn curls. Stella was a knockout. Ted executed an exaggerated bow. "Stella, you are ravishing," he said smoothly. Taking her hand, he lifted it to his lips. "None of the other girls here can hold a candle to you. You take my breath away, and if Harry here weren't my nearest and dearest friend, I wouldn't trust myself."

Harry shook his head, grinning. "What a bunch of hokum."

Stella's cherry-red lips curved in a smile. "*I* like it. You should take notes, Harry!"

Ted handed Stella a cup of hot cider. She eyed him speculatively through the steam. "What I can't understand is why a suave fella like you doesn't have a date for the first Gamma Delt bash of the season."

"There's only one Stella Rivers on campus," joked Ted, "and Harry Watson snapped her up before I got a chance to."

Stella tossed her reddish curls and laughed. "Now that *is* a bunch of hokum," she said. "C'mon, Harry, give me the scoop on why Ted Wakefield, star reporter, doesn't have a date. You have a tragic romantic past, right? There was a girl, a striking brunette. No, a platinum blonde! Her father was a Milwaukee beer baron, but the family company went bust because of Prohibition, and when you found her, she was selling cigarettes on a seedy Chicago sidewalk. You fell for her hard and wanted to lift her out of the gutter, but she was too proud." Stella giggled at her own silliness. "Am I close?"

Ted smiled but didn't comment. A tragic romantic past . . . that wasn't exactly it. But there were things about himself that he hadn't told any of his college friends, even Harry. Ted had distinctly mixed feelings about his family history. With time, he had come to sympathize with his mother. But he couldn't help feeling a lingering sense of shame about his illegitimate birth. As a result, he'd decided to keep the secret of his parentage to himself. Which meant that while Ted and Harry were practically constant companions, Harry didn't know nearly as much about Ted as Ted knew about Harry. It was safer, Ted often thought, not to let anyone get too close. Maybe that was why he didn't encourage the attentions of the many attractive Rosse coeds who made it clear they'd like to get to know him better.

Getting no response from Ted, Stella turned to Harry. He lifted his shoulders. "Don't look at me. I think the man's just choosy." He pulled her close. "Just like me."

With another wink at Ted, Harry sauntered off toward the dance floor with his date. Ted flipped the first round of well-done steaks onto a platter and threw on the next batch. He looked in at the dancers, suddenly feeling a bit wistful. He couldn't help being envious of Harry, not because Harry had Stella, but because Harry had confidence. Everything about Harry was top-drawer. Harry was born to go to a college like Rosse, to join a fraternity like Gamma Delta Iota. Whereas Ted, despite his social and academic success, was always secretly conscious that he was somehow different.

* * *

163

"Nice serve!" Ted shouted after Harry aced him. "Keep playing like this, and you'll be top seed on the team before the season's over!"

It was a crisp autumn day and the two, dressed in V-neck sweaters and baggy white trousers, were playing a brisk game of lawn tennis. Harry had won a spot on the college team, and Ted was improving rapidly thanks to his friend's tips.

Harry served again. This time Ted returned the ball with a slicing backhand.

"Not bad yourself!" Harry charged to the net. A rapid volley ensued, with Ted finally taking the point by lobbing the ball over Harry's head to the baseline.

Harry dropped his racket and grabbed a towel that was draped over the net. He swabbed his forehead. "Let's call it a tie, old chum. If I let you run me around like this for much longer, I won't cut much of a figure on the dance floor with Stella tonight. And I'd make sure to inform her that she should hold you personally responsible for my inadequacy!"

Ted chuckled. "There's a compelling threat."

Together they strolled to the corner of the court where they'd left their jackets. Harry slipped his on, then patted the pocket. "Just remembered—I have something to show you," he said to Ted. He pulled out an envelope. "It's a letter from Samantha. I've told you about my gorgeous sixteen-year-old twin sisters, Samantha and Amanda, haven't I?"

"Only about a thousand times!"

Harry grinned. "Well, they're simply the most fabulous girls in the world. And if you think I talk your ear off about them, you should hear what I've told *them* about *you*."

"What have you told them?"

"Nothing but the facts. And I sent a snapshot of the two of us. My sister returned the favor. Here, take a look at this." Harry removed a photograph from the envelope and handed it to Ted. "Tell me she won't be a movie star someday!"

Ted whistled. The girl in the picture was breathtakingly beautiful: a jazzy-looking, icy-blond flapper with a pouting, sensuous smile and a playful, inviting sparkle in her eyes. If she looked this good in black and white, what would she be like in person? "Is this Samantha or Amanda?" he asked.

"That's Sam. Amanda still wears her hair long," replied Harry. "Sam hasn't been able to talk her into bobbing it yet."

Ted turned over the snapshot. On the back, Samantha had written a message—a message to him. She'd signed it *Kisses from Samantha* in handwriting that was as rich and curvy as she was. "She really wants to meet me?" Ted said in disbelief.

"She's dying to," confirmed Harry. "And she's commanded me to twist your arm until you promise to stop in Detroit for a visit with my family on your way home to Chicago for the holidays."

"You don't have to twist my arm." Ted returned

to studying the girl in the photo. "I'd drive a few miles out of my way to meet Miss Samantha Watson!"

"And her equally charming twin sister, Amanda," Harry reminded him.

"Double the reason for a detour."

"You and Samantha are bound to hit it off." Harry was clearly pleased at the prospect of a liaison between his best friend and his younger sister. "She loves jazz and she can dance all night."

"Sounds like the girl of my dreams." Ted waved the photo. "Mind if I keep this?"

"She's probably hoping it'll end up under your pillow."

Ted pocketed the photo, intrigued. There was something about Samantha Watson. . . . Suddenly, he had a strong, exciting intuition. The beautiful girl in the photograph was going to have a big impact on his life.

Harry stumbled off to the bedroom, undressing as he went. He tossed his scarf on a chair, his raccoon coat on the couch, his necktie over the bedroom door. Still standing in the study room of their apartment, Ted went to the window and opened it a crack, letting the brisk February air flood the room. It had been another late night at the Back Room, and he was ready to hit the sack himself. But there was some mail lying on his desk that he'd been waiting for a private moment to read.

As soon as he heard Harry snoring, Ted sat down at his desk and pulled an envelope from under a textbook. Lifting it to his nose, he closed his eyes and breathed deeply of the delicate, unforgettable fragrance the writer had dabbed on the stationery. *Amanda* . . .

Ted didn't open the letter right away. Instead, he gazed out the window. The snow had turned to rain, as if the season couldn't decide whether it was spring yet or still winter. It didn't matter to Ted, who was reveling in the warmth and immediacy of his memories. In his mind, it was December again, and the moonlight was bright on the new snow and on Amanda's angelically beautiful face.

Sometimes Ted couldn't believe his good fortune. Harry's sister Samantha was as much fun as Harry had promised. While visiting the Watsons that past December, Ted had enjoyed dancing up a storm with her and talking to her about Fitzgerald's novels and motion picture stars like Charlie Chaplin and Clara Bow. But it wasn't Samantha Ted had fallen for during his holiday visit. To his surprise, it was her twin sister, Amanda, who had turned out to be the girl of his dreams.

What was it about Amanda? A smile touched Ted's lips as he pictured her in his mind. Amanda equaled Samantha in beauty, if not in flash and dazzle; her hair was like spun gold, her eyes a deep blue-green like a mountain pool, her creamy skin as soft and inviting as velvet. But more attractive were

Amanda's inner qualities: she was warm, gentle, poetic. Ted recalled the evening a few days before Christmas when he, Harry, and the twins had gone to a local roadhouse to hear some jazz. At the Watsons' home later that night, as the rest of the household slept, Ted had wandered downstairs to find Amanda curled up on the sofa in her robe, her silky hair loose about her shoulders, writing a poem by the light of the moon. She had been shy about her poetry, but at his urging, she'd read some of it to him. Then it had been as if they were spellbound. Somehow they had found themselves in each other's arms, sharing a deep, long, magical kiss.

In that moment, an incredibly deep connection had been forged between them. Both felt as if they'd known each other for much, much longer than a single weekend. The bond had been strengthened through their correspondence. Since Christmas, Ted had lived for Amanda's letters. Each time she wrote, she was more open about her feelings for him, more passionate.

Eagerly, Ted broke the seal on her latest letter. He read it quickly, then reread it more slowly, savoring each word, the grace of her handwriting, the perfume of the stationery.

Amanda had good news. *I finally told Sam about our correspondence,* she'd written. *She was a little miffed, but for the most part she's taking it well.*

Because the whole Watson family had assumed that Ted was interested in Samantha—Samantha herself included—Ted and Amanda had been conducting their romance in secret. Ted hadn't told Harry that he exchanged letters with Amanda, and Amanda made sure she was the first one to the mailbox each afternoon. Ted had pressed Amanda to come clean with Samantha, feeling it was best to be honest. Amanda had been hesitant, afraid to hurt her twin's feelings.

But all's well that ends well! Ted thought, relieved. He felt good knowing that he and Amanda were doing the right thing by Samantha, of whom he was genuinely fond. Now there was only one smudge on Ted's conscience.

As he put pen to paper to begin a letter to Amanda, Ted frowned. There was one aspect of that evening at the jazz club in Detroit that he didn't take pleasure or pride in recalling: the fact that he'd been untruthful with Harry and his family about his background. C. C. Earl, a jazz musician Ted knew well, had been playing at the roadhouse. At one point, Earl had joined Ted's party and recounted the hard-luck story Ted had once told the musician when he was trying to persuade Earl to grant him an interview. It had been a nice piece of fiction, featuring a grandfather who'd struck it rich during the gold rush and a dwindling family fortune that forced Ted to make a living by his pen. Amanda and Samantha had found the story terribly romantic and they admired Ted greatly for working

169

his way through school, so Ted had let them believe it.

Later, Ted had considered telling Harry and Harry's family who he really was. But somehow, in the luxurious setting of the Watsons' elegant home, Ted had lost his nerve. The Watsons were high society. They were too well-bred ever to say so, but might they not think less of him if they knew his true family history?

No. Not Amanda, Ted thought. Though she was wealthy, she cared for him because of who he was inside. He could trust her. Someday he'd open up to her, find a way to tell her the truth.

In the meantime, he could only count the days until he was with her again—that, and fill page after page with heartfelt expressions of love. *Dear Amanda,* Ted wrote rapidly. *The night is cold, but I am warm with dreams of you. . . .*

Seventeen

1926. Detroit.

"I'm sorry, Ted." As Amanda Watson looked up at him a shadow clouded her usually bright blue-green eyes. "I guess I'm just not in the mood for dancing tonight."

"Me either," Ted confessed. C. C. Earl was playing at the Café Car and the band was as hot as always, but Ted was too tense to enjoy himself. Taking Amanda's hand, he led her back to their table. "C'mon, let's blow this joint."

The situation was almost comical, Ted thought as he and Amanda put on their coats and stepped out of the steamy, smoky club into the cool spring night. Deciding to make a weekend trip to Chicago in his new secondhand coupe, Ted had written ahead to Amanda to let her know that of course he would stop in Detroit to visit her. Ted's arrival, however, had apparently come as a complete surprise to her. After months of agonizing separation, Amanda hadn't even been home to meet him —she'd stayed after school to work at the newspaper office! His letter must have been lost in the mail, Ted figured. What was worse, though, was that not only had Mrs. Watson and Samantha known nothing about his proposed visit, but they'd also known nothing about Ted's relationship with Amanda. Samantha had gone with Ted to pick up her twin, but instead of directing him to the high school, she'd taken him to the local lover's lane and tried to kiss him. Ted didn't like to remember the pain and outrage in Samantha's eyes when he had rejected her attentions and told her that his heart belonged to another—her twin sister.

Ted and Amanda walked to Ted's car in silence. When Ted opened the passenger door for Amanda, he noticed a sparkle of tears in her eyes. "I'm sorry," she said in a small, remorseful voice. "I ruined our weekend. I ruined everything!"

"Amanda." Leaning back against the side of the car, Ted pulled her into his arms. Amanda rested her cheek against his chest and he stroked her hair, now cut in a chin-length bob like her sister's. "You didn't intend for things to work out this way. You just wanted to spare Sam's feelings."

"And look what happened!" Sniffling, Amanda put her hand in Ted's jacket pocket, searching for his handkerchief. "Because of my supposedly good

172

intentions, Sam is even more hurt than she would have been if I'd been up-front from the start."

And you don't know the half of it, Ted thought. He'd spared Amanda the more intimate and disturbing details of his encounter with Samantha that afternoon.

"She'll never forgive me," Amanda continued, this possibility inspiring a fresh bout of tears.

Ted couldn't deny that both his and Amanda's friendships with Samantha were in serious jeopardy. In addition, he suspected that he looked like a bit of a cad in the eyes of Mr. and Mrs. Watson. They must think he was simultaneously wooing both of their daughters. The whole thing made Ted terribly uncomfortable. He almost wished he'd just stayed in Rosse and studied that weekend.

The Watson home was dark when they pulled into the driveway. Ted reached for a light as they stepped through the side door, but Amanda put a hand on his arm to stop him. "Don't," she whispered. "It's nicer in the dark."

Amanda wound her slender arms around his neck and began kissing him passionately. Bending, he scooped her up in his arms and carried her to the living-room couch, where they'd shared their first kiss a few months earlier.

"Maybe Sam will be angry at me forever, but do you at least forgive me?" Amanda asked Ted.

"Of course." He kissed the tip of her nose, then gently brushed each of her eyelids with his lips.

Maybe Amanda had made an error in judgment by not telling Samantha of her and Ted's feelings for each other, even though she had written Ted to say she had. But Ted knew her intentions were solid gold. He'd never known anyone with a heart so gentle and loving, anyone as unselfish and pure. He was so lucky to have found her! It must have been fate that made him and Harry roommates.

"I love you, Amanda."

"And I love you," she murmured. Their mouths met again; desire swept away the earlier worries of the day. It felt so good to hold Amanda close, to feel her heart beating against his through the delicate silk of her peach-colored dress.

"Maybe we should say good night," Ted said, his voice husky.

Amanda drew back with a small sigh. "I suppose you're right."

He could tell she was reluctant to leave the comfort of his arms. "Everything will turn out A-OK," Ted promised. "I'll wager that in the morning everything will be back to normal in the Watson household. A good night's sleep is what we all need."

"I hope that does it!" Amanda agreed, pulling Ted close for one last embrace.

So much for a good night's sleep! Ted thought as he and Amanda sped back to the Café Car in his coupe. Gripping the steering wheel with one hand, he lifted the other to rub his sleep-bleary eyes. He'd just drifted off when Amanda had woken him. Apparently, a messenger had come by the house— Ted's friend C. C. Earl was in some kind of trouble and needed his help. Without a second thought, Ted had thrown his clothes back on.

Now, as they approached the Café Car, Ted caught his breath sharply. Trouble wasn't the word for it! "Whoa! What's going on here?"

Amanda was also gaping at the scene. The entrance to the club was barricaded off, and by the blinding glare of floodlights, Ted could see a crowd of people milling about excitedly.

He braked alongside the barricades. Immediately the car was approached by two heavyset men in dark suits. "Miss Amanda Watson?" one of them asked. Ted's eyebrows shot up in surprise. How did the man know her name?

"Yes, that's me," Amanda said hesitantly.

"Agent Samson." The man flashed a badge. "Perhaps you'd like to step out of the auto."

Amanda started to open the door on her side of the car. Ted put a protective hand on her shoulder. "Is there a problem, sir?" he asked.

"Not for this young lady." Agent Samson helped Amanda out of the car. "I'd just like to thank her for doing her duty and bringing you to us."

"Me? To you?" Ted looked up at Amanda through his open window. "Amanda, I thought Earl sent for me."

To his surprise, she didn't meet his eyes. Instead, she looked at Agent Samson. "We hear you've been financing your college tuition with some illegal money," Samson said.

Ted's confusion was growing by the second. He had absolutely no idea what the agent was talking about. Since when was it illegal to write for a newspaper? "Excuse me?"

"You know what's in this car as well as we do," Samson snapped.

The next thing Ted knew, he was being dragged forcibly from the coupe by two other agents. "What's going on?" Ted demanded. "What does this have to do with Miss Watson? If you do anything to hurt her . . ."

"The only person who's hurt me is you."

Ted stared. It was Amanda who'd spoken, and she was crying. *This must be some kind of bad dream,* Ted thought. But no. The floodlights were real, and the agents, and Amanda's tears. "Amanda, why are you crying? I don't understand what's going on here."

"Maybe she's crying because her boyfriend turned out to be a crook," said Agent Samson.

"A crook?"

"Yeah. Now, how's about you open up the trunk for us so we can take a look at what you got in there?"

Ted opened the trunk; he could think of no reason not to. He knew it was empty except for his tennis racket and a spare tire—nothing to interest the FBI. But when the lights hit the contents of the trunk, Ted gasped in surprise. It was full of bottles! And not just any kind of bottles. Liquor bottles.

Ted was so stunned he barely heard Agent Samson's words. ". . . a crime to be transporting intoxicating drink . . ." Then the agent addressed Amanda. "Thanks for making us wise to this guy."

That got through to Ted. "You *knew* what was in my trunk?" he asked her. "You told them that I had . . . ? But what about Earl?"

"This isn't about Earl, Ted." Amanda sniffled. "It's about you running bootleg liquor."

The questions crowded Ted's mind. How had the bottles gotten into his trunk? When had Amanda discovered them? And why, why hadn't she confronted him first, before going to the police? They loved and trusted each other. How could she have been ready to believe the worst of him?

"Amanda, you don't think I really put this stuff in here, do you? Why didn't you say something to me? I would have told you I didn't know a thing about it."

"And you'd expect me to believe you? The same fellow who took my sister up to Overlook Valley and . . . oh, I can barely say it . . . tried to—to seduce her!"

For a split second, it was Samantha Ted was seeing, not Amanda. Samantha's rage when he'd rejected her kisses, Samantha's brooding silence for the rest of the day . . . But obviously she hadn't been completely silent. She'd told the story to her sister—only it was the wrong story. Ted could almost understand why Samantha would lie. She'd been deeply hurt. But how could Amanda have believed her?

"You've got it all wrong," Ted told Amanda, who was now sobbing. He reached out for her, simultaneously wanting to shake her and to fold her close to his heart.

One of the agents seized Ted's wrists and handcuffed him. "Amanda, believe me," Ted called as he was dragged to a waiting car. At that moment, he didn't care that he was being arrested. It didn't matter what the Feds thought of him. But Amanda just had to be on his side! "I never made a move for your sister. And I didn't put the bottles in my car."

"Sure you didn't," Agent Samson scoffed. "They just walked in there by themselves."

"Please, sir. Somebody else must have planted those—" Suddenly Ted froze. No. It couldn't be. She loved him. She might be hurt on her twin's behalf, but she would never turn on him so completely. She couldn't have so little faith in him. She would never go that far. . . .

Ted faced Amanda. His voice dropped almost to a whisper. "Did you do this because you thought I made a play for your sister?"

Amanda stared back at him, her eyes now dry. She didn't answer.

It was like looking at a stranger. Where was the Amanda he'd come to know, to love, to trust? How could she have been so quick to accept Samantha's accusation without even giving Ted a chance to tell his side of the story?

"You can't be the girl I fell in love with," Ted cried as he was pushed into the unmarked car.

Still Amanda did not speak. She simply stood and watched as the Feds drove him away.

Ted sat on the edge of the hard cot, his head in his hands. He hadn't moved for hours, not since the Feds had shoved him into the windowless Detroit jail cell. Was it morning yet? He didn't know, and didn't care.

He sat up, however, when Officer Joe Johnstone unlocked the door to his cell. "I've got good news for you, pal," the burly, white-haired cop announced. "You're off the hook and free to go."

"I am?" Ted jumped to his feet, his eyes lighting up with sudden hope. Maybe Amanda had relented and made a plea on his behalf! "What happened?"

"The Feds couldn't make the charges against you stick." Johnstone swung the door wide so Ted could pass through. "It was too clearly a setup."

Ted's shoulders slumped again. The light died in his eyes. He walked slowly from the cell. "A setup.

I guess that's right. The girl I love—" Ted paused to correct himself. "The girl I *loved* set me up."

"Tough break, kid," Johnstone commiserated, handing over Ted's wallet and car keys. "If you want my advice, in the future stay away from the flashy dolls. They only cause trouble."

Ted just nodded, too dispirited to speak.

Outside the station, he found his car parked at the curb. Ted climbed into the driver's seat and sat for a moment with the engine idling. Where was he going to go? He was too upset to go back to the Watsons' for his belongings. He had nothing more to say to Amanda.

Swinging the coupe onto the street, Ted hit the gas and headed for the highway to Chicago. He didn't care that by exceeding the speed limit, he was risking another brush with the law. He was too eager to leave Detroit far behind him.

The Lincoln Park apartment was empty. Sarah had left a note. She and her neighbor, a middle-aged widower named Joe, were on an "outing," but Sarah wrote that they'd be back in time for dinner and hoped Ted would be in town so he could join them.

Dejectedly, Ted wandered into his old bedroom. Opening the desk drawer, he took out two treasures: the gold ring that had belonged to his English grandfather, Theodore Wakefield, and the journal kept in the 1880s by his half-Indian grandmother, Dancing Wind.

Ted studied the design on the ring. It was an unusual family crest, a many-petaled rose. He slipped the ring on his finger, enjoying the smooth, well-worn feel of the gold. Sitting alone in the empty apartment, a strange sensation of timelessness enveloped Ted. He'd never felt this lost and confused, not even on the night when he had discovered the truth about his parentage and run off to Rosse on the midnight train. *I'm back where I started and it's nowhere good,* Ted thought morosely. What had he accomplished in the years on his own at college? He still didn't know who he was. As for what he wanted to do . . . In addition to sounding the death knell for his love for Amanda, the previous night had poisoned his love of jazz. He didn't have the heart to return to Ohio and resume his writing and his studies, or to face his roommate, Harry.

Ted flipped through the brittle, yellowed pages of Dancing Wind's diary, wondering about the woman who had filled the volume with the tiny, slanted script. All at once, something occurred to him. Maybe part of the reason he felt like a stranger to himself was because he was a stranger to his family history, which had been hidden from him all the years he was growing up. There were so many questions that Sarah had never been able to answer. Theodore Wakefield, Dancing Wind . . .

who were they, really? Where did he, Edward Wakefield, come from?

A sudden inspiration infused Ted's mind and body with new energy. *I won't go back to Rosse, but I won't stay in Chicago, either,* he decided. He had a car and enough cash to pay for gas. He'd journey west to learn more about the grandparents he had never known, to learn about his roots. *And maybe I'll learn something about myself in the process.*

Eighteen

1926. Swift River, Oregon.

Ted hit the brakes when he saw the painted wooden sign swinging in the wind: Last Chance Lodge. Smiling wryly, he swung the battered coupe into the lane leading to the rustic log structure. Last Chance Lodge—it sounded like the perfect place for a dusty, road-weary traveler who had come to the end of a three-month, cross-country odyssey.

The mud-spattered car showed the wear of the journey west, and so did Ted. He was leaner; his skin was tanned a deep copper; his strong chin was dark with five days' growth of beard. Instead of the neat trousers, V-neck sweaters, and blazers of his college days, he sported a well-worn pair of dungarees, leather cowboy boots, and a miner's shirt. *Harry Watson wouldn't know me,* Ted thought as he

183

climbed out of the coupe and shook his long legs to get out the kinks. *Amanda wouldn't, either.*

Three months had taken the edge off Ted's bitterness but hadn't erased it entirely. There were times, though, when he couldn't believe that he'd ever been a student at Rosse College, belonged to an elite fraternity, fallen in love with and been betrayed by a faithless beauty. Since that night in the Detroit jail, Ted had covered thousands of miles of road. He'd seen mountains and deserts; he'd looked out across the endless blue expanse of the Pacific Ocean.

Ted's mother had wired him some money from his savings account; Ted had also written to Harry, asking his former roommate to forward his belongings to Chicago. But other than those brief contacts, Ted's past life was far removed from him in time and space.

Grabbing his suitcase from the back seat, Ted entered the Last Chance Lodge. *Not exactly the lobby of the Palmer House,* he observed, but then the Cascade mountain town of Swift River was a long way from Chicago. It looked to Ted as if the lodge's check-in counter also served as the local bar. A few scruffy characters were perched there on stools, cradling mugs of something golden that looked suspiciously like illegal beer.

"I'd like to rent a room," he announced to no one in particular, since it wasn't clear who, if anyone, was in charge.

A grizzled mountain man in grimy jeans and the top of a pair of red long johns hopped to his feet. "The honeymoon suite is occupied," he joked, "but I've got another room I think'll do you. A cot and a camp stove, shower and latrine out back, five dollars a week."

Ted stepped forward to shake the man's hand, getting a strong whiff of alcohol as he did so. "I'll take it. Thanks, uh . . ."

"Dick Dawson." He gave Ted's hand a thorough wringing. "I can't give you no key because there ain't no lock on the door."

Ted laughed. "I've got nothing to lock up anyway."

"Then take a load off, son." Dick patted a stool. "I'll throw in supper—pork and beans, my world-famous sourdough bread, and a mug of cold brew —if you sit awhile and tell us where you've been and where you're heading."

Ted was glad to. He was bone-tired, hungry, and thirsty. And even, he had to admit, a little lonely. "Well, it's a long story," he warned the men.

"They got no place to go!" said Dick. The others guffawed.

"It all started in Chicago," Ted began, deciding not to share the more painful and still confusing details of his history, such as Amanda's betrayal and the setup in Detroit. "I was aiming for California, the Napa Valley, where my parents grew up. On the way, I stopped in Nebraska and in the Rocky

Mountain ghost town where my great-grandfather, Jake Webster, looked for gold. He found a few nuggets but never struck it rich."

Dick plunked a heaping plate of pork and beans and a huge hunk of bread in front of Ted, then slid a mug of beer his way as well. "There's many a man out this way that can tell the same story," he remarked.

Ted paused for a few bites. After a moment's hesitation, he took a sip of beer. Then he continued his account. Arriving in Vista, he'd visited Theodore Wakefield's Manor Farm, now owned by strangers who were clearing out the fruit trees to make room for a vineyard. Ted had also looked up his paternal grandparents, the Brookes, only to find that they'd sold their livery stable and moved from the area not long after the death of their son Edward, Ted's father. "The last stage of my quest is to track down the Awaswan Indian tribe," Ted concluded, draining the mug. "They lived in California originally, but according to government records, they were relocated to Oregon in the 1860s."

"You've found 'em," said Dick. "The reservation is just five miles up the valley. There ain't no roads, though. You'll have to hoof it."

Ted hadn't realized he'd come so close to the reservation. There were still a couple of hours of daylight left. . . . Ted pushed back his empty plate. "Can I borrow a horse?"

Ten minutes later, Ted and a mule named Pete

were trotting along a pebbly path skirting the Swift River. Pete wasn't the most elegant animal, but he knew the trails; he was footsure and reliable. "You can't get lost with Pete," Dick had promised Ted. "He'll bring you home at sunset, whether you want to come or not."

For the first few miles of the ride, the river cut through a narrow gorge. Water rushed on one side of the trail while granite cliffs rose straight on the other. Soon, however, the valley widened into a broad expanse of lush green. It was here that the Indian reservation was located.

Ted hadn't known quite what to expect—tepees and feather headdresses, perhaps, like in the movies. Instead, he saw a village of small log cabins that looked a lot more comfortable than his room at the Last Chance Lodge. There were plots of land planted with vegetables, and paddocks and pens for horses, pigs, goats, and chickens. Ted dismounted and led the mule toward the settlement. Two little boys with fishing poles scampered across the path, darting curious glances in his direction. "Can you tell me where Ten Horses lives?" Ted shouted after them.

According to Dick, Ten Horses was an Awaswan chief who knew as much tribal lore and history as anyone. The boys pointed to a cabin and ran off. Tethering Pete, Ted approached the cabin and knocked tentatively. A deep voice called out something in a language Ted didn't understand.

Assuming it was Awaswan for "come in," he pushed the door open.

The one-room cabin's windows were small, and the interior was somewhat dim and smoky. When his eyes adjusted to the shadows, Ted detected two figures seated on a woven rug. One, an elderly man, beckoned him forward with a gnarled hand. Stepping closer, Ted was surprised to see that the second figure was a young white woman with a small notebook on her lap and a pencil in her hand.

Both the man and the girl stood up. Ted explained his intrusion. "My name is Ted Wakefield," he said, addressing the chief. "I'd like to speak with you, Ten Horses. I was hoping to learn something about my great-grandmother, Owl Feather, who was born among your people."

The old man peered at Ted, his gaze hawk-sharp. "Yes," he murmured in English, "I see it. In your eyes, I see the Awaswan. Sit with us."

The girl, who was dressed like a cowboy in dungarees and a flannel shirt, remained standing. "Ten Horses, I'm leaving now," she said. "We can talk more tomorrow, if you have the time."

"I have time for you, my daughter," Ten Horses replied.

The girl left the cabin with a backward glance and smile at Ted. Watching her, Ted was momentarily distracted. She was beautiful, with sky-blue eyes, wheat-blond hair hanging in a glossy braid down her back, and long, slim legs. He shook his head to clear it of her image. He hadn't come out west to find love, he reminded himself. As a matter of fact, after what had happened with Amanda, he was through with romance altogether.

He took a seat at Ten Horses's side. "Owl Feather," Ten Horses mused, reaching for a pipe.

"She was probably born in the eighteen-forties," said Ted. "When she was a young woman, she left the Awaswan to marry a white gold prospector named Jake Webster. She never returned to the tribe."

"Yes." The chief nodded. Ted's heart leaped. "Her story is known to me. Others have forsaken the tribe to become white people, but Owl Feather's departure is remembered because she had been promised to the chief for his bride."

Ted was surprised. He didn't think Dancing Wind had known this part of her mother's history. "You see," continued Ten Horses, "Owl Feather's father was Redwood Spirit, a medicine man of legendary powers, the spiritual leader of the tribe. It was believed that a union between Redwood Spirit's most beautiful daughter and Chief Fist-of-Thunder would bring new strength and luck to the tribe, which was then experiencing the first encroachments of the white man. When Owl Feather ran off with her white husband, Fist-of-Thunder was furious. Redwood Spirit had many other children, and he offered to give the chief another of his daughters. But the chief wanted no one but Owl Feather."

"And she was gone," said Ted.

Ten Horses sucked on his pipe. "There are those who say the tribe's ill fortune dates from Owl Feather's departure."

Ted shifted uncomfortably. He hadn't expected his great-grandmother's tale to be so dramatic. Maybe his particular connection to the tribe made him a less-than-welcome guest.

"But now Owl Feather's great-grandson has come back to us, along with Paper Voices," Ten Horses mused. "Perhaps this means our luck will turn again."

"Paper Voices?" asked Ted.

"Julia." Ten Horses nodded at the door. "Go now. She waits for you."

Ted hesitated; he had more questions. The chief seemed to read his mind. "Return tomorrow and you can meet the other descendants of Redwood Spirit."

"Thank you, I'll do that."

Not knowing how to bid goodbye to an Awaswan chief, Ted bowed and then left the cabin. Walking back to where he'd left the mule, he saw that Julia was indeed waiting for him, as Ten Horses had predicted.

Without preamble, Julia held out her hand. "Julia Marks. Did Ten Horses have any information for you, Mr. Wakefield?"

"Did he ever!"

Julia smiled. "He knows absolutely everything. He's been a gold mine for me. By the way, are you heading back to town? Because if you are, I could use a lift. I hiked out this morning," she explained, "and didn't mean to stay this long."

Ted nodded. It was nearly sunset; if she went on foot, she wouldn't reach town until well after dark. "Ol' Pete can probably carry us both. But I'm going to have to exact a toll."

"A toll?"

Ted's eyes twinkled. He'd strike a deal with her like the one Dick had made with him earlier. "A ride to town for a story."

Julia put her hands on her hips. "What kind of story?"

"Oh, how did Dick Dawson put it? 'Tell me where you've been and where you're going.'"

"Dick Dawson?" Julia burst out laughing. "You're not staying at the Last Chance, are you?"

Ted grinned. "The finest accommodations in town."

"I like roughing it, but that's too primitive even for me," she said. "If you get a hankering for indoor plumbing, try Miss Mittelstadt's boardinghouse half a mile up the road from Dick's. And as for your toll, I'm happy to oblige you. Stories are my line."

Ted mounted Pete and helped Julia swing up behind him. "Stories are your line, eh?"

Without any urging from Ted, Pete set off for

home at a brisk trot. "That's right," Julia confirmed. "I'm a journalist."

"You don't say! Why, so am I. At least, I was," Ted corrected himself.

"Really?" Julia looped one arm around his waist for balance. "What kind of writing do you do?"

"I was a columnist for a couple of different mid-western newspapers. I covered the jazz scene."

"Why the past tense?" Julia asked.

"The toll," Ted reminded her. "Your story first!"

Julia laughed. "You won't get off the hook entirely," she warned. "Let's see . . . it all started in New York City. That's where I grew up. My father's a Wall Street financier. I'm an only child."

Ted put two and two together. "You're filthy rich, huh?"

Julia laughed, clearly amused by his frankness. "You got it. I certainly can't complain. Daddy's always given me everything I wanted, everything money can buy. I've been very lucky."

"But it's not enough," Ted guessed.

"No, it's not. You see, I always wanted to be a reporter," said Julia. "And when I graduated from high school last spring, I looked for a job. I didn't *have* to work, but I didn't want to just live the high life in Manhattan, sponging off my father. I wanted to earn my own way."

"Well, you came an awful long way to find something to report on," Ted observed. "Isn't there any news in New York these days?"

"There's plenty. But every city paper I went to would take one look at my résumé, or rather my name, and assume there was only one thing I was capable of covering—the social scene." Ted could hear Julia's indignation, and feel it in the arm circling his waist. Without thinking, she gave him a little squeeze to punctuate her words. "Ugh! Can you imagine writing about nothing more important than who wore what and danced with whom at the most recent debutante ball?"

"Nope."

"Well, neither could I. I realized I had to get out of New York, for a while at least, if I didn't want to be pigeonholed just because my name is Julia Marks. So I headed west. I figured that maybe out in this big country I'd find a big story—one that would establish my credentials so I could get jobs covering foreign events or serious domestic issues."

Ted was filled with admiration for her boldness and ambition. "Have you found it? The big one, I mean."

"I'm onto something, but I'm not sure yet how big it's going to be. Here's the background." Julia told Ted that she'd come to Swift River to investigate allegations that the United States government had reneged on nineteenth-century treaty promises regarding land and mineral rights for a number of Indian tribes, including the Awaswan. "I've gotten my hands on some official documentation, and the Indians themselves are ready with oral testimony.

But there are still a few pieces of the puzzle missing."

They reached the Last Chance. "Let me ride you to the boardinghouse," Ted offered.

"No, no," Julia insisted as she jumped down from the mule's back. "I'm fine from here."

Ted dismounted, and they stood for a moment looking at each other. Julia seemed to be summing him up with her intense blue eyes. "I paid your toll, Mr. Wakefield," she said. "Now how about doing something for me?"

"Name it."

"Consider getting back in the journalism business and giving me a hand breaking this story. That is, if you're planning to stay in Swift River for a while."

With her curiosity and journalistic ambition, her beauty and zest, Julia reminded Ted a little of both Amanda and Samantha. But she was also distinctly Julia Marks. Promising himself he wouldn't get involved with her, he realized he had nothing else to do right now, nowhere else to go.

"Will we share author credit?" Ted asked, his eyes twinkling.

Julia smiled. "My name comes first."

Ted put out his hand to shake. "Deal!"

Nineteen

"I happen to know that Dick cooks nothing but pork and beans morning, noon, and night," Julia greeted Ted. "So I brought you some of Miss Mittelstadt's sweet rolls."

Ted eyed the flask Julia carried strapped over one slender shoulder. "And coffee, I hope. Dick's is a little . . . strong."

She laughed. "That's because he never cleans the pot!"

Before parting the night before, the two had agreed to meet at the start of the river path the next morning at sunrise. Now they sat down cross-legged on a flat rock by the river's edge. Julia unwrapped the rolls. "Yum," she said. "I already ate a few of these back at the house, but I worked up an appetite walking over here. I think I'll have another."

Ted bit into a roll, chewing with a blissful expression. "That settles it. I'm checking out of the Last Chance and into Miss Mittelstadt's."

Julia uncapped the flask of coffee and handed it to Ted, wondering if he'd take this opening to tell her a little about himself. *He knows practically my whole life story. But I don't know anything about him other than the fact that he's absolutely the most handsome and intriguing man I've ever met,* she thought, stealing a glance at his rugged profile.

But Ted didn't expand on the subject of his life in Chicago, and Julia decided not to question him. She had faith that he would grow less reticent after they'd spent some time together. Besides, there were plenty of other things to talk about, namely the story she was investigating.

As soon as they polished off the rolls, Julia hopped to her feet. "C'mon. I'll fill you in on the situation while we walk to the reservation. I do my best thinking when I'm on my feet and moving."

"A good trait for a journalist," Ted remarked.

They hiked briskly along the rocky path. "The problem started a year ago, when a government-backed company began mining some land that supposedly was part of the Awaswan and Yakima reservation," Julia began. "The village you saw yesterday is only a small part of the total reservation acreage. The Indians had also been given what appeared to be useless land in the Cascade foothills. But then an exceptionally rich vein of iron ore was discovered in the area. Rumor has it there may even be oil there."

"But if the land legally belongs to the Indians . . ."

"That's just the problem," said Julia, stepping over a tree that had fallen across the path. "When the Indians went to the local government office for help, Frank Foster—the official liaison between the tribes and the government—told them the treaty had been lost. So they scraped together enough money to send Ten Horses to Washington to appeal to the federal Bureau of Indian Affairs. But it turned out there was no copy of the treaty on file in D.C., either."

"Sounds fishy to me!"

"Mighty fishy," Julia agreed. "Ten Horses's journey made national news—that's how I came to write to Ten Horses and the Yakima chief, Bear Paw, offering to help. All I've gotten so far, though, is the Indians' oral testimony that the land and any mineral rights traditionally belong to them. And unfortunately, the only surviving nineteenth-century papers documenting the actual treaty negotiations reveal that at the time, the government was considering a couple of different land packages for the tribes, one of which didn't include the area in question. Of course, that's all the evidence the government thinks it needs now to steal the land back." Julia's eyes flashed. "If only I could find out what became of the treaty!"

Ted stopped in his tracks. "I've got it."

Julia stared at him. "Got what?"

"Frank Foster's the key. He knows what happened to at least one copy of the treaty—he may even have it in his possession, despite his statements to the contrary."

"But how do we get our hands on it?"

"You've tried the honest approach. Now it's time to play the game Foster's way." Grabbing Julia's hand, Ted pulled her back toward town. "Let's go!"

"I don't think I can say it," Julia told Ted as he parked his coupe in front of the regional office for Indian affairs in Parkersburg, ten miles from Swift River. "He'll know I'm bluffing."

As they stood on the sidewalk Ted put his hands on Julia's shoulders. "Do you trust me to do the talking?"

She looked up into his deep, earnest eyes. "Yes," she said without an instant's hesitation.

"Then let's do it."

Inside, they breezed past the startled receptionist and marched straight into Frank Foster's office. Foster looked up in surprise. When he saw Julia, his face folded into a peeved frown. "What do *you* want?"

"The truth," Ted said promptly. "We're onto the scheme, Foster."

Foster narrowed his eyes. "What do you mean?"

"The treaty," Ted answered. "What would you

say if we told you that a third copy had been made and we have it?"

Foster blanched visibly. "There was no third copy."

Ted patted his backpack. "Bear Paw, the Yakima chief, has had one all this time. It was passed down to him by his father, and his father before him. It's the real thing, Foster. Signed and sealed in 1877 by President Grant himself. If you don't believe me, why don't we compare it to your copy? There's no point lying anymore—we know you have it."

Foster opened a drawer in his desk and removed a plain, unlabeled folder. "Show me what you've got first," he ordered, resting his hands on top of the folder.

Ted stepped to Foster's side, pretending to unbuckle his backpack. While Foster's eyes were on Ted, Julia darted forward and grabbed the folder. Then the two turned and ran for the door. Foster yelled in outrage, but they didn't stop until they reached the car, which Ted had left idling. Jumping in, Ted stepped on the gas, pushing the pedal to the floor. Julia gripped the edge of the seat as they roared off.

In moments, they'd left the center of Parkersburg behind. Julia's hands were still shaking from the excitement, but she managed to open the folder. And there, resting right on top of a few other papers, was a yellowed piece of parchment. The treaty!

"We got it!" she yelled.

Ted flashed her a triumphant grin. "Talk about teamwork."

"Oh, Ted, I couldn't have done it without you." Julia threw her arms around his neck.

The car nearly swerved off the road. "Whoa, watch it!" cautioned Ted, but Julia noticed he didn't seem to mind her nearness. "Yes, you could have done it, and you would have," he went on. "I'm just glad I was there to help you deal with a scoundrel like Foster." Ted turned off the paved road onto a dirt road running along a steep cliff above the Swift River. "Now that we have the treaty, what's the next step?"

"I think we should take it right away to—" Julia stopped. Did she hear the sound of another engine? She twisted in her seat to look back through the rear window. Out of nowhere, a black car had appeared, and it was coming up behind them fast. "That driver should be more careful on such a dangerous road," she commented. "If he doesn't watch out—"

Crash. There was a sound of crumpling metal. The other driver had rear-ended Ted's car! The black car fell back slightly, then accelerated. Again, it crashed into the back of the coupe!

"My God, what's he trying to do?" Julia cried fearfully.

"Force us off the road." Ted's voice was grim and his knuckles white as he fought to keep the damaged coupe on course. "It looks like Foster isn't going to give up that treaty without a fight."

Trembling, Julia looked behind her again. There were two men in the car, but both wore hats pulled low over their eyes. She couldn't tell if either of them was Foster. "Maybe we should pull over."

Instead of braking, Ted gunned the engine. "No one's taking your story away from you!"

A wild chase ensued. Their sudden acceleration took the other driver by surprise, and for a moment, Julia thought she and Ted would get away. But the other car was more powerful. Soon it was on their tail again. And the road was growing narrower, rougher, and steeper all the time.

Suddenly, there was a screeching, scraping sound. The black car was pushing its way alongside the coupe—pushing Ted and Julia closer to the edge of the cliff. "We're going over!" Julia screamed, squeezing her eyes shut.

Ted braked and yanked on the steering wheel with all his might. Julia was hurled against the car door. She opened her eyes, expecting to find herself staring down the cliff to the raging river below. Instead, she saw that their car had jackknifed, but was still on the road. It was the other automobile that was plunging headlong down the cliff!

With a sick feeling in the pit of her stomach, Julia watched the black car somersault. It landed at the river's edge, upright but incredibly crumpled. Could anyone survive such a crash?

Setting the emergency brake, Ted jumped from the car. Julia climbed out after him. "Ted, where are you going?" she called as he began skidding down the steep grade to the riverbed.

"Whoever's in there needs help!" he shouted back.

Julia scrambled after Ted, clutching rocks and plants to keep her footing. She was still only half-way down the cliff when Ted reached the wreck. She saw him wrench open the car door and pull out the limp bodies of two men. Quickly, Ted dragged the men one by one to the shelter of a large boulder a short distance away. His action was not a moment too soon. Julia flung up her arms to protect her face as the car exploded.

"Foster and his cohort tried to kill us, but you saved their lives," Julia said, her eyes glowing with admiration. "You're really something, Ted Wakefield."

It was evening, and Julia and Ted were eating a home-cooked supper in the candlelit parlor of Miss Mittelstadt's boardinghouse.

Ted sipped his cider. "I didn't do anything out of the ordinary, Julia. Anyone would have acted the same way."

"That's not true and you know it. Most people would have panicked. Because of your courage, those men are alive—and in jail. You did a very noble thing."

"Noble?" Ted smiled crookedly. "Not a word I would use to describe myself." He looked into Julia's eyes. He seemed to be on the verge of some kind of confession. She held her breath. "Julia, I'm not a knight in shining armor. I think you should know what kind of man I really am."

"I know what kind of man you are. I saw you in action today."

"But actions aren't all that matters. A man is made up of more than that—things like background, and family."

Ted seemed to be watching closely for her reaction. "Maybe some people think that way, but not me," Julia said. "I'm not a better person just because my family is wealthy and we have a name in New York. I couldn't respect someone who prejudged me on that basis. And that's not how *I* judge people."

Julia put a hand on Ted's arm as she spoke. "It doesn't matter to me whether you're a prince or a pauper, Ted," she whispered. "I admire you, plain and simple."

And I'm falling in love with you, plain and simple! she added silently.

"I've finished what I came for," Ted told Julia a few days later as they cast their fishing lines into the river. "I learned a lot of Awaswan lore from my distant cousins that I can pass on to my children one day."

Julia bit her lip. "So it's time to go?"

Ted nodded. "I guess I've stayed away from home long enough. It's time."

Say it, Julia silently commanded herself. *This is your chance. Don't blow it!* "I'm finished, too. My parents are expecting me in D.C. in a week— they're visiting friends there. I'll present my evidence to the Bureau of Indian Affairs, then head back to New York to get the story in print. Are you . . . are you reenrolling at Rosse?"

"No. I don't know what I'm going to do next," Ted admitted.

Julia took the plunge. "Then come with me," she urged. "Come to Washington! You'll love it. It's a wonderful city. And the Vaughns, my parents' friends, have a fabulous estate with tennis courts and stables, and we could go to the museums and monuments, and see a play, and I bet there are plenty of jazz clubs—"

Ted held up a hand, laughing. "Whoa! That's enough. It sounds great. But I'm not sure I could handle all that culture and civilization after a whole spring and summer of living out of my automobile!"

"Well, if it'll make you feel any better, you can camp out in the backyard, and I'll serve you pork and beans in your tent," Julia teased.

Ted smiled. Narrowing his eyes, he studied her face. "You really want me to come with you?"

Julia nodded, wondering if her eagerness was overwhelmingly apparent. Could Ted tell that she'd fallen head over heels in love with his warm brown eyes, his mysterious intensity, his rare but rich laughter? Was it so obvious that she'd never met a man who interested her more?

"Well . . ." Ted considered her offer. "It's a nice invitation. I'd like to travel some more, see more of the country. And I'd enjoy your company. I accept."

"I'm so glad!" Julia couldn't tell whether Ted had agreed to her proposal because he had nothing better to do or because he was as interested in her as she was in him. It didn't really matter, she decided. After cracking her first big story, she felt confident that her future would be marked by success. She planned to put all her energy into this next assignment: winning Ted Wakefield's heart.

Twenty

"This sure is an easier way to travel than the way I got out here," Ted declared.

He and Julia had met in the narrow corridor outside their adjoining sleeping berths and were now seated in the elegant dining car of the transcontinental train. The view from the window was dramatic. The tracks carved through jagged peaks: On one side, a white-capped mountain towered, and on the other, a river boiled down a deep gorge.

"The mountain roads must have been brutal on your auto," Julia remarked, stirring a sugar cube into her coffee.

"They certainly put it to the test," Ted agreed. "I was almost sorry to sell the beast back in San Francisco. We covered a lot of ground together."

"The beast?" Julia laughed. "Is that how you'll refer to me someday? 'I was almost sorry to part with the beast in D.C. We covered a lot of ground together.' "

Ted grinned. "No, this time around *I'm* the beast. You're the beauty."

She shook her head, still smiling. "I guess I'll have to be satisfied with that."

A waiter in a crisp white coat delivered their breakfast. Julia dug into her omelet with relish. Ted lifted his fork, but didn't begin eating. A memory came to him, from far back in the past. So far back, in fact, that it wasn't even his own memory—it was his mother's. "You know, this isn't the first time I've ridden a train east from San Francisco."

"It's not?" Julia looked up from buttering a roll. "I thought you had always lived in the Midwest."

"My parents were from California. My mother didn't move to Chicago until after I was born." Ted studied Julia's sweet, expectant face. Suddenly, Ted wanted to tell her everything there was to know about himself. He'd always kept so much hidden from his friends—even from Harry, even from Amanda. How would it feel to know that one other person really knew him?

"I thought I was pretty gutsy, cutting loose from school and driving out west by myself. But when she was even younger than I am now, my mother took the train from San Francisco to go to a city she'd never even seen with a newborn baby and no husband. She wasn't even a respectable widow.

207

She was an unmarried girl who'd been kicked out of the house by her father."

Julia's blue eyes grew round. Ted could see that she was trying to imagine being in such a predicament. "That *is* gutsy."

Ted was filled with a sudden rush of affection for Julia. She was always beautiful, but to Ted she'd never appeared more beautiful than she did at that moment.

"In deference to society, she raised me as her orphaned nephew." Ted smiled wryly. "So there you have it, Julia. The life story you've been waiting for. What do you think?"

Under the table, Julia touched his foot with her own. "I think that if that's the only reason you've been holding back from—" She stopped, her cheeks suddenly flooding with color. Then she laughed at her own embarrassment. "I'm the one who should be worried about what you think about my being so forward! Well, Ted, I guess the secret's out, if it ever was a secret. I like you—I like you very much. And I'd like to get to know you better."

Ted smiled. He liked her forwardness. *Honesty* was another word for it. He knew she hadn't invited him to travel to D.C. with her just because she didn't want to eat alone in the dining car. *I'd better be straight with her—completely straight,* Ted decided. It wasn't fair to lead her on. "Let me tell you another story."

In a clipped voice, Ted told Julia about the affair

with Amanda, his love for her and her betrayal. After he finished, Julia was silent for a moment. "Do you—do you still have feelings for her?" she asked at last.

"Not the kind of feelings you mean," he said. "But other feelings, as a result." *Bitterness, disillusionment . . .* he thought silently. "Julia, I—I value your friendship. I'm glad we're getting to spend more time together. But I'm just not looking for . . ." He didn't complete the sentence. He didn't have to; his meaning was clear.

If she was disappointed, she covered it well. "Don't say another word about it," she said brightly. "I understand completely. We'll be wonderful sightseeing companions, you and I. We'll have a ball in D.C."

Ted hoped so. But he couldn't help wondering if it would really be possible for him and Julia to be just friends.

"I don't know when I've ever danced so much!"

"I feel like I'm still whirling," Julia breathed. Bending, she slipped off her high heels and ran in stocking feet across the midnight-dark lawn of the Vaughns' estate.

Ted ran after her. "Your hair is falling down," he told her.

"Oh, let it fall." Lifting one bare arm, Julia released the jeweled clip that was coming loose. She

209

shook her head, and her long, wheat-blond hair fell shimmering about her shoulders.

She heard Ted catch his breath. There was a look in his eyes she'd never seen before. "Your hair—it's like moonlight," he said.

Julia gazed at him, her own eyes glowing. *Touch it—touch me,* she thought.

The night air was warm, but Ted's hands were warmer still. He touched Julia's shoulders, lightly at first. Then, grasping them, he pulled her to him. She closed her eyes and lifted her face to his, her lips burning for his kiss. She'd waited so long for this.

Finally, Ted's mouth was on hers. Her body melted against his as he kissed her hungrily. "Haven't you wanted this all week?" she murmured. Ted's lips were traveling down the curve of her throat. "I have. All the time we were playing tennis or horseback riding, going for walks— haven't you wanted this?"

"Yes." He wrapped his arms even more tightly around her. "Yes."

Joy flooded Julia's heart. Ted was drawn to her as much as she was to him. Maybe he hadn't been looking for love, but he'd found it—it had found them. He couldn't deny it now. "I love you, Ted. Do you love me?"

Ted had placed his hands on either side of her face, preparing to kiss her again. Now he dropped his hands and stepped back from her. "Yes . . . no. I mean . . . oh, Julia."

Suddenly she felt cold. She crossed her arms over the front of her sleeveless beaded dress. *He just got carried away, carried away by the dancing, the moonlight,* she realized, crushed. *He's still not really interested in me.*

"You're shivering." Ted removed his jacket and draped it around her bare shoulders. "Come on. Let's go in."

"A remarkable monument to a remarkable man," said Ted as he and Julia gazed up at the seated marble figure in the Lincoln Memorial.

"It brings tears to my eyes every time," Julia added.

From the Lincoln Memorial, they strolled alongside the reflecting pool toward the Washington Monument. Ted looked at Julia out of the corner of his eye. The tailored green linen suit she was wearing made the most of her slender, curvy figure; a tiny matching hat was perched on top of her pile of blond hair, a few silky strands of which had been teased free by the warm summer breeze.

"Let's rest our feet," Julia suggested.

They sat down on a shady bench. Julia hooked her arm through his and leaned lightly against him. *The way a good friend would,* Ted thought. He felt a pang of guilt. Their passionate encounter the previous night had ended on an awkward note. But he knew Julia still had hopes; he could see it in her eyes.

I should never have let it happen, Ted thought. But remembering Julia's kisses, his heart pumped a little faster. She'd been right. He *had* wanted it. But when she'd told him she loved him . . . Ted hadn't wanted that. He hadn't been ready for that. He *did* have feelings for her, but they weren't as strong as hers were for him. It wouldn't be fair for him not to love her wholly, as she seemed to love him.

"Julia, I'm leaving town tomorrow," he announced abruptly.

Her eyes widened. "So soon?"

"The Vaughns have been wonderful, but I don't want to take advantage of their hospitality."

"Where will you go?"

"Home to Chicago." Disappointment shadowed Julia's face. "But then I'd like to try New York for a while," he added. "I want to start writing again and I could use a new scene."

"Well, there are plenty of newspapers and jazz clubs in New York," Julia said, turning her head away from him.

He took her hand. "Julia. Look at me."

She did, revealing tear-filled eyes. "I can't say I'm happy you'll be leaving." She hesitated. "I've told you how I feel about you, Ted. But I don't know what *you* feel for me. I'm not sure you know yourself," she challenged.

Ted shook his head. "No," he said simply. "I do know. I—I love you, too, Julia. And I wish I could be feeling it all for the first time, the way you are, feeling it with my whole heart and soul."

"But you're not. So what?"

Ted frowned. "So what?"

Julia folded her arms across her chest. "So what?" she repeated. "You had a bad time because of Amanda. What are you going to do about it? Just give up on love altogether? You might as well give up on life!"

"Well, I—"

"Now you look at me, Ted. I'm pretty, I'm smart, I like hard work and adventure. Most of all, I love you. With my whole heart and soul. Are you going to hold that against me?"

Ted touched her face. "No. No, of course not."

"I'd make you the perfect wife and you know it."

"You left out how forward you are," Ted whispered, almost laughing now.

He hugged her, and she pressed her cheek against his. "I'm not Amanda," she whispered. "It could be different for us, Ted."

As he held Julia close Ted realized that he wasn't afraid anymore. He could love Julia in spite of what had happened with Amanda. "I know," he whispered back.

Twenty-one

1927. New York.

"It's perfect," Julia raved as she and Ted strolled about the first floor of the empty brownstone. "Look at the size of this kitchen!"

"It's bigger than our whole apartment," Ted agreed.

Julia put an arm around his waist. "But you haven't minded being so cramped and cozy, have you?"

He smiled down at her. "What do you think?"

Oblivious to the real estate agent, who'd moved on to the dining room, where he was extolling the quality of the crown molding, Julia and Ted shared a long, sweet kiss. Julia loved the little studio apartment where she and Ted had lived since their autumn wedding. But she couldn't deny that it would be wonderful to have more living and working space.

"And upstairs . . ." the agent droned on.

Julia and Ted trailed after him. "You know, the price is right," Ted said to her under his breath. "If you really like it, maybe we should go ahead and make a bid."

Julia nodded. The brownstone needed a little work, but the price was reasonable, and it was within walking distance of both their offices. "Just think," she said, giving Ted a squeeze. "A home of our own!"

Ted squeezed her back. "Everything's going our way, darling."

It really was, Julia thought. Immediately after their wedding, they had plunged into city life, determined to take New York by storm. Ted's impressive portfolio had landed him a position at *The New Yorker* magazine. Julia's luck had been just as good. After printing her story about the Swift River Indian reservation, the daily *New York Chronicle* had hired Julia to cover events and issues of local interest. She had her very own column—"Citywatch," by Julia Marks-Wakefield. Now Ted was talking about taking classes at Columbia University in hopes of completing his bachelor's degree.

"Two roomy bedrooms," the realtor pointed out when they reached the top of the stairs.

"And look at this little room here!" Julia pulled Ted into a small room with one big, sunny window.

"Hmm," Ted said, considering. "Just right for a study."

"Just right for a nursery, I think," said Julia.

"Well, yes, someday. But for now—" He broke off and stared at her. Julia, standing by the window, smiled at him. "Julia, you're not . . . ?"

She nodded. "I am. We are!"

"Julia!" Ted crossed to her side in two long strides. "I'm—I'm—we're—oh, hurrah!"

Picking her up, he lifted her high in the air. Julia squealed with laughter. "How's that for a scoop?" she asked him. "Extra, extra, read all about it!"

He set her back on her feet. Before he folded her in his arms, she saw that his eyes were sparkling with happy tears. "We make quite a team, Julia. And I think this is going to be our best story yet."

The door to the hospital room was ajar. Ted nudged it with his toe because his hands were full —he was holding a large bouquet of red roses and a big stuffed bear. Julia didn't notice him at first. But Ted didn't mind at all.

Sitting up in bed, Julia cradled a newborn baby in her arms. Her eyes were fixed on the tiny, perfect face. Ted watched her laugh with joy as the baby screwed up his eyes and opened his mouth in a wide yawn. He took this as his cue. "Good morning, family," he said, stepping into the room.

Julia looked up. "Hello, darling. You're just in time for our post-breakfast burps."

"Excellent! That's when I find both of you at

your most charming." He pulled a chair up to the bedside. "May I?"

Gently, Julia handed the swaddled baby to Ted. Gazing down at his son, named Robert after Julia's father, an overwhelming feeling of awe, gratitude, and love swept over Ted. He and Julia had made a wonderful life together in the first year of their marriage, but nothing they'd made was as wonderful as Robert.

"We're so lucky," Ted said, putting his finger in Robert's tiny hand to test his son's grip. "We have everything we could ever want, don't we?"

"I don't." Julia reached for a newspaper on her bedside table. "Take a look at this." She tapped page three, where "Citywatch" was printed. A guest columnist was filling in while Julia was on maternity leave. Ted knew it rankled his wife to have someone else covering her beat. "Have you ever seen poorer writing?" she demanded. "They would be better off just dropping the column until I can be back on the job!"

Ted returned the baby to Julia's arms. He skimmed the piece. "Actually, this isn't half bad. I like her style."

She swatted him with the newspaper. "You would. She usually writes about the music scene!"

Ted laughed heartily. His laughter trailed off a moment later, however, as he flipped through the paper. Julia leaned over to see what had caused his sudden soberness.

Julia read the headline out loud. " 'Hollywood Starlet Samantha Watson Dies.' " She clucked her tongue. "What a sad story. She was so glamorous, and so young. To die in childbirth! How awful for the poor husband and the little baby."

A lump in his throat, Ted closed the paper. The article hadn't mentioned Amanda, and he didn't see any reason to tell Julia about the connection. *Poor Sam*, Ted thought. *Poor Amanda*. And Sam's husband, Jack Lewis. *How must he feel, losing his wife at what should have been the happiest time of their lives? What if I'd lost Julia?* He leaned over and gave her a tender kiss. He really did feel like the luckiest man in the world.

Twenty-two

1937. New York.

Julia walked home from work, a bounce in her step
and a smile on her face. She had spring fever from
the balmy March air and she was giddy from the
glass of champagne she'd drunk at the office party
the *Chronicle* had given in her honor. No one had
been happier than Julia herself to toast the two
thousandth appearance of "Citywatch" by Julia
Marks-Wakefield. *And wait until I tell Ted about my
next assignment!*

Although the Great Depression had brought un-
employment to many, even to Ted for a brief period, Julia's position at the *Chronicle* had remained
secure. In fact, her career had grown by leaps and
bounds; her bold investigating and compelling style
made "Citywatch" the most-read column in the
newspaper. It was Julia who had exposed the shifty
dealings of the banks and Federal Reserve Board

prior to the fateful stock market crash of 1929; Julia who had ventured alone into the unsavory part of the city where homeless, jobless people lived in pathetic shelters constructed from scraps of wood and cardboard boxes, so she could tell the "Hooverville" residents' story in their own moving words.

Thank goodness for Franklin Delano Roosevelt, Julia reflected. The Depression was passing, slowly but surely. Ted now worked for the Works Progress Administration overseeing a WPA music program that offered classes and free concerts for the public. He loved the job, not least because he loved being able to give work to his many down-on-their-luck musician friends.

He'll be so happy for me, Julia thought, running up the steps of the brownstone. *And Robert will be, too!*

She draped her coat on the banister and tracked the voices into the kitchen. Nine-year-old Robert was helping his father peel potatoes. "Hello, boys!" Julia sang, tousling her son's brown hair. "What kind of culinary magic are you conjuring up tonight?"

Ted grinned. "Something pretty fancy. Mashed potatoes and meat loaf."

"Now, I wonder who selected that menu?" Julia tickled Robert. "We'd eat that every night if it were up to you, right, kiddo?"

Robert's dark eyes crinkled with laughter as he

twisted away from his mother's hands. "Right, Mom."

"You're in a good mood," Ted observed.

"I am, and I'll tell you why." Removing the peeler from Ted's hand, Julia took his arms and placed them around her waist. "Guess who's been offered the reporting assignment of a lifetime?"

Ted pretended to ponder the question. "Let's see . . . could it be Julia Marks-Wakefield?"

"Of course it could be! Oh, Ted, you won't believe it. The *Chronicle* wants to send me to Germany!"

"Germany?"

"Where's that?" asked Robert.

"It's in Europe," Julia told her son. "And I'll explain all about it in a moment. Germany, Ted—just think of it!" She gazed up at him, her eyes glittering with excitement. "I would observe the Nazi government and its *führer*, Adolf Hitler, in action."

Ted squeezed her. "It's the foreign assignment you've been waiting for."

"Isn't it a thrill? And Ted, if I do well," Julia continued, her tone suddenly solemn, "I'll probably be offered the foreign-correspondent position in Berlin."

As she had expected, this angle took Ted's breath away. His arms dropping, he sat down abruptly on one of the stools by the counter. "Berlin," he said simply. "Julia."

"I won't be committing myself to anything long-term if I take just the one trip," she hurried to say. "We'll have time to talk it over. I wouldn't accept any offer, no matter how tempting, without being sure that it was the right thing for us all."

"It will be hard for me and Robert to lose you, even for a short time," Ted told her.

"I know." Julia took her husband's hand. With her other hand, she reached for her son. "It will be hard for me to be away from you, too. But, Ted, it's so important that I go." Her voice grew passionate. "The situation in Europe is explosive. Hitler is re-arming his country. I'm determined to see for myself how far Hitler has taken his anti-Semitic theories. Ted, this could be the big one! The story I've been looking for ever since those early days in Oregon."

Ted had been watching his wife carefully as she spoke. Now he put a hand on either side of Julia's flushed, pretty face. "Of course you have to go. For yourself and for all of us. The story is what matters."

"Thank you, Ted," Julia whispered.

Robert was tugging at the sleeve of her silk blouse. Julia looked down into his wide, apprehensive eyes. "Germany's far away, isn't it, Mom?" he said, trying to sound brave.

Kneeling, Julia hugged her son reassuringly. "It is indeed. But I'll be back soon, and I'll write you every day. I'll be back," she repeated.

*　*　*

"Do you think she's there yet?" Robert asked Ted as they ate dinner one evening in late March. Robert had selected the menu; once again it was meat loaf and mashed potatoes.

Ted looked across at his son. For some reason, the dining room table seemed big and empty without Julia sitting there between them. "She'll be stepping off the boat in France any minute now," he answered. "Then she'll take a train to Germany. The countries are right next to each other—it won't be a long trip."

"I wish we could have gone with her, to take care of her." Robert pushed a few peas around on his plate with his fork, his small forehead creased in a worried frown. "Those Germans are bad people, aren't they?"

"I don't think the German people are bad. But their *führer* is, and I'm afraid he's leading the country in a dangerous direction."

"When will we hear from her?"

Ted knew that for the young boy, each day his mother was gone felt like a year. For Ted, too, time had been passing much more slowly since Julia's departure. "Soon," he promised Robert. "She'll telegraph us right after the *Normandie* docks. And then the letters will start coming."

"They'll be great," Robert predicted confidently. "Mom can really write."

223

Ted smiled at the note of pride in his son's voice. "She sure can," he agreed.

The letters came, and they were as lively and interesting as Ted and Robert expected. First, Julia wrote about the transatlantic passage on the *Normandie,* and then about the train journey to Berlin. In entertaining detail, she described the people she had met, the adventures she had had, the sights and sounds and smells of foreign places.

Reading Julia's letters became a cherished ritual. One afternoon late in April, father and son fixed their usual snack of bread-and-jam sandwiches and hot tea. With great ceremony, Robert tore open the envelope and handed the letter to his father.

Ted cleared his throat and began to read. When he came to a difficult word or concept he would stop to explain it as best he could to Robert. This letter had many such difficulties; since she'd arrived in Germany, the content of Julia's letters had grown more serious.

The atmosphere in Berlin is grim, Julia wrote. *Each day, I witness or get word of additional Nazi atrocities. Anti-Semitism is widespread. Hitler plans to assert the dominion of the Aryan "master race" and to expand the German* lebensraum—*space for living—throughout Eastern Europe.*

The news was indeed disturbing. Ted put down the letter for a moment to take a few bites of his sandwich.

"I don't understand why Mom's worried," Robert said. "If the Germans just want a bigger living room . . ."

Ted smiled wryly at his son's translation of the term *lebensraum.* "It's more than just that. Here, I'll read some more."

Julia went on to report that the rest of Europe's attitude toward Hitler was anxious but disbelieving. *They still think he will become more moderate, but I don't agree,* she proclaimed in her bold, loopy script. *The evidence is everywhere. The Nuremberg Laws forbid Germans to have commerce with or marry Jews. Jews are now classed as "subjects," not "citizens," of the nation and are denied many rights.*

While they finished their sandwiches, Ted tried to remain cheerful in front of his son. But when Robert ran outside to play stickball with a friend, Ted reread the letter, his concern growing. He did not like to think of Julia in such a dangerous country, taking risks to acquire the information she needed to document her report. No, Ted thought, story or no story, he wouldn't be at ease again until Julia wrote to tell them she was coming home.

In Julia's next letter, she touched on many of the same issues detailed in her previous correspondence. But Ted was struck by something odd in her style. Instead of her usual directness, she was evasive, only hinting that she'd discovered something particularly horrifying. At the end of the letter, she explained her reticence. *I fear the government cen-*

sors, she wrote. *It's possible that my letters are being screened, so I must be discreet. They can't censor this, however! I love you, Ted. I love you, Robert. And I'll be home soon—details of my travel plans to follow!*

The next letter arrived, the last letter, and in it Julia announced that she would soon be leaving Germany to travel home to the United States by airship. But that was the only information on the page that Ted could decipher—the letter had been heavily censored. He stared at the heavy black marks blotting out Julia's words. What had she written that was so dangerous to the German authorities?

Ted and Robert circled May sixth, the date of Julia's return, on the calendar. Finally, the day came, and they were on their way to Lakehurst, New Jersey, where the dirigible would dock and its passengers would disembark. On his lap, Robert held a fluffy white kitten with a blue bow around its neck, a welcome-home present for his mother; he himself wore a brand-new baseball cap.

They parked the car at the edge of a field and walked to where a small crowd had gathered to await the arrival of the *Hindenburg.* Robert could barely contain his excitement. "Is Mom really flying home on a giant balloon?" he asked.

From his jacket pocket, Ted removed a newspaper clipping with a photograph of the *Hindenburg.*

He showed the picture to Robert. "It's a giant balloon with a rigid frame," Ted explained. "It's filled with hydrogen, which is lighter than air. See?"

Robert examined the photograph. "And it can fly across the ocean?"

"Yep." Ted tucked the clipping back into his pocket. "The *Hindenburg* has crossed the Atlantic more than twenty times. Look!" He pointed. In the distance, a long, cigar-shaped airship sailed into view. The *Hindenburg!*

Clapping, Robert jumped up and down. "Hi, Mom!" he yelled.

Ted laughed. "She can't hear you yet."

Holding their breath, they watched as the massive dirigible eased up to the landing tower. In just a few minutes, Julia would step out onto the platform. Ted's heart pounded. He couldn't wait to hold his wife in his arms again.

His eyes fixed on the airship, Ted thought he saw a flicker of something like lightning. An instant later, the *Hindenburg* burst into flames!

There were cries and exclamations from the onlookers. "Dad, what's wrong?" Robert cried, frightened.

Ted didn't have time to answer his son's question. Shoving Robert into the arms of a horrified woman standing nearby, he sprinted across the field toward the flaming airship.

Suddenly, there was a deafening explosion, then

another. The impact threw Ted to the ground, but he leaped to his feet again. "Julia!" he shouted as he ran toward the disintegrating *Hindenburg*. "Julia!"

Twenty-three

Ted sat on the living room couch holding Julia's journal in his hands and staring into the glowing embers of the fireplace. The house was quiet. He had just tucked Robert into bed and he prayed that, for once, his son would sleep through the night without being woken by one of the terrible nightmares that had haunted him since the horrific accident and Julia's death.

Set on the coffee table facing Ted was a framed photograph of Julia—the last picture he'd taken of her, at the moment she'd boarded the *Normandie* to leave for Europe. She was wearing a navy suit, the square-shouldered jacket belted snugly at her slender waist and the trim skirt showing off her shapely legs; over one arm she carried a travel bag and cape. She was turning to smile and wave goodbye at her husband and son. *For the rest of our lives, that's all we'll have,* Ted thought. *That one final smile. Why, oh why, did I let her go?*

His anguish was so deep it verged on anger, even hatred. He stared down at the journal, his eyes burning. If it hadn't been for her *Chronicle* assignment, she would be alive at that minute. The stupid notebook! It had been rescued from the undamaged hold of the *Hindenburg* and forwarded to Ted; Julia was lost, but the journal survived. Where was the justice in that?

Ted fought an urge to hurl the small book into the fire. Instead, he opened it gingerly. At the sight of Julia's familiar handwriting, tears sprang to his eyes. The script was large and loopy; she always wrote too fast, her hand never quite able to keep up with the speed of her thoughts. Ted stroked the page, aching from the wish that he could be touching Julia herself, not just her words.

As he began to read the journal, however, his expression changed from one of sorrow to disbelief. Julia's hastily scribbled notes were shocking. *German Jews are being forced to live in horrendous conditions,* she wrote. *In some instances, their property is seized and they are arrested on trumped-up charges and sent to work camps. It seems as if the Nazis want to get rid of them altogether. Certainly they don't want the Jews to have any economic or political presence in Germany.*

Quickly, Ted turned the page to another entry. *It is not only German Jews who are in danger,* Julia had continued. *According to my sources, Hitler has expansionist designs—his eye is on Austria. Conditions for the Jews, however, continue to deteriorate. All but the Nazis live in great fear of what Hitler will do next. Why?*

Ted closed the journal. At that moment, he heard footsteps on the staircase. "Dad?" a fearful voice called out.

"In here, son."

Robert, dressed in pajamas, hurried into the living room. "In my dream, everything's on fire. Mom's on fire and you're on fire and there's nothing I can do."

Ted put his arms around his son, who was trying manfully not to cry. "I'm here with you, Bob," he said. "We're both all right."

Robert buried his face against his father's chest. "Why'd she have to die, Dad? I wish she would come back."

"I wish that, too, son," Ted said. "I wish that, too."

It was a cold autumn evening, and Ted's breath came in white puffs. Pausing at a street corner on his way home from work, he handed a few coins to a paperboy, who slapped the latest edition of the *New York Chronicle* into his palm. Ted flipped the paper open and read as he walked.

The headline was printed in large, ominous type: "Thousands Arrested During 'Kristallnacht' Riots."

In horror, Ted read the story of what had happened recently in Germany on the date that had been dubbed Kristallnacht, "the night of broken glass." Synagogues and stores had been looted and burned, people injured and killed, and no one knew exactly how many Jews had been arrested and sent to camps.

Europe teetered on the verge of war; no one could deny it any longer. Hitler had forcibly annexed Austria, and Czechoslovakia and Poland were braced for attacks. German Jewish refugees had begun to pour into New York, bringing horror stories of conditions in Germany and of the daily outrages committed by officers of Hitler's monstrous army.

Tucking the newspaper into his briefcase, Ted turned down the street where Robert's friend Jason Hoch lived; Robert was playing at Jason's until dinnertime. *Kristallnacht* . . . Ted shuddered at the horror of it. And mixed with his dismay was a sense of bitter irony. He remembered reading Julia's Berlin journal many months ago. Hadn't she predicted this state of affairs?

A grim smile twisted Ted's lips as he rang the Hochs' bell. In a strange way, what was a disaster for the free world was a triumph for the journalist Julia Marks-Wakefield. Her final story had been confirmed. At long last, she would indeed have broken "the big one."

Twenty-four

1943. New York.

Robert strode into the Navy recruitment office with his chin up and his back straight, hoping he looked relaxed, confident, and a couple of years older than he actually was. It helped that he'd inherited his father's height and broad shoulders.

He joined the line of other young men there to enlist. Soon it was his turn. "I'd like to sign up," he told the elderly man behind the desk.

"That's the spirit, son," the man declared. "Uncle Sam needs you. Have a seat right here. The first step is to fill out these forms. Then you'll head over to Room C for your physical."

Robert wasn't worried about the physical. He was healthy and fit—the doctors wouldn't find anything wrong with him. The hard part was going to be filling out the forms. Carefully, he printed his name and social security number, then his home address and his father's name for next of kin. Only one space in the personal information portion of the application remained blank: date of birth.

July 10, 1925, Robert wrote, pressing hard with the pen, as if that would make the date look more legitimate. Most of it was true, anyway—only the year was a little off. And Robert suspected that the armed forces were so eager to sign up new recruits that they wouldn't question his application.

What does it matter, anyway, if I was born in 1927 instead of 1925? Robert thought as he capped the pen. What mattered was that he wanted to fight for the cause of world freedom. It was his duty.

An hour later, Robert was back out on the sidewalk. His thick brown hair was noticeably shorter; around his neck was a set of dogtags; he held a duffel containing his boot-camp assignment and a sailor's uniform. *I did it!* Robert thought jubilantly. Striding up the street, he was so euphoric that he barely felt the pavement under his shoes. The very next day he'd leave for boot camp in Virginia; within months he'd actually be "over there," helping the Allied forces defeat its enemies in Europe or the Pacific!

As he got closer to home, however, Robert's mood changed. There was still one major hurdle to tackle.

Robert took the steps of the brownstone two at a time. Inside, he headed straight upstairs to his bedroom. He dumped the uniform onto his bed, then removed the jingling dogtags. Changing into athletic attire, he folded the recruitment papers and slipped them into his pocket.

He found his father, also dressed for exercise, chugging a glass of apple juice in the kitchen. "Tennis or basketball?" Ted asked.

"How about just a run in the park?" Robert suggested.

"Fine with me," said Ted. Then he noticed his son's hair. "Got your football-season haircut a little early, eh, son?"

Robert ran a hand over his crewcut self-consciously. "Uh, yeah."

Outside, the two stretched for a few minutes, then jogged toward Central Park. It didn't take long to work up a sweat; it was a warm August afternoon. Entering the shade of the park was a relief, and the two men settled comfortably into stride.

Robert, meanwhile, was racking his brain for the right way to begin what he knew would be a very intense conversation. "How was class today, Dad?"

Ted now taught music history and journalism at New York University in addition to contributing freelance articles to magazines. "No one concentrates very well when it's hot, including the professor," Ted replied. "That's the problem with summer school."

Robert decided to take advantage of the fact that his father was huffing and puffing slightly.

235

"Reading the newspaper today, I thought about Mom," he began. "If she were alive today, I bet she'd be in the thick of things in Europe, reporting the events of the war."

Ted shot a glance at his son out of the corner of his eye. "You're probably right."

"Dad, I want to fight for the cause."

"We've been over this before," Ted said, panting. "You're much too young to enlist, Robert. Besides, the war will be over any day now."

Ted didn't sound convinced of this last statement. Robert jumped on it. "You know that's not true, Dad. The war against Hitler is in its most crucial stage. And what about the Pacific?" In addition to the brutal land battles on the European front, Allied forces were also engaged in a deadly effort to regain the Pacific islands from the Japanese. "My country needs me," Robert persisted. "If Mom were here, she'd let me go."

Ted's expression grew pained. "Your mother believed in fighting injustice, it's true. But she was a wife and mother as well as a journalist. I think if she were here, she'd feel the same way I do about this. She'd ask you to wait until you're eighteen. And then, if the war is still going on—"

"I'm not going to wait."

Ted stopped. He bent forward, his hands on his knees, sucking in air. "What did you say?"

"I said I'm not going to wait."

Ted straightened. The two men were the exact

same height; he looked his son in the eye. "You enlisted already, didn't you? I should have known."

Robert knew there was no going back. The moment of reckoning had come. His heart pounding, he took the papers from his pocket. "I enlisted in the Navy this afternoon. I leave for Virginia first thing in the morning."

Ted's face, already flushed from exercise, darkened further with anger. "You enlisted without my permission?"

"Because I knew you wouldn't *give* me your permission."

"And for good reason!" Ted exclaimed. "Robert, you're only sixteen! You're not old enough—"

"I'm old enough," Robert interrupted, "and I'm going. There's nothing you can do to stop me, Dad!"

Ted stared at his son. "Oh, yes, there is," he said tightly. "I have a good mind to go down to the recruitment office and tell them the truth about your age." He grabbed Robert's shoulders and shook him hard. "Do you know what you're doing? Do you know the risk you're taking? This isn't a parade, Bob. It's not all marching bands and handsome uniforms. It's a bloody, vicious war."

Robert stood his ground. "I know what it is, Dad," he said quietly.

Ted dropped his hands. His face looked tired and gray. "Do you know the risk you're taking?" he repeated, his voice hoarse. "You could lose your life."

"It's the risk every soldier takes."

"Then go." Ted waved his hand and turned away from his son. "If you're set on killing yourself, just go!"

"Dad, listen to me. Please—"

But Ted had taken off down the sun-dappled path at a dead run. With a lump in his throat, Robert watched his father disappear into the trees.

Robert awoke at dawn. He ate a quick breakfast and washed up in the bathroom, making as little noise as possible. There was no sound from the master bedroom; his father must still be asleep.

The night before, Robert had waited anxiously for his father to come home from the park. It had been well after dark when he'd finally heard his father's footsteps in the hall, but Ted had marched straight to his bedroom without a word and slammed the door. Now, as Robert stuffed a few personal belongings into his duffel bag, he wondered if he would even see his father again before he left.

Just then there was a knock on the door. "Come in," Robert called.

Ted stepped into his son's bedroom. There was a moment of silence. Then he said, "Bob, I'm sorry about the scene yesterday."

"It's OK, Dad. I understand how you must feel about this."

"No, I don't think you do." Ted sat down on the edge of his son's bed. "When your mother died, I was devastated. If it hadn't been for you, I don't think I would have cared much about living. You mean the world to me."

"I know, Dad."

"I don't want you to fight," Ted went on. "I can't bear the thought that I might lose you. Part of me wants to deny that all this is happening. Last night I thought it might be easier if I just pushed you away from me. But then I remembered my mother's story. Her father had lost his wife and his son; Sarah was all he had left. And he loved Sarah so much that when she did something he didn't approve of, he pushed her away. He told her to go, and she did. He never saw her again, although I have to believe that he lived to regret his action."

Robert bent his head.

"Here." Ted held something out to Robert. "Take this."

It was a gold ring. Robert turned it in his hand, examining the strange design. "That's the Wakefield family crest," Ted explained. "The ring belonged to my English grandfather, my mother's father. I never did meet him, but apparently he was a strong man, with strong opinions."

"In a word, stubborn." Robert's brown eyes crinkled with laughter. "It's in the blood, then."

"It's in the blood," Ted agreed. He stood. "But I think his stubbornness helped him live a long, full life." His voice broke. "I wish the same for you."

Robert stepped to his father's side. The two men embraced.

"Thanks, Dad."

"Do your job and come back safely."

"Don't worry, Dad. Of course I'll come back," Robert said confidently.

Twenty-five

1943. The South Pacific.

Ensign Robert Wakefield stood on the deck of the steel-gray aircraft carrier *Richmond*, his feet braced against the rolling motion caused by high seas. The carrier rammed into a particularly big wave; Robert was dashed from head to toe with salty spray. He knew he should probably take cover if he didn't want to get soaked to the skin, but he couldn't tear himself away from the awesome sight of Admiral William Halsey's South Pacific Command task forces in full steam out of their base at Brisbane, Australia. In every direction, the ocean was dark with massive ships: carriers, cruisers, destroyers, minesweepers, transports. *What an incredible display of power,* Robert thought proudly.

Basic training at boot camp had been grueling. In October, he had received his instructions: He was being assigned to the *Richmond,* which was being sent to join the Sixth Army of the United States, the spearhead of General Douglas MacArthur's strategic offensive to recapture the Solomon Islands and the Philippines from the Japanese. Robert was assigned to the communications division. He wiped the water from his watch. It was 0900 hours, time to report to his superior officer at the communications center.

Five other new recruits were already assembled, standing at attention in a room papered with charts and crowded with telegraph machines, radios, typewriters, desks, and file cabinets. Robert gave Captain Danforth a crisp salute. Danforth nodded.

"You know the situation," the captain began without further delay. "The Japanese had the upper hand in the islands since December of forty-one, when they bombed Pearl Harbor, but we regained the initiative with the Battle of the Coral Sea, Midway, and Guadalcanal."

Danforth stepped over to a large wall chart of the Pacific. Using a pointer, he indicated two sets of push pins, one red and one blue. "We're now about to initiate a two-pronged offensive against the Japanese." He tapped the blue pins. "Admiral Nimitz's Pacific Fleet will push west across the central Pacific. Meanwhile, we"—he pointed to the red pins—"will move up the coast of New Guinea, eventually pushing the Japanese all the way back to the Philippines. I won't pretend it's going to be a picnic, men," Danforth went on. "Fighting in the islands is very different from the land battles in Europe. But we will advance. We will triumph."

The new recruits cheered.

"Gentlemen, you've arrived just in time to see some action," Danforth concluded. "I hope you're ready for it!"

"It's not all good news, is it, Ensign?"

Robert, seated at the wireless, looked up at Captain Danforth. He knew his face had blanched as he recorded the message that thirty American soldiers had just been killed in a thwarted attempt to land on a nearby Japanese-occupied island.

No, it hadn't taken Robert long to learn that it wasn't all good news in the communications center of the *Richmond,* or to learn that his assignment was by no means a restful one. Simultaneously, the communications staff had to keep in touch with every ship in Halsey's fleet, with ground units on the newly recaptured islands, with Nimitz's fleet in the central Pacific, and with various side operations in the region. And although Robert's wasn't a combat position, lives depended on his doing his job well. Misinformation, an error in the slightest detail, could lead to disaster.

"You're picking things up fast," Captain Danforth observed now. "So I'm going to foist another duty on you."

"I'm glad to help in any way, sir," Robert said.

243

"There's a group of female prisoners of war on Mindanao Island. You know Mindanao?"

"It's a large island in the southern Philippines, a key island, sir."

"Right. They're army nurses and nurses' aides captured when the Japanese took the island. When the fleet reaches the Philippines, we'll take the first possible opportunity to capture the garrison holding them and liberate the prisoners."

"Where do I come in?" asked Robert.

"We have a POW contact who transmits signals to us from an illegal radio," Danforth explained. "She keeps us informed about conditions on Mindanao and the state of Japanese preparedness."

Robert was impressed. "Wow, she's taking an incredible risk."

Danforth nodded. "If her captors find out what she's up to, she'll be shot," he said bluntly. "This is the frequency she transmits on." Danforth jotted some figures on Robert's notepad. "I've been taking her signals personally, but from now on you will do it. Her code name is Pacific Star. We hear from her once a week, usually in the morning."

"I'll be ready for her," Robert affirmed.

Captain Danforth strode off to check up on the rest of his team. Robert sank back in his chair. As he enjoyed a rare moment of quiet, he found himself thinking about Pacific Star, wondering what such a brave woman must be like, and looking forward to her next communication.

*   *   *

Another steamy morning dawned on the island of Mindanao. Eighteen-year-old Hannah Weiss and her four fellow prisoners paced the small dirt courtyard of the cement military complex, built for use by American troops but currently in the control of the Japanese.

The orange sun topped the roof and blazed down on them. "I've stopped keeping track of the number of days that have passed since we were captured," Joan Madden said with a sigh.

Hannah hooked her arm through that of her friend. "I know how many days it's been." Her deep green eyes crinkled as she smiled. "Do you really want me to tell you?"

Joan laughed. "Not really!"

"A year and a half." Pretty Debbie Houghton shook her blond curls. "I can't believe I'm spending the prime of my life in a prison camp."

"That's what you get for joining the Army in order to meet men," Pam Baird teased.

"I did not join the Army to meet men!" Debbie protested. "At least that wasn't the *only* reason."

Hannah laughed along with the others. They had to laugh and joke about their situation; it was the only way they could bear it.

"You all should be in a more cheerful mood," remarked Nettie MacAllister. "It's washday, remember?"

"Nettie's right," said Hannah. "We do get out of this place once a week. It could be a lot worse."

The others nodded. Their living conditions were really quite fair, considering the fact that the Japanese considered them an evil enemy. They were fed twice a day and the rations were generous; they had the run of a sleeping cell, a bathroom, and the outdoor courtyard; once a week they were escorted by a guard to a neighboring building where they washed their clothes, then hung them on lines to dry. While the clothes were drying, the women were allowed to stroll under the palm trees or swim in a nearby stream.

The brief spell of relative liberty was only one reason Hannah looked forward to washday. The other reason was that on washday, she sent her weekly status report to the aircraft carrier *Richmond*. Those moments of contact with the outside world helped keep her hope alive that someday she and the others would be rescued.

By ten A.M., the five were ready and waiting impatiently for their washday escort. Hannah's slim figure was wrapped in a belted robe, and her long, wavy auburn hair was tied back with a piece of string. Like the other POWs, she carried a bundle of sheets, towels, uniforms, and undergarments to be laundered. Finally, the girls heard the heavy door of their cell being unbolted from the outside. A Japanese soldier gestured to them with his rifle. Hannah had picked up enough Japanese during the past year and a half to understand the words he spoke to them. "Come, and don't be slow."

It was certainly funny, Hannah reflected as she and the others stood over the large sinks working the soapsuds into the laundry with their hands and chattering almost gaily. To think that something as tedious as doing wash could under certain circumstances become a pleasure! When she was growing up in southern California, she'd been an expert at palming household chores off on her older brother, Sam. Now, doing laundry was the high point of the week. If only it were possible to ignore the presence of the hawk-eyed armed guard . . .

When they finished rinsing out their things, the soldier marched them back outside. Soon the clotheslines were draped with dripping garments. As she hung her last towel Hannah caught Debbie's eye. Debbie wrinkled her nose, but she nodded. It was her turn to distract the guard while Hannah sneaked off to make her radio transmission.

Hannah, Joan, Nettie, and Pam waded into the narrow stream. On the other side, near a stand of tall reeds, was a large rock where they liked to sit and sunbathe. Debbie, meanwhile, hung back. "The other day, I saw a water snake," Hannah heard Debbie say in English to the guard. "Are they poisonous?"

The guard understood only a few of her words. He questioned her in Japanese. Debbie began trying to translate her remark. Soon she had tricked the unwitting soldier into giving her a Japanese vocabulary lesson.

That was Hannah's cue. As the other three reclined on the rock, dabbling their feet in the cool water, Hannah strolled along the bank, pretending to examine the exotic tropical plants that grew there. Stepping behind the reeds, she ducked down. She lifted a flat rock, then clawed at the damp earth. Underneath the rock a radio wrapped in plastic was buried.

Quickly, she unwrapped the radio and raised the antenna. Adjusting the frequency, she held it to her mouth and spoke softly. "Ironman, come in."

There was some crackling static. "Pacific Star?" an unfamiliar male voice said over the radio.

For a split second, Hannah almost shut the radio down. Who was picking up her signals?

But the man hastened to reassure her. "Pacific Star, this is Sea Eagle in the communications center on the *Richmond*. I'm your new contact."

Hannah breathed a sigh of relief. "You gave me a start, Sea Eagle!"

"Sorry about that." His tone gave Hannah a distinct feeling that if she could see his face, he would be smiling. "Pacific Star, what's the situation there? Are you all right?"

"We're fine. You can report, though, that there seems to be some troop buildup. The soldiers are drilling a lot more than usual." She described some of the drills in more detail.

"They think Mindanao will be the first point of attack when the American fleet reaches the Philippines, eh?" Robert speculated.

"Possibly," Hannah said. She had nothing more to report of a military nature, so she ventured a personal question, to satisfy her curiosity. "Did you just join the crew of the *Richmond?*"

"Been on board three days."

"Seen any action?"

"We shot down two Japanese planes today. It was pretty hairy," he admitted. "I suppose you've seen a lot worse than that, though. How long have you been a prisoner?"

"Since May of forty-two, when the Allies surrendered the Philippines. I'd only been in the Army Nurse Corps as a nurse's aide for a few months." She forced a laugh. "If I'd known what was in store for me, I would have stuck with high school and the cheerleading squad."

"You mean you were still in school when you joined up?"

"I was only sixteen," Hannah confirmed. "I lied about my age. Now, don't spread that around!"

"You must have felt strongly about the cause we're fighting for."

"I did—I do," Hannah said fervently. "The war . . . it's not a far-off and distant thing for my family. We're Jewish, and I have cousins in Austria.

We've received no word from them in the past couple of years and are afraid they've been sent to Nazi work camps."

"That's terrible!" Robert exclaimed.

"This whole war is terrible," Hannah agreed. "I felt I had to do something. I couldn't just sit by and wait for news, safe and comfortable at home while other people were fighting . . . and dying. A lot of the boys I knew from school were enlisting, and I decided to do the same."

At that moment, Hannah heard a low whistle—the signal from the other girls that it was time to hide the radio and reappear before the guard became suspicious. "I have to go," she said quickly. "I'll talk to you next week. Over and out."

Robert signed off. Hannah reburied the radio, sweeping bits of grass around the rock so her tampering would not be visible. Then she grabbed a handful of bright wildflowers and walked back to the stream.

Twenty-six

1944. The South Pacific.

Sometimes I feel like I've been in the service forever, Robert thought as he and his bunkmate and fellow communications officer Jason Carter made their way along the narrow, low-ceilinged corridor of the ship to the mess. He'd been at sea for seven long months, and the life of a sailor, the combination of monotonous routine and constant danger, was wearing him out. Breakfast was the usual that morning: reconstituted eggs, gloppy oatmeal, and coffee so strong and thick Robert thought it could probably hold its shape without the cup.

"OK, think about this," Jason commanded, his elbows on the table and a utensil in each hand. "It's morning on the farm in Wisconsin. My mom's the best cook in the state, by the way. We start with a plate of fresh eggs—fried, with yolks as big as golf balls. Then sausage, four or five juicy links. Mom

251

makes that herself. Then cinnamon bread right out of the oven, and fried potatoes, and a tall glass of foamy fresh milk and—"

"Stop!" Robert groaned. "How am I supposed to eat this stuff now? Besides, you didn't really eat like that every morning, did you?"

"Every morning of my life," Jason confirmed. "You work hard on a farm. I've been taking it easy since I joined the Navy."

"Right." Robert laughed dryly. "This is a real vacation. 'Get away from it all! Put on your grass skirt and sail the Pacific on the *Richmond*!' "

Jason grinned. "Speaking of grass skirts, today's washday, isn't it?"

Robert lifted his coffee cup to his mouth, hoping the steam would hide the flush he felt creeping up his neck. "It might be."

"Hey, I'm not going to give you a hard time," said Jason. "I'm glad you've gotten in good with that girl. Maybe you can put in a good word for me with her friends."

"The Japanese?" Robert joked.

"No, the other female POWs, of course. They're going to be ready for a good time when they get off that island, and I'd love to be the one to show it to them."

Robert dug into his tasteless scrambled eggs, pretending he was eating one of Mrs. Carter's prizewinning farm breakfasts. He supposed he didn't really mind Jason kidding him about Hannah. He probably deserved it for letting himself get so attached to a girl he'd never even seen.

With every month that passed, Robert was more eager than ever for the armed forces to reach their goal of liberating the Philippine islands—and Hannah. Each time they communicated over the radio, Robert felt closer to her. Talking in a code they'd developed together over the past few months, they had managed to tell each other their real names as well as other details about their lives. When Hannah had an extra minute, they'd talk about their families and homes and friends; what they wanted to do when the war was over; which band was better, Jimmy Dorsey's or Benny Goodman's. Robert looked forward to Hannah's transmissions so much that sometimes he almost forgot her messages were considered crucial for strategic purposes.

Robert and Jason finished their meal and reported to the communications center just in time to learn from Captain Danforth that the fleet was preparing to attack a nearby Japanese-occupied island a day earlier than originally planned.

An announcement came over the loudspeaker system. The crew was to man battle stations. "Get ready," said Danforth. "We're going in!"

As the *Richmond* fell in line with the other ships zeroing in on the island, the atmosphere in the communications center grew tense. Robert was on the wireless with an officer from the carrier *Springfield* when the booming of guns began.

"They've landed," Jason said grimly.

Robert tried to imagine what it must be like to be one of the marines going in on the ground to recapture the island, which was in the process of being bombed from the air by planes taking off from the *Richmond* and the *Springfield*. Suddenly, there was a jolt; Robert was flung from his seat.

"We've been hit!" Captain Danforth shouted.

Sirens began wailing. A lieutenant rushed in to inform the captain that it was not a serious hit. It was bad enough, though, to warrant the announcement that followed. "All able-bodied men report on deck immediately!" the voice crackled over the loudspeaker. Robert, Jason, and the others sprinted for the door.

On deck, they found two planes burning from the Japanese strafing. As some members of the maintenance crew hurried to carry below the sailors injured in the explosion, another tossed Robert a hose. "Help us put this fire out!"

Obediently, Robert trained the hose on the flames. The sky above was buzzing with planes, both American and Japanese. One aircraft seized Robert's attention. It was a Japanese plane, and it was heading straight for the *Springfield*. Robert waited for the plane to fire its guns and then swoop back up into the sky, but it didn't alter its course. "It's going to hit the boat!" he shouted.

The plane nosedived right into the *Springfield*.

There was a series of massive explosions; the carrier began to list badly.

"They're sinking," Robert exclaimed in disbelief. The Japanese pilot had given his life to destroy an American ship.

The *Richmond* altered course in order to aid the sinking ship. No sooner had they come within range, however, than the whining buzz of a plane's engine was heard. It grew louder and louder. Another pilot was targeting the *Richmond*. There was a blast of antiaircraft guns. The Japanese plane suffered a hit but didn't veer off. "Run for cover!" Robert yelled at Jason, diving behind a gun turret.

The impact of the plane jolted the ship from bow to stern. Crumpled steel and broken bodies flew through the air. Robert, protected by the turret, was unharmed. But many of his crewmates had suffered a different fate. When he ran forward to help the wounded, the first body he stumbled over was Jason's.

"Jason!" Robert fell to his knees next to his friend. He slipped an arm under Jason's shoulders. Jason's head lolled back on his neck. His eyes were wide open, their expression surprised. His limp body was riddled with shrapnel. He was dead.

Robert slumped in his chair in the communications center, resisting the urge to drop his head onto his arms. He was bone-tired; this had been the longest day of his life.

The *Richmond* had only been damaged by the kamikaze plane, and finally, after a hair-raising skirmish, the American forces had routed the Japanese from the island. *Another battle won, but at what cost?* Robert thought dully. So many men were dead. Never again would Jason reminisce about the farm and his mother's cooking.

Thinking about Jason, Robert remembered that that day had been Hannah's day to use the secret radio. She had probably tried to signal him, but received no response. If anything could make him feel better, it would be the sound of Hannah's voice. If only he could contact her at will. How could he go another week without speaking to her?

At that moment, the telegraph machine behind Robert began clattering. He spun in his chair and began decoding the message. It was incredible news on the European front. At long last, Allied troops had landed on the beaches of Normandy. The liberation of France from Nazi occupation had begun!

Robert showed the bulletin to Captain Danforth, who gave him the nod to make a general announcement. Solemnly, Robert relayed the news to the rest of the crew. When he finished, his back was a little straighter as he sat at his post. The sacrifices being made were tremendous, but Robert believed —he had to believe—that ultimately the cause was worth it.

* * *

"Why the double guard?" Joan whispered to Hannah as the five women marched across the compound to the building where they did their wash.

Out of the corner of her eye, Hannah glanced nervously at the two Japanese soldiers. "Everything's getting tenser around here," she whispered back. "They know the Americans are almost here."

"Thank God!" breathed Joan. "Oh, Hannah, do you think we'll be rescued soon?"

"Any day now," Hannah predicted.

It was September, and Hannah knew from her last communication with Robert and from the continued buildup of Japanese forces on Mindanao that Halsey's fleet was closing in. *Mindanao is their next stop!* Hannah thought happily as she plunged her hands into the soapy water of the washtub. Soon they would be free. Soon she would walk on free soil . . . phone her parents . . . and finally meet her contact on the *Richmond*, Robert Wakefield.

Hannah was lapsing into a daydream about Robert when the conversation between the two soldiers caught her attention. In almost two and a half years, she'd learned quite a bit of Japanese, far more than her captors could have guessed. Now, although she pretended to be listening to the chatter of Nettie, Pam, Joan, and Debbie, she focused on the words of the guards.

"Twenty more planes arrive today," the first

guard informed the second, "and more will come tomorrow."

"Is it really a good idea to leave the central Philippines so weak in order to reinforce southern islands like Mindanao? What if Mindanao isn't the first American objective?"

"But of course it is!"

"You only say that because it's what our commanding officer believes," the second soldier sneered.

"He knows better than you," the first rejoined. "And if you know what's good for you, you won't question his policy."

Hannah bit her lip. She knew that what she'd just heard could be of great interest to the approaching American fleet. It was more important than ever that she make contact with Robert that day. But how was she going to sneak off with two soldiers on guard?

Nettie had the same question. While the women were hanging their laundry to dry, she hissed at Hannah, "How will you get to your radio today, Hannah?"

"I don't know, but I must. Help me, girls! We need an idea. It's going to take more than a little idle conversation to distract these two."

"I have an idea," said Pam. "When we're wading in the stream, I'll pretend to slip and fall and hit my head on a rock. I'll fall with my face in the water, and Joan and Nettie will start screaming that I'm drowning. Both guards will come running. That's when you go to work."

"But you'll have to make it fast," Debbie cautioned. "The way things are around here, if you get caught today of all days . . ."

Hannah didn't want to think of what the Japanese would do to her—to all of them. She couldn't think about it, or she'd be too scared to go through with her mission. "It's a good plan," she praised Pam. "Let's go for it!"

The moment came, and Pam performed her part like the best actress on Broadway. Drawn by Debbie and Nettie's shrill cries, the two guards rushed to the fallen girl. Hannah, who'd strolled in the opposite direction, dashed behind the reeds. Her heart pounding, she signaled the *Richmond. Please be there, Robert,* she prayed. *Please be fast!*

"Pacific Star?"

"Sea Eagle!" she exclaimed. "I have urgent news." Quickly, she relayed the contents of the conversation she'd overheard. As she spoke she suddenly realized the implications of the information she was passing along. It might encourage the armed forces to shift their strategy; they might postpone the rescue of the POWs on Mindanao. But Hannah knew she couldn't think of her own welfare first.

"Sea Eagle, I can't talk any longer. We're under heavier guard than usual."

"Be careful," Robert begged.

"I will," Hannah promised. "Over and out."

Her hands shaking, Hannah rapidly reburied the radio. She rose to her feet just as a Japanese soldier rounded the stand of reeds. Hannah gasped, putting her hand to her heart. The soldier lifted his rifle, pointing it right at her chest. "What are you doing?" he barked.

"I saw a pretty little salamander," she said in broken Japanese. "I was trying to catch it to show my friends, but it ran into the reeds."

"Didn't you hear the shouts?" the guard asked her.

Hannah tipped her head to one side, playing dumb. "What shouts?"

The soldier grabbed her arm roughly and dragged her back to the stream. Hannah knew she would have some bruises, but she didn't care. She was too thankful that he hadn't noticed the disturbed earth at her feet, where the radio was hidden.

"You are too much trouble. No more walks by the stream," the guard muttered as he herded the women back to their cell.

Hannah's heart contracted painfully. By good fortune, she had succeeded in getting a message to Robert that day. But would it be the last time she ever heard his voice?

Twenty-seven

Something was going on, Hannah and the other POWs sensed. Suddenly, they were virtually unguarded. Where had all the planes and soldiers gone?

Months had passed since Hannah's last conversation with Robert, and she could only guess that the army had indeed attacked the Philippines at a more vulnerable point in the central islands. Certainly Mindanao wasn't a target—yet.

"It's January first, 1945," Nettie announced one morning. "Happy New Year!"

"What's so happy about it?" Joan grumbled. "It's the third New Year's Day that's come and gone since we've been imprisoned. I don't think that's anything to celebrate."

"It's also the last New Year's Day we'll spend here," Hannah said. "We'll be rescued soon."

"You don't know that for sure," Pam reminded her.

It was true. Their Japanese captors had been very closemouthed lately. Hannah hadn't overheard any news from them, good or bad.

"Let's find out for sure today," Hannah said. "It's been so long since we've been allowed to walk outside. Maybe they'll let us go to the stream if we ask nicely."

"If the Americans *have* invaded, keeping an eye on us should really be the least of their worries," Debbie agreed. "It's worth a try."

The women were surprised by how easy it was. When Debbie made the polite request, their guard just shrugged and unbolted the padlock. "Don't go far," he ordered, waving them off with his rifle.

It was the most freedom the five had had since their capture. They ran laughing to the stream, their hair flying in the breeze. With the garrison force greatly diminished, their guard was doing double duty; he hung back, watching them with only one eye.

"Maybe we should try to escape!" Pam cried excitedly as they splashed into the stream.

Debbie pointed to the forbidding barbed-wire fence in the distance. "How do you plan to get over that, fly?"

"We could dig under it," Pam suggested.

"And get shot in the process," Joan said. "No, thanks."

"We can't risk it," Hannah agreed. "But as soon as I talk to Robert, I'll be able to give you good news about the plans to rescue us, I promise!"

While the other girls lounged on the grass alongside the reeds, Hannah crawled to the flat stone. It had been so long since she'd visited the spot. Was the radio still there? Would it still work? Her heart pounded thankfully when she found it, intact and operable. But as she adjusted the frequency to radio Robert, another misgiving came over her. What if something had happened to *him*? What if his carrier had been hit, even sunk? Holding her breath, Hannah waited for what seemed an age for someone to answer her signal. *Please, let him be there,* she prayed. "Star? Pacific Star?" a male voice said at last. "Is that you?"

"Sea Eagle!" To Hannah's surprise, her eyes filled with sudden tears.

"Oh, Star, I thought you were . . . you haven't been hurt, have you?"

"No." Hannah laughed through her tears. "I'm fine. We're all fine! And you?"

"I'm fine, too. The battle for Leyte finally ended. We lost a lot of men."

"Oh, Sea Eagle, isn't this war almost over?" Hannah asked.

"Yes," Robert promised. "Soon we'll come for you." There was a new note in Robert's voice. "I've been in agony waiting to hear from you, wondering if you were still alive."

"It's been hard for me, too," Hannah confessed. "For a while, they stopped letting us go outside. Now, though, the compound is practically empty of soldiers. I think they'll be less strict with us from now on."

"We took the Japanese by surprise up here," Robert said. "They had to pour reinforcements into the area—from your garrison among others, I bet."

"Sea Eagle, I should go," Hannah said reluctantly. "But I'll radio again soon."

"Pacific Star, I—I think about you all the time. I'll be waiting to hear from you. But be careful."

"I will. And you be careful, too."

"Over and out."

Hannah replaced the radio, her cheeks pink from the warmth of Robert's words. It was absolutely crazy, but she couldn't deny what was happening in her own heart, and what seemed to be happening in Robert's as well. They'd fallen in love over the wireless.

Time passed slowly, but it was bearable for Hannah because she could contact Robert regularly now that the guards, preoccupied with other matters, had grown lax. One day in early March, the five women hung their wet laundry and then strolled away from the compound along the stream. Debbie and Pam tossed a coconut back and forth, pretending it was a football. Nettie and Joan picked

264

flowers. Hannah slipped behind the reeds to radio Robert.

"Good news!" he greeted her. "Manila is back in American hands!"

"Is it over then?" Hannah asked hopefully. "Have the Japanese surrendered?"

"Not yet," Robert said. "We still have to eliminate the last Japanese resistance in the southern islands. My ship's heading south again now."

"The southern islands . . . you mean here?"

When Robert assented, Hannah's heart pounded with a mixture of exultation and fear. Finally, the war was coming to Mindanao!

At that moment, she heard shouting from the direction of the compound. Soon another sound became audible: the distant buzz of planes. Debbie darted around the stand of reeds and grabbed Hannah's arms. "Come on!" she yelled. "We have to take shelter! Those are American planes, and I think they're going to bomb the base!" Hannah didn't even have time to say goodbye to Robert. Dropping the radio, she kicked the stone over it and ran after Debbie and the others.

The girls never even made it back to the compound. As they watched in amazement, a host of trucks and tanks rumbled by them, flanked by foot soldiers—the entire population of the base, Hannah guessed. Seeing the girls, an officer gestured sharply with his rifle. The five fell into line. Pam clutched Joan's arm fearfully. Debbie and Nettie clasped hands. "What's happening?" Debbie cried.

The grim-faced troops paid no attention to her. Hannah spotted the soldier who'd been their guard that morning. "Please, where are we going?" she asked him.

"The American army is attacking," he replied in terse Japanese. "We are abandoning the base to retreat into the mountains, where we can make a better defense."

Abandoning the base! Hannah glanced back longingly at the reed-fringed stream. If she'd only known! She would have risked detection in order to smuggle the radio away with her. Now there was no way she could retrieve it. A feeling of dread crept into Hannah's heart, freezing the blood in her veins. From this moment on, the POWs were cut off from all communication with the outside world. The Japanese troops were dragging their prisoners into the jungle to make their last stand, and Hannah knew they would fight to the death.

Twenty-eight

Hannah and the other POWs ran through the black jungle. Hannah was weak from hunger and fatigue. The fighting between Japanese and American troops had been going on for days, and there was time for neither eating nor sleeping. But every time she or another one of the girls stumbled, they were brutally jabbed in the back with a rifle. Hannah concentrated on each step. She feared falling—she feared being shot where she lay.

Suddenly the night was torn open by a deafening explosion. A shell burst within fifty yards of them! For an instant, the dense jungle was as bright as midday. Hannah could see the fear on her friends' faces, and the fury and terror on the faces of the Japanese soldiers. When the girls hesitated, they were prodded forward once again. "Go! Go!"

Hannah dashed forward into the smoke. Another

shell exploded, this one even closer than the last, then another and another. She put her hands to her ears and screamed. She couldn't even hear the sound of her own voice above the unrelenting roar of gunfire and shells.

All at once Hannah's guard halted. The POWs had been following in the wake of a larger division of soldiers, but somehow, in the smoke and confusion of the unexpected attack, they'd become separated.

As the five Japanese guards huddled, discussing what to do, Hannah, Pam, Debbie, Nettie, and Joan threw their arms around one another.

"What's that?" Pam suddenly screamed, pointing into the jungle behind Hannah.

Hannah whirled. Soldiers charged toward the girls through the smoke, their rifles pointed! *They're going to shoot us,* Hannah thought, astonished at how calm she suddenly felt. It seemed inevitable somehow.

She closed her eyes, waiting for the bullet to tear into her flesh. But instead of a bullet, she felt a hand. A man's hand, strong but gentle, on her arm.

Hannah blinked. The soldier grasped both her arms, shaking her. She stared at him, at his eyes, bright blue in his smoke-blackened face, and his hair, corn-yellow in the light of the exploding shells. And his uniform. The uniform of a United States Marine!

"Come on," the marine said. "Let's get out of here!"

Now it was the turn of the five Japanese guards to be herded at gunpoint, by American soldiers. And although Hannah and the other girls were running again, they were running to freedom.

"Have you ever seen so many good-looking fellas in one place at one time?" said Debbie, flopping back on the bed with a sigh of pure happiness.

Hannah laughed. "I think we're in heaven," she agreed. Since setting foot on the U.S.S. *Calhoun,* they'd been treated like royalty. The handsome young officers were open in expressing their admiration of the brave and beautiful nurses. They showered the girls with small gifts and flowers, and fought over who would get to carry their trays and sit next to them at meals. The former prisoners reveled in the attention, but no one more than Debbie, who seemed to be making up for three years of lost flirting in one day.

"Captain Steadman was so nice to turn his quarters over to us," remarked Pam, curling up in a comfortable armchair.

"The best part was getting these new uniforms." Joan smoothed the crisp khaki skirt over her knees. "And getting our hair cut for the first time in ages."

Nettie giggled. "Even if it was by the ship's barber!"

Hannah touched her neatly bobbed auburn hair.

It *had* been a delight to get rid of those unfashionable long curls!

Joan observed the gesture. "Imagine if you'd had to meet Robert looking like a female Robinson Crusoe," she said slyly.

"You must be so nervous!" Pam guessed. "After a year and a half, you're finally going to *see* Robert when we reach Manila tomorrow."

"I am nervous," Hannah admitted. "We're . . ." *In love,* she wanted to say. Because it was true. Though they'd never said so explicitly, Hannah loved Robert and she felt sure that he cared deeply for her, too. "But what if we're disappointed when we actually meet? What if we don't have anything to talk about? What if he doesn't like me in person as much as he does over the radio?"

"He'll adore you," Nettie assured her. "You're sweet, pretty, and smart. What more could a boy want?"

"And if you don't like him as much in person, there are plenty of other guys to choose from," Debbie pointed out.

Hannah didn't feel she could explain to Debbie and the others why she wouldn't want any other guy. The attachment formed between her and Robert over the past year and a half was wonderful and rare. But Hannah suspected that because of its uniqueness, it was also fragile. Could any man live up to the picture she'd painted in her mind of Robert Wakefield?

* * *

Hannah resisted the urge to chew her nails as the *Calhoun* cruised into the harbor at Manila. Robert was taking shore leave from the *Richmond;* he'd be waiting for her at the dock when she disembarked.

"How do I look, girls?" she asked her friends after anxiously checking her reflection one last time in the mirror.

"Utterly adorable," Nettie said.

"Like a picture," gushed Pam.

Joan adjusted Hannah's cap. "There. Just right."

"Sergeant Butler gave me this." Debbie displayed a bottle of perfume, then spritzed Hannah with it. "Now you smell as delicious as you look!"

Hannah took a deep breath. "I guess I'm ready."

"Good luck, Hannah!"

The gangway was crowded with sailors eager to begin their shore leave, but all gallantly stepped aside for Hannah. She almost wished they wouldn't; she felt exposed as she walked down to the dock. *How will I know him?* she wondered, her mouth suddenly as dry as sawdust.

Then she saw him. Though the dock teemed with men in uniform, one sailor stood somehow apart. He was tall and broad-shouldered, with dark hair, a strong jaw, and brown eyes that seemed to jump out of his sun-bronzed face. His gaze was trained intently upon her as she approached.

271

Hannah held out her hand, her cheeks flooding with color. "Robert?"

"Hannah. At last!" He took her hand, gripping it tightly. For a moment, they stood staring into each other's eyes, mesmerized. Hannah was surprised to find that all her nervousness had faded the instant Robert took her hand. *But maybe I shouldn't be surprised,* she thought. *He's not a stranger, after all.*

Robert didn't release her hand. Instead, he pulled her toward him and wrapped his arms around her. In front of all those people, he bent his head to hers and kissed her on the mouth.

The sinking sun, poised just above the horizon, bathed the bay in glimmering orange and silver. Robert had a transistor radio strapped over one shoulder. It was tuned to the Armed Forces Network, which was broadcasting the swinging big-band sound of Kay Kyser and his orchestra. As they walked along the sand with their arms around each other, Hannah rested her head against Robert. She felt utterly comfortable and at peace, as if she and Robert had known each other for years. Which in fact they had, even though it had been only a month since the day they'd joined up in Manila.

She laughed suddenly. "What's so funny?" Robert asked.

"I was just remembering how a month ago, I was almost afraid to meet you. My expectations were so high. I didn't think any mortal man could meet them!"

"I was a big disappointment, eh?"

Stopping, they turned to face each other. Hannah slipped her arms around Robert's waist and looked up at him, her eyes full of love. "No," she said. "As it turned out, my expectations didn't even come close."

They shared a deep kiss as warm as the summer evening. "Hannah, what do you want to do when the war's over?" Robert asked.

"Go home to California, I guess," she replied. They resumed their stroll. "Spend time with my family. I've missed them so much! And I'd like to finish school, become a nurse or even a doctor. How about you?"

"I'll probably visit my father in New York. We'll have a lot to catch up on. And I want to go back to school, too. But I'm not sure I want to settle in New York permanently. Hannah, I was thinking that maybe—"

At that moment, a loud *boom* echoed across the water. It was followed by a second boom, then another and another. "What is it?" Hannah cried. "Is it another attack?"

"I don't think so." Robert frowned. Then his frown transformed into a jubilant smile. "Look, Hannah!" He pointed. The firing of guns continued, but now it was joined by the sound of people celebrating. On every ship in the bay, Hannah and

Robert could see people in motion, waving their arms and tossing their caps in the air.

"The surrender," Hannah guessed. "Finally, Japan has surrendered!"

Robert nodded. "It has to be. Hannah!" Grabbing her around the waist, he whirled her around on the sand. "The war is over!"

They twirled until they were both dizzy and laughing. Hannah could hardly believe it. The war in Europe had ended earlier in the year. She had been praying that her family would hear from her missing Austrian cousins. And now, finally, the war in the Pacific was over as well. *We'll be going home,* she thought with profound gratitude. *We'll all be going home.*

"You'd better get back to the ship," Hannah told him.

"I'd better," Robert agreed. "But you're coming with me."

"Why on earth?"

"I just had a great idea of how we can celebrate the end of the war," he told her. "You know our friend, Captain Danforth?" Hannah nodded. "Well, he has a certain power, by virtue of his rank, that I think we should take advantage of without further delay."

Hannah was puzzled. "What are you talking about?"

"As a ship's captain, he has the power to perform marriages." Robert smiled at her astonished expression. "So, what do you say, Hannah? Will you marry me or not?"

She stared at him. "Have you gone crazy?"

"I've never been more sane and sober." Clasping both her hands in his, Robert dropped to one knee in the sand. "Hannah, please marry me," he begged, his tone now serious. "You've already made me the happiest man on earth. Become my wife and make it official."

Hannah looked down at Robert. She was only nineteen years old, and she and Robert had been together for only a month. But they had been through so much together, and Hannah's heart was overflowing with a love she knew would last for the rest of her life. She had to say yes.

She smiled. "I just thought of something else I want to do when the war's over," she said by way of a reply. "I want to introduce my family to my wonderful new husband."

As the celebratory boom of guns continued across the bay, Robert pulled Hannah down to the sand to seal their engagement with a kiss.

Twenty-nine

Sweet Valley, California.

"I can't believe you're a grandfather!" Sarah Wakefield-Mayne said to her son, Ted.

"I can't believe *you're* a great-grandmother," Ted countered with a smile.

"What I can't believe is that everybody came all this distance for the holidays," said Hannah, bouncing her infant son on her knee.

Ted swooped the baby from Hannah's arms and held him high in the air. Little Ned laughed with delight. "Well, we Edward Wakefields have to stick together!"

Hannah glanced at her husband, a soft smile touching her lips. Robert looked so happy. She knew nothing gave him more pleasure than to see how much his father and his son enjoyed each other. *This is what life is all about,* Hannah thought. *The continuity of generations. Parents lov-*

276

ing and caring for children so they can grow up and have children of their own.

As if she'd read her daughter's mind, Lise Weiss sat down on the couch next to Hannah to give her a hug. "We have a wonderful family, don't we?"

"I feel so lucky," Hannah told her mother. "It's great to have everybody finally together in one place at one time."

"Right. And it's about time, too. You and Robert cheated us out of having a family reunion at your wedding," her mother teased.

Hannah smiled. "We just couldn't wait. Did you really mind that we didn't have a traditional wedding?"

"Of course not. What mattered most to your father and me was that you came home safely. And that you decided to live in California, near us."

"I love living close enough to visit a lot. I only wish Robert's relatives weren't so far away." Ted was still living in New York, and Robert's grandmother Sarah and her husband, Joe, lived in Chicago.

Hannah looked across the living room to where her older brother, Sam, and his wife, Ruth, were playing with their baby, Rachel, who was the same age as Ned. "I think Ned and Rachel will have a lot of fun growing up together."

"We're lucky to have them," her mother said, a sad note in her voice.

Hannah thought she knew why. "Are you thinking about Uncle Karl and Aunt Berthe, Mom?" she asked softly.

Hannah's Austrian-born mother had come to America as a young woman. But her older brother Karl, a university professor, had raised his family in their homeland. During World War II, his entire family had been sent to Nazi concentration camps. Miraculously, Karl and his wife had survived, but their children, Hannah's cousins, had perished at Auschwitz.

Taking a handkerchief from her pocket, Hannah's mother wiped her eyes. "I hate to think of them growing old alone, with no children or grandchildren."

Hannah bent to kiss her mother's cheek. "Maybe that's why these babies seem especially precious to us. Someday I hope Karl and Berthe can come to America for a visit. I would love Ned to know his great-aunt and great-uncle."

At that moment, Hannah's father, Larry, emerged from the kitchen carrying a chocolate-frosted cake. "Come to the table, everybody!"

At the table, the two babies grabbed for the cake with eager fists. Robert laughed as his young son smeared frosting all over his face. "What a mess!"

Hannah looked up and met her husband's eye. For a moment, they gazed at each other, communicating silently. Hannah had a feeling Robert was thinking the same thing she was—how lucky they were to have such a wonderful life.

After returning to the States as newlyweds, Hannah had gone to school to become a registered nurse. Robert had gotten a job with the telephone company and was taking night classes at the nearby College of Southern California. They had a lovely home in Sweet Valley, an idyllic town right on the Pacific Ocean. Best of all, they were raising a happy, healthy son.

Robert lifted his glass. "I'd like to make a toast."

The other adults lifted their glasses as well. Little Ned and Rachel, in imitation of their elders, lifted small chocolatey fists.

"To peace and prosperity throughout the world," Robert began.

"Cheers!" the others cried.

"And to the best family a man could have."

Just then, Ned took a tiny handful of chocolate cake and hurled it at his cousin. With a gleeful squeal, Rachel retaliated in kind.

Hannah grinned at Sam and Ruth. "I have a feeling these two are going to keep us on our toes for years to come!"

Thirty

Early 1960s. Sweet Valley, California.

"If I've told you once, I've told you a thousand times, Hank." Sixteen-year-old Rachel Weiss put her hands on her hips and gave Hank Patman her most disgusted look. "I do not want to go out with you!"

Hank had cornered her after school in the parking lot of Sweet Valley High. She didn't like to be so blunt, but he'd been pestering her for weeks. She hoped he'd finally get the message and leave her alone.

Instead, Hank stepped closer. Rachel backed up and found herself pressed against the trunk of one of the leafy shade trees bordering the lot. "I like your style," Hank said with a nauseatingly smug smile. "I like a girl who speaks for herself."

"Well, I like a guy who actually listens when a

girl speaks," Rachel retorted. "Don't you ever take no for an answer, Hank?"

"Sometimes," he said. "But I usually get what I want eventually."

Rachel wasn't sure why Hank was pursuing her with so much determination. They had absolutely nothing in common—they hadn't had a single pleasant conversation in all the years they'd been going to school together! And she certainly wasn't rich, like the debutante types Hank hung around with at the country club.

"I've got to go," Rachel said, trying to sidestep Hank. "I'm meeting Ned and Seth—"

"I can't believe you waste your time hanging out with those deadbeats," Hank drawled.

"Deadbeats!" Rachel's eyes flashed with indignation. "Ned happens to be my cousin, and Seth is my friend. And they're both a million times nicer than you'll ever be!"

"Well, nice just doesn't make it in this world. You deserve better than that." Hank cast a disdainful eye toward Seth's battered jalopy, which was parked nearby. "I could *really* take you places, Rachel. I know how to show a girl a good time."

"Well, you've shown this girl that it's a good time to say goodbye!"

Rachel tried to push past Hank. He grabbed her arm. "Say yes instead, Rachel. I like that word a lot better."

Pulling her toward him, Hank tried to kiss her. "No!" Rachel exclaimed.

At that moment, someone gave Hank a hard shove. "Lay off her, Patman," Ned Wakefield warned.

Rachel breathed a sigh of relief. Hank was an athletic guy himself, but he knew better than to mess with tall, broad-shouldered Ned.

Recovering his balance, Hank glared at Ned, his eyes cool with anger. "Mind your own business, Wakefield. We were just talking. I'll see you around, Rachel," he said to her.

"Unfortunately," she replied.

Hank sauntered off. Ned turned to his cousin. "Rachel, are you OK?" he asked, his brown eyes warm with concern.

She gave herself a shake. "I'm fine. Just fuming! Hank Patman is so arrogant, it's beyond belief!"

"Forget about that rat," advised Seth, walking up to them. He opened the door of his jalopy so she could climb in. "Think good vibes. Think about the perfect wave. It's out there somewhere, and I'm going to catch it!"

"Nope, it's gonna be mine," Ned vowed as he jumped in after Rachel, squeezing her between him and Seth.

As Seth revved the engine Rachel relaxed. The old jalopy, surfboards stashed in the back, sputtered to life. "Can't you share the perfect wave?" she wondered aloud.

Ned laughed. "Good old peacekeeping Rachel!"

"That's not such a bad role to play, is it?"

"As long as you don't let people push you around," Ned said.

"I just try to be fair and give everybody a chance, everybody but Hank Patman, that is. He just had his last chance with me!"

"Too bad you always have to see him and his jerky friends at student council meetings," remarked Seth as he turned onto the road heading for the beach.

Rachel grimaced. "Tell me about it," Ned said with feeling. The cousins had a lot in common. Having grown up together, they were more like brother and sister. And one thing they shared was a hearty dislike for their snobby classmate Hank. But Seth was right—they had to deal with Hank Patman whether they liked it or not. All three served on the Sweet Valley High student council, Rachel as secretary, Ned as vice president, and Hank as treasurer.

"Hank and his friends are the worst," Rachel said. "At the meeting during lunch today, we argued the whole time about what kind of music to play at the next dance."

"All the kids at school want to hear the cool stuff," Ned told Seth, "the Beach Boys and the Beatles. But Hank and his drippy, out-of-date, conservative—"

"Uncool, unhip," Seth contributed.

"—uptight, totally square friends want to play this hideous old music. You know, the kind of stuff our parents listen to. Count Basie and his orchestra, that sort of thing. And there might actually be enough of them to outvote us."

"Man, I'm boycotting the dance if they play Perry Como or something like that!" Seth declared.

"I hope we'll be able to strike a compromise," said Ned. "Rachel the peacekeeper's working on it."

Rachel wrinkled her nose. "Lucky me!"

There were lots of perfect waves that afternoon, and Ned was pretty sure he and Seth caught them all. After a few hours of surfing, they rejoined Rachel on the beach.

Halfway home, Seth pulled the jalopy over to the side of the road. "I'm starving. Let's pick up something to eat at this farm stand."

The three hopped out. While Seth and Rachel picked through bins piled high with oranges and grapefruits, Ned rested his suntanned arms on top of a fence. He watched as a couple of migrant workers unloaded bushels of fruit from the back of a pickup truck. *Those guys don't look any older than me,* he thought.

The workers hauled the baskets toward the stand. "Want some help?" Ned offered to one of them.

"No, I can manage," the boy answered.

When the truck was empty, the workers sat down in its shade to rest for a few minutes. The boy Ned had spoken to perched on the fence not far away. Ned tried again, but this time he addressed the boy in Spanish, having guessed that the boy was Mexican. "My name is Ned Wakefield. I'm sixteen. How old are you?"

"Sixteen, too." The boy smiled shyly. "I'm Salvador."

"Where do you live, Salvador?"

Salvador pointed to some dilapidated shacks on the far side of a melon field. "That's my family's home for now. Until they run out of work for us here."

Ned was pretty sure he'd never seen Salvador at Sweet Valley High. "Do you go to school around here?"

Salvador seemed surprised by the question. "I don't go to school."

"You don't go—" At that moment, Ned heard a loud whistle from Seth, who was trying to get his attention. "Well, see you," Ned said.

Salvador lifted his hand. "See you."

Back at the jalopy, Rachel was already peeling an orange. She doled out sections. Ned took a piece. "Hey, do you guys know anything about why migrant worker kids don't go to school? That guy back there was our age. He shouldn't be working all day—he should be getting an education."

"I bet he's supposed to be in school, but his

family needs the money so they have him work instead," Seth guessed.

Ned thought about this as Rachel played with the radio dial. She found a Beach Boys song and she and Seth started singing along. Ned joined in, but only halfheartedly. Somehow, his joy in the perfect afternoon had been tainted. It didn't seem fair that kids like Seth and Rachel and him should be having so much fun, while other kids like Salvador had to work all day in the hot sun.

Hannah Wakefield placed the steaming casserole on the kitchen table. "How was the surfing today?" she asked her son.

Ned shrugged. "It gets boring after a while."

His father pretended to be shocked. "Don't tell me you're abandoning your sacred quest for the perfect wave!"

"It's just starting to seem like a silly way to spend my time, that's all," said Ned.

The three sat down at the table. Hannah studied her son's face as she served the casserole. "Did something happen at school today, honey?"

"Actually, something did happen, but not at school." Ned told his parents about his encounter with Salvador. "Do the migrant workers really earn so little money that they can't afford to let their kids take time out to go to school?"

Robert considered the question. "To tell you the truth, Ned, I don't think it's by choice that someone like Salvador isn't in school. I believe the children of migrant workers are forbidden to attend the Sweet Valley public schools."

Ned was amazed. "But why? They live here, don't they?"

"Yes and no," said Robert. "From what I understand, even though the migrant workers spend a large part of the year in the area, they aren't considered legal residents. They're allowed into the country to work, but that's all."

"That's not fair!" Ned exclaimed. "They might live in a shack instead of a mansion like the Patmans, but they still live here. They should have the same rights as everybody else."

"I agree," his mother said.

"Can't anything be done about this, Dad?" Ned asked.

"Of course, if people care enough to take action."

"I think the case should be presented to the town council and the Board of Education," Ned declared. "I know!" His eyes burned with sudden inspiration. "The student council can put together a petition. We'll tell the mayor and everybody else that we want the migrant kids to be in our classes and clubs and on our sports teams. We want them to be treated just like us. Our voices should carry some weight, shouldn't they?"

"They should, son," Robert replied. "I hope they do."

* * *

"If the whole student council doesn't endorse the petition, it won't carry nearly as much weight." Ned pounded his fist on the conference table for emphasis.

Hank Patman leaned back in his chair, a smug smile on his face. "Maybe not. But the fact is, I don't endorse it, and neither does Kent, Stan, or Shirley."

"Can't they speak for themselves?" Rachel demanded.

"Speak for yourselves," Hank instructed his cronies.

"I agree with Hank," announced Stan. He was echoed meekly by Shirley and Kent.

Rachel stifled a groan. It was absolutely sickening, the way those three played up to Hank. Thanks to their spinelessness, the student council was in a deadlock over Ned's proposal.

"Well, there are six of us and only four of you," Ned pointed out. "Majority rules, right?"

"Not always, fortunately," said Hank. "A student council endorsement has to be unanimous."

Ned looked for help to Mary Baker, the student council president and one of his allies on the issue. Mary shrugged helplessly. "I'm afraid Hank's right, Ned. We'll just have to send the petition out over our individual names."

Hank pushed his chair back, preparing to leave the after-school meeting. Stan, Kent, and Shirley followed suit. "Good luck with your petition," he said snidely.

Rachel couldn't restrain herself any longer. "What is wrong with you anyway, Hank?" she cried. "Life has given you so much. How can you begrudge some poor innocent children something so basic as a decent education?"

"Because those poor innocent children you're suddenly so fond of don't contribute anything to this town. Why should Sweet Valley spend money on them? They don't pay taxes."

"Neither do you!" Rachel countered.

"I don't, but my father pays plenty," said Hank. "Look, Rachel." Hank leaned close to her, and Rachel took a giant step backward. Hank didn't even seem to notice her repulsion. "If you want my advice," he said, "don't bother signing your nutty cousin's stupid petition. It's not going to get anywhere."

"I think you're wrong," Rachel said hotly.

"We'll see." Hank sauntered from the room.

"You Patmans don't own this town, you know!" Ned shouted after him.

Hank looked back, flashing another one of his insufferable smiles.

"I can't believe it," Ned said to Rachel a week later. "I can't believe that rat Hank was right."

They were sitting on stools at the ice-cream parlor. Hoping to cheer him up, Rachel had offered to treat her cousin to a giant root-beer float. But Ned just poked at the ice cream with his spoon, watching it melt into the soda. He didn't have any appetite.

"I just don't get it," Ned went on. "You'd think the more well-off people are, the more generous they'd be. How can someone like Alexander Patman exert so much influence on the town council?" It seemed as if few town policies were made without the approval of Hank's father, head of one of Sweet Valley's founding families and president of both the town council and the Board of Education.

"Like father, like son," Rachel said. *"Blech!"*

"Things just shouldn't work that way," Ned stated. "People like the Patmans shouldn't determine what's right and what's wrong, what gets done and what doesn't, just because they're rich. And money shouldn't be the only consideration when it comes to taking action! I'll tell you, Rachel, they beat us this time, but I'm not giving up. Alexander Patman didn't take us seriously, but a few of the other council members did. And if you can reach people, you can teach people. Someday things are going to be different!"

Thirty-one

*1960s. Campus of the College
of Southern California.*

"Not another tie-dyed tapestry!" Rachel shouted
over the music as her roommate Judy entered their
dorm room. Rachel was sitting on the tapestry-
draped sofa, sewing patches on a pair of torn and
faded blue jeans. "You've already covered the walls
and the ceilings and our beds. What's left?"

Judy shook out the psychedelic cloth and draped
it around herself. "Our own bodies! I thought we
could cut skirts and scarves out of it."

Rachel's other roommate, Barbara, stuck her
head out of the bedroom of the two-room suite.
"Admit it, Judy, you're as sick of tie-dye as we are.
You just can't resist that scruffy guy who sells T-
shirts and stuff on the corner!"

Judy smiled dreamily. "He is scruffy, isn't he?"

"Oh, no," Rachel groaned. She put a hand to the

beaded headband around her forehead. "She's in love!"

Still swathed in tie-dye, Judy bounced onto the couch next to Rachel. "I am. And we have a date, sort of," she informed her roommates. "We're going to hang out together at the SPAN meeting tonight!"

There were a lot of clubs and organizations on campus, but Rachel hadn't heard of this one. "SPAN?"

"Students for Progressive Action Now. It's a new awareness-and-activism group," Barbara explained. "There are signs up all over the dorm."

Students for Progressive Action Now—it sounded interesting, Rachel thought. "Maybe I'll check it out," she said.

As a favorite Rolling Stones song came on the radio, Rachel couldn't help thinking how much fun campus life was turning out to be. She'd only been at the College of Southern California for a couple of months, but already she had a lot of wonderful new friends, and every day she was exposed to all sorts of new ideas. What she learned in class was only part of it; it seemed to Rachel that some of her most educational experiences took place outside of the classroom. There were just so many things to care about—civil rights, women's liberation—and students all over the country had decided that they weren't going to spend all their time with their noses in books. Everyone agreed that awareness and activism were where it was at.

When the song was over, Barbara turned down the volume on the radio. "Do you mind?" she asked her roommates. "I'm going to try to study until dinner."

"We're mellow," Rachel assured her. "Hey, you know who'll probably be at the SPAN meeting? My cousin, Ned. It's just the kind of thing he digs."

Barbara forgot about studying for a moment. "Then I'm definitely going. Anything to catch a glimpse of the cutest, grooviest guy on campus."

Rachel laughed. She was always amused by the way her female friends responded to her handsome, dynamic cousin. "I'm afraid a glimpse is all you're going to catch," she told Barbara. "Ned doesn't seem to have time for dating. All his energy goes to his causes."

"Too bad!" said Barbara.

Rachel trimmed a piece of flowered fabric to use as a patch and thought about her cousin. Ned didn't even seem to know he was good-looking—he just wasn't concerned with that sort of thing. *Too busy trying to change the world,* she thought fondly. Sometimes she was a little sad that she and Ned didn't get to spend as much time together as they had in high school. Their dorms were only a stone's throw apart, but they took completely different classes—Ned was prelaw, while she was interested in history and sociology. She'd probably never see him if she didn't bump into him at rallies and concerts.

The door to the suite was ajar. Now someone pushed it open all the way. "Can I come in, folks?"

Rachel looked up. Her jaw dropped. "Becky?" she asked, by no means sure that the girl standing in the doorway was her hallmate, Becky Foster.

"It's me!" Becky floated into the room, the tiny bells on her gauzy Indian-print cotton skirt jingling.

Rachel glanced at Judy, who raised her eyebrows. Rachel knew her roommate was thinking the same thing she was: Since when had Becky Foster, a snooty debutante, become a flower child? Instead of wearing one of her usual conservative, elegant outfits, Becky was letting it all hang out. Over the long flowing skirt she wore an embroidered peasant blouse; around her neck were strings of iridescent beads, and matching earrings dangled from her lobes; her glossy black hair fell loose to her shoulders; her feet were bare.

"What's up, Becky?" Rachel asked cautiously. Becky didn't usually hang out with them. Early on, Becky had tried to strike up a friendship with Rachel. But once she had found out that Rachel couldn't or wouldn't help her get to know Ned better, Becky had dropped Rachel like a stone.

"Don't call me Becky. My name is Rainbow now."

"Rainbow?" Rachel could see her roommates trying hard not to giggle.

Becky-Rainbow nodded seriously. "I've recently

discovered that I have Native American blood," she explained. "I'm one-sixteenth Indian."

"So where does the rainbow concept come in?" Barbara wondered.

"Because of my Indian heritage, I feel I am a prism of personality." Rainbow lifted her chin with a proud expression. "With many hidden colors and talents."

A prism of personality? Rachel thought she might gag. She'd never heard such garbage. A giggle exploded from Judy, who started coughing to cover it up.

"Anyway, I just dropped in to make sure you were all coming to the organizational meeting of SPAN tonight. And did I hear you mention that your cousin's planning to go?" Rainbow asked Rachel.

Rachel couldn't believe it. Rainbow must have been eavesdropping! "We'll be there. Why?"

"I'm one of the coordinators of SPAN," Rainbow answered.

"You helped start SPAN?" Barbara said in disbelief. "You're the one who put up all the posters about awareness and activism?"

Rainbow nodded as she glided toward the door. "See you there."

When Becky was gone, the three roommates stared at one another. "Tell me I imagined that whole scene," Rachel demanded.

"It was for real," Judy told her. "But whether Becky's for real, that's another story."

"I don't see how she could go through such a complete transformation overnight," Barbara said doubtfully. "One day she's the snobbiest, most self-centered, most conniving girl on campus, and then the next day she's suddenly the high priestess of hippiedom!"

"Maybe we're making too big a deal out of this," Judy said. "It's possible Becky has a genuine interest in becoming an activist. People can change."

Rachel had serious doubts, but she decided to keep them to herself. She believed in giving people a chance, and there was no proof that Becky had ulterior motives. *No proof yet,* Rachel thought as she resumed stitching the patch on her jeans and humming along with the radio. But something about Rainbow's seemingly casual question about Ned made her wonder.

The SPAN meeting convened at sunset on the lawn outside the student union. Ned spotted his cousin, wearing hip-hugger jeans and a psychedelic tank top, sitting cross-legged at the front of the gathering. He himself had on a tie-dyed T-shirt and cutoffs, and he wore his shoulder-length brown hair in a ponytail.

He made his way to Rachel's side and dropped onto the grass next to her. "What's shakin', Rach?" he greeted her.

"Hi, Ned! I was wondering when you'd show up."

"I was rapping with a couple of other prelaw students about starting an alternative law society on campus," he explained. "I lost track of the time."

At that moment, a beautiful black-haired girl who'd been sitting nearby rose to her feet. Lifting one graceful arm, she waved for quiet. A hush fell over the chattering groups of students.

"My name is Rainbow." The girl's soft, musical voice made Ned think of a mountain stream. "And these are Joshua, Candy, and Lenny. We're going to share with you some of the goals we hope SPAN can achieve. Then we want *you* to stand up and speak to us about the issues you feel need progressive action now."

Ned elbowed Rachel. "Hey, I think I know her. She's in a couple of my prelaw classes."

"I know her, too. She lives in my dorm. And her name isn't *really* Rainbow," Rachel said disparagingly. "It's Becky Foster. As in daughter of ultra-conservative Judge Leonard Foster and society queen Mimi Foster."

Ned stared at Rainbow. She definitely looked familiar from class, but he felt as if he were seeing her for the first time. He couldn't believe he hadn't taken more notice of her before.

Rainbow and the other SPAN leaders presented their agenda, then opened up the meeting as promised. People took turns tossing out ideas, many of which Ted thought were great. It really looked like SPAN was going to turn out to be a group with spirit and substance.

He turned to his cousin, surprised to see that she looked skeptical; he'd expected her usual enthusiasm. "Don't you dig SPAN, Rach? Rainbow's really on your wavelength. Women's issues seem to be her top priority."

"I doubt that," Rachel muttered under her breath.

"What?"

"Oh, nothing." Rachel pulled her long hair over one shoulder and began braiding it. "You know, Ned, you should try to talk to Becky—er, Rainbow after the meeting."

Ned nodded. "I'd like to find out what inspires her."

"I bet it will be *very* enlightening," Rachel predicted. "Well, I'm off to the library."

As the gathering broke up Ned crossed the lawn to where Rainbow stood jotting down names and phone numbers of people who wanted to help plan activities. "Put my name in there," he said. "I'm Ned Wakefield."

A radiant smile illuminated Rainbow's face. "I know who you are. You're in Professor Kalben's American government class, right? And Professor Young's Introduction to Legal Process. Those classes are killers, huh? I'm glad you want to get involved with SPAN."

"I think you have some great ideas," Ned told her. "I admire people who don't just sit by when they see that there's something wrong with society."

"We have a duty to take action, don't we?" Rainbow's big brown eyes smoldered with passionate conviction. "A duty to our planet and to every man, woman, and child living on it."

"You're right, but a lot of people don't think that way."

"Maybe it's my Native American ancestry," Rainbow mused. "I feel somehow connected to the earth and its creatures."

"Hey, my great-great-grandmother was half Awaswan Indian."

Rainbow gasped. "I'm a descendant of the Awaswans, too."

Ned shook his head. "Wow! What a coincidence."

"I think it's more than a coincidence." Rainbow stepped closer to him. Ned noticed that she smelled like jasmine—warm, sweet, and sensuous. "Some kind of cosmic force has brought us together, Ned. We were meant to work together in the cause of justice."

Ned was mesmerized. Sometimes he felt shy around girls—girls other than his cousin, that is. But Rainbow wasn't just beautiful, she was committed. He felt incredibly drawn to her. "I hope you'll let me help you get this group off the ground," he said. "In fact, why don't we get together tomorrow night and talk about it?"

Rainbow's lips curved in a pleased smile. "I'd like that."

"The snack bar at nine?"

"I'll be there. And Ned?" She touched his arm as he started to turn away. "Bring your government books, OK? Maybe we could talk about that paper assignment."

"Sure." Ned tossed her a goodbye wave. "Keep the faith."

"Stay cool," she returned.

Shouldering his ragged canvas backpack, Ned headed toward the library. The western sky was streaked with sunset colors. *The colors of the rainbow.* Ned laughed at himself for having such a corny thought. He wasn't usually the romantic type. Between studying and extracurricular activities, he didn't have much time for romance. But he had a feeling he'd be making time for it in the very near future.

Thirty-two

Dressed in her bathrobe, Rachel walked down the dorm hall carrying a towel and a plastic bucket containing soap, toothpaste, and shampoo. In the bathroom, she took up a position at one of the sinks and turned on the tap. *Man, am I beat!* she thought as she splashed her face with cold water. *Getting up for a nine A.M. class on Friday morning sure is a drag when you've stayed up until all hours partying the night before!*

As she patted her dripping face with the towel, Rachel heard a familiar—and detested—voice greeting her. "Good morning, Rachel," Becky cooed sweetly.

Rachel made a face into her towel. Then she lowered the towel to give Becky a cool stare. "Hi, Becky."

"Rainbow, remember?" Becky said with a smile,

seeming to take pleasure in Rachel's unfriendliness.

"Rainbow. Of course." Rachel squeezed some toothpaste onto her toothbrush. "And how is your prism of personality this morning?"

Rainbow laughed airily as she ran a comb through her black hair. "Oh, I'm just fine. No, make that fantastic," she amended. "I had the best night of my life last night. Want to hear about it?"

Rachel didn't really. She knew that Rainbow had spent the evening with Ned—she'd seen them together at the party. Rachel had hoped that when Ned spoke with Rainbow he'd figure out that she wasn't for real, but apparently it hadn't happened that way. Just the opposite, in fact.

Rainbow didn't wait for Rachel to reply. "I danced for hours barefoot under the stars with your very own cousin, Ned Wakefield," she said. "I've been trying to catch his eye since the first day of school, and it looks like I've finally got him."

"You had one date, and I happen to know my cousin's very independent. I wouldn't say you've *got* him."

"Oh, no?" Rainbow's lips pursed in a smug, self-satisfied smile. "You should have heard the things he was whispering in my ear last night."

Rachel frowned at Rainbow. "Why are you so interested in Ned, anyway? I wouldn't think he's your type. Wouldn't you have more in common with someone like Hank Patman?" Rachel said, naming the most stuck-up boy she could think of.

Rainbow laughed. "Oh, Hank's OK if you're looking for someone to shower you with diamonds and drive you around in a flashy car. But that's not what I'm after."

"What are you after?" Rachel asked.

Rainbow didn't answer the question directly. "I knew Ned was the one for me on the very first day of Intro to Legal Process. We discussed a case, and Ned made some comment that Professor Young said was brilliant. Brilliant," Rainbow repeated. "I'd already seen for myself that he was gorgeous. So he became the obvious choice."

Rachel was still baffled. "The obvious choice for what?"

"A boyfriend," Rainbow said, dabbing face lotion on one smooth cheek.

Rachel gaped at her. Rainbow caught her eye in the mirror. "You have to go after what you want in this world," she continued. "You can't settle for second best if you want to get anywhere. And I have plans. I plan to follow in my father's footsteps. I plan to attend the best law school in the country. It's certainly going to be convenient," she added nonchalantly, "to have a boyfriend who can help make sure I graduate with honors."

Rachel couldn't believe her ears. This was the girl who'd been spouting off about women's liberation at the SPAN meeting! "Is that what this—this

—prism of personality stuff is all about? You just wanted to get to Ned so you can use him?"

"Did I say that? I didn't say that." Rainbow gave Rachel an innocent look. "Don't be so uptight, Rachel." She bent toward the mirror and began applying dark liner to give her eyes a slanted, exotic appearance. "As long as your cousin's happy, what do you care? Live and let live!"

Rachel grabbed her bucket and stomped from the bathroom in disgust. Rainbow was an utter fraud . . . and she had her claws deep in trusting, idealistic Ned. *Somebody has to tell him the truth about her,* Rachel realized, *and it looks like it's going to have to be me.*

Rachel wandered through the crowd at the outdoor concert on the quadrangle, oblivious to the music and the revelry. She couldn't relax until she got a chance to talk to Ned. Judy grabbed her and pulled her into a crowd of people, their arms waving and their long hair tossing, but Rachel escaped. Then she spotted Ned.

"Hey, Ned!" she called.

He turned. "Hi, Rachel. Some party, huh?"

"Some party," she agreed with false enthusiasm, bobbing up and down to the beat as if she were having a good time. "But it's not as wild as the one last night. I saw you hanging out with Rainbow. I suppose you were talking about SPAN."

"We talked about everything under the sun and

moon," Ned said. "You wouldn't believe how much we have in common, Rachel."

Yeah, right, she thought grimly. "Did you talk about your prelaw classes?"

"As a matter of fact, we did. We rapped about the paper topic for Kalben's course. She came up with some great ideas."

Rachel would have bet anything that the great ideas had been all Ned's. Becky had probably just manipulated the conversation to make it look like she was contributing.

"I've never met anyone like her," Ned continued, not picking up on his cousin's doubtful silence. "We share all the same dreams and values. She's like a soul mate."

"Hmm. That's interesting." This was worse than Rachel had expected. "I'm actually a little surprised you two got along so well. I had the impression Becky was a very different kind of person. I mean, at the beginning of the semester she was hanging out with Hank Patman's crowd."

Ned narrowed his eyes. "What are you trying to say?"

"Oh, I don't know. Maybe just that Rainbow isn't exactly what she seems."

He shook his head. "I'm disappointed in you, Rachel. I thought you were more generous than that. It's true Rainbow comes from a privileged family a lot like Hank's, and her father is an ultraconservative judge. But in my opinion that just makes her political commitment even more admirable. She wants to practice a very different kind of law than her father does. She wants to change things. As for being rich, she told me she's decided to renounce all earthly possessions so she can be unburdened in her search for spiritual fulfillment."

"And you believed her?" Rachel burst out.

Ned's eyes flashed. "Yes, I believed her. I believe in taking people at their word, in trusting people." A pained note deepened his voice. "I can't believe you'd be so cynical. I thought you'd be happy for me, Rach."

Rachel bit her lip and remained silent. She was afraid to offend Ned further, and if she said anything more she knew she would. She wanted to be happy for her cousin, she really did. And if Ned had met the right girl, she would have been. But Becky Foster wasn't the girl for Ned—Rachel was sure of it.

Ned and Rainbow lay on the grass under a tree on the quadrangle. A feeling of deep peace filled Ned's heart. "I'm so happy with you," he told her.

"I'm happy with you, too." Rainbow kissed the tip of his nose. "This has been a wonderful two weeks."

The two had been together constantly since their first date. They met for meals, studied at adjacent carrels in the library, held hands at rallies and concerts, and just plain hung out. With every day, Ned grew more attached to Rainbow, more absorbed in his feelings for her. "Are you sure going steady isn't too old-fashioned for you?" he asked. "It's not the hip way to handle relationships these days. Seems like nobody sticks with an 'old man' or 'old lady' for more than a couple of days."

"I'm not into the love-the-one-you're-with stuff." Rainbow smiled. "Unless, of course, I happen to be with you."

Ned kissed her. Rainbow kissed him back for a few seconds, then pushed him away gently. "Come on, you promised you'd help me rough out my paper for Intro to Legal Process."

"Your paper?" Ned sat up and ran a hand through his rumpled hair. He looked at the clock on the student union. "We can do it tonight. Right now I think we should gather all the members of SPAN and go to the rally. Our presence and solidarity could really have an impact."

Rainbow sighed. "I'd love to go the rally with you . . . what rally?"

"The rally to persuade the school administration to officially denounce the U.S. role in Southeast Asia! Everybody's talking about it."

"Of course," Rainbow said. "*That* rally."

Ned jumped to his feet, extending his hand to Rainbow. "You round up the girls in your dorm, and I'll get the guys from mine. The rally starts at four. I'll meet you there."

An hour later, Ned and a bunch of his

dormmates crossed the quadrangle on their way to the administration building. As they walked they were joined by dozens and dozens of others also heading to the rally. Arriving at the administration building, Ned caught his breath. It was an amazing sight. Hundreds of students and members of the faculty were gathered on the broad steps of the building. Some carried protest signs, and others were giving inspirational speeches through bull-horns. "Power to the people!" Ned shouted, thrusting his fist in the air.

He scanned the crowd for Rainbow and spotted her lingering at the fringes. "We're going to block the entrance to the building so no one can come or go without hearing us out," he told her, seizing her hand. "C'mon!"

She hung back. "It's kind of crowded up there. . . ."

"I'll keep you from being crushed," Ned promised.

Reluctantly, Rainbow followed Ned to the door of the administration building. The steps were packed with students holding hands to create an unbreakable human chain. Whenever an administrator appeared at the door, the students pressed forward, stamping their feet and chanting, "U.S. out of Southeast Asia!"

"Look, it's the president of the college," Ned said.

The president had appeared at the door. "Clear

the steps!" he boomed. "Send a committee if you want to address a grievance. I won't negotiate with a mob!"

Rather than abating, the chanting increased in volume. The president retreated. The students pressed forward and some began pounding on the door.

Suddenly, Ned heard the piercing shriek of police whistles behind him. "Clear the steps!" a cop bellowed through a bullhorn. "Bring the protest down to the lawn!"

Ned was willing to heed this suggestion, and so were many of the students around him. But they were so closely packed together, they couldn't move quickly. Confusion developed as many students attempted to retreat while others continued pushing forward. "Cool it," Ned urged his fellow protesters.

"Let's get out of here," Rainbow pleaded, tugging at his hand.

But before they could move more than a few inches, they were assaulted by a smothering cloud. Tear gas! His eyes stinging, Ned wrapped his arms protectively around Rainbow, who was bent over, coughing. There were cries and shouts; through his tears, Ned saw that the police had entered the crowd, wearing gas masks and using their billy clubs as prods to herd students away from the building.

It happened in the wink of an eye. Ned saw a fist

fly. An angry protester had lashed out at a cop! Someone shoved heavily against Ned and he shoved back, trying to preserve his balance. The fight escalated rapidly. Concerned with shielding Rainbow from the fray, Ned didn't have time to react when he was grabbed from behind and his arms were pinned. Before he knew it, his wrists were in handcuffs. "Hey, what's going on?" he demanded.

All around him, students were being handcuffed and shoved down the steps to police vans. "You're under arrest for disturbing the peace and defying police orders," the cop snapped.

"I wasn't doing anything wrong!" Rainbow cried. "Take these things off me!"

Her protest went unheeded; she was herded into the van along with the others. "I can't believe this is happening," she said fearfully as the van sped off. "What are they going to do to us?"

"Just take us to the police station and book us. We won't have to stay long," Ned assured her.

"Take us to the station and book us? You mean we're going to *jail*?"

"I won't let them separate us. They probably won't keep us more than a night, anyway. There are plenty of witnesses to testify that we were trying to move peaceably away when the police gassed us."

"I'm not spending a minute in jail, much less a night," Rainbow declared.

"I'll be with you," Ned reminded her. "I'll make sure you're safe."

"Oh, right. I'm really going to rely on you!" Rainbow snapped. "You're the one who got me into this mess in the first place!"

Ned's eyebrows shot up. "*I* got you into this? How?"

"By dragging me to that stupid rally! I should have known something like this would happen. This is what I get for hanging out with long-haired, hippie fanatics, most of whom haven't taken a bath in a month!"

Ned stared at Rainbow. He felt as if he were looking at a stranger. Was this the girl he'd fallen in love with? "If you feel that way about them, if you feel that way about *me* . . . why did you get involved with SPAN? Don't you believe in Students for Progressive Action Now?"

"You must be kidding," Rainbow said. "That's a bunch of baloney. You're suckers to think you're going to change anything with your little marches and rallies. Look how far you got today! I can't believe I thought you could help me get ahead. All you did was help me see the inside of a jail!"

Ned shook his head, baffled. "I don't get it." He lowered his voice so the other students in the van, who were talking about calling lawyers as soon as they got to the station, couldn't hear. "I thought we shared something, Rainbow. I thought we saw the world in the same way. I thought we cared about the same things." *I thought you cared about me*, he could have added but didn't.

"Well, you thought wrong. And I thought wrong, too. I thought it would be cool to hang out with a guy like you." She laughed harshly. "And let me assure you, you've shown me a good time."

Ned narrowed his eyes, trying to get her in focus. For the first time, he saw beyond the feathers and the beads, the silky hair, the velvet-smooth skin. Rainbow, whoever that was, disappeared, and he found himself looking at Becky Foster, whoever *she* was. But Ned still didn't get it. He recalled his argument with Rachel. His cousin had tried to warn him; she'd suspected that Rainbow—Becky, rather—was putting on an act. But what could have motivated her? "Why did you lead me on, *Becky*? Why did you pretend to be someone you're not, feel something you didn't feel?"

"I thought we could help each other get someplace we both wanted to go," she replied. "And look where we ended up. In jail! But as for leading you on, did I really, Ned?" Her gaze was steady and completely without warmth. "It seems to me I didn't have to try that hard. You saw what you wanted to see in me."

Struck by the unexpected and undeniable truth of her words, Ned fell silent.

When the twenty arrested students climbed out of the van at the police station, Rainbow quickly pushed her way to the front. "I'm Becky Foster," she informed the officer behind the main desk. "My father is Leonard Foster. *Judge* Leonard Foster. I'd like to use the phone immediately."

Ned watched in disbelief as Becky was ushered into a private office. Ten minutes later, her father arrived at the station. Ned heard the chief of police apologize to Judge Foster for the "misunderstanding" and promise him that Becky would be released immediately.

A few minutes later, Becky waltzed from the police station with her father. *She sure didn't hesitate to take advantage of his influence,* Ned thought ironically. *So much for wanting to be a free spirit, a different kind of lawyer than her dad!* She didn't even give a backward glance to Ned, whom she left behind to be charged and booked.

As he waited for a chance to call his parents, Ned's anger grew. But now he wasn't just hurt and angry that Becky had used him to get good grades. He was mad at himself for being duped. Ned gritted his teeth, remembering the papers and assignments he'd helped her with. He'd been so smitten, he'd almost compromised his academic integrity. How could he hope to become a political leader when he'd let the first pretty girl who blinked her eyelashes at him and told him what he wanted to hear make a fool of him?

If I want to be effective in the future, I'll have to stick to business, Ned determined. He wouldn't be fooled again.

Thirty-three

*1960s. Campus of the College
of Southern California.*

"It's great to have you back on campus," Ned told
Rachel as they walked across the quadrangle. "I
missed you last year."

Rachel had spent her junior year in Vienna, doing research on the pre–World War II Austrian
Jewish community of which her father and Aunt
Hannah's relatives had been a part. She was going
to write up her research for a senior honors thesis.
"I sent you more letters than everybody else com-
bined," she said, kicking off her flipflops and dropping her backpack in the shade of a large oak.

"I know. But it wasn't the same as really talking
to you."

Rachel sat down, hugging her knees. "Maybe
you should have gone away junior year, too."

"I thought about it," Ned admitted, lying back

on the grass. "A change of scenery might have been cool. But there's so much work to be done right here. I kept pretty busy. I got to ditch the dorm scene, anyway. Vince, Seth, Danny, and I have a great pad in a house off campus. You have to come by soon."

"Do you still enjoy it as much as you used to? The protests and the rallies and all that?"

"Sure. The movement is more urgent and exciting than ever. But that's not what you really want to know about, is it?" Ned grinned at his cousin. "What you're really wondering is whether I've finally found a girlfriend or whether you should take another shot at fixing me up with one of your roommates."

Rachel laughed. "I've tried that too many times! If you're determined to be a lone wolf, I'm not going to be able to change you."

"I'm not determined to be alone, Rach. It's just happened that way."

Rachel was skeptical. After Rainbow, Ned had continued to attract girls like a magnet, but as far as she knew, he hadn't dated a single one.

"Yeah, well, I guess I just want everybody to be as happy as I am."

While she was in Vienna, she'd fallen in love with another American studying abroad. She and Paul had backpacked all over Europe together. It had been a magical year, and the best part of it was that Paul went to UCLA, so they could see each other every weekend now that they were back in the States.

"Well, the way you found Paul just goes to show that you can't look for love. It just happens, right?"

"I suppose." Rachel took a cheese-and-bean sprout sandwich from her backpack. "But you have to be open to it. You have to *let* it happen."

Ned didn't reply. She handed him half the sandwich. Ned's dedication to the movement and to his prelaw studies was all very well and good. He achieved success at just about everything he put his mind to, and she admired him intensely. But Rachel couldn't help feeling that for all his involvement in cutting-edge politics, Ned was missing out on one of the most important experiences the world had to offer. As she bit into her sandwich Rachel wondered if her cousin would *ever* open himself up to love—the thrill, the risk, the joy, the pain—again.

It had been a long time since Ned had taken time out to go surfing, and this afternoon it had felt good. A few hours of riding the waves had tired out his body and cleansed his mind. He felt completely refreshed.

Now he rested his board against a dune and sat down in the sand, staring pensively out over the blue Pacific. Down the shore he could hear the muted sounds of a beach party: Janis Joplin on a portable radio, shouts and laughter as an energetic volleyball game got under way.

The school year's almost over, Ned thought. It was hard for him to believe that his college years were coming to a close. He'd applied to law schools and had already been admitted to a few programs. But something was holding him back from accepting any of the offers. It was such a big decision. Was he really choosing the right path?

Reflecting, Ned noticed a girl with long sun-streaked blond hair standing at the water's edge. He thought he recognized her as a C.S.C. student —she was probably part of the party down the beach. He watched her curiously, trying to read the language of her slim, tanned body. Bending, she picked up a stone and hurled it at an incoming wave. She threw another stone, then another. *Boy, she's mad at somebody!* Ned thought.

Having vented her anger on the water, the girl waded into it, up to her knees, then her thighs, then her slender waist. She dove under the curl of a wave and began swimming out to sea with strong, graceful strokes. Farther and farther she swam. Ned stood up, shading his eyes against the afternoon sun. "Hey, that's far enough," he heard himself say out loud.

As if she'd received his message, the girl stopped swimming. He could see her floating peacefully on her back, her face to the sky. *She's OK,* he told himself, settling back on the warm sand. But he kept his eye on her; the nearest lifeguard was a hundred yards down the beach.

After a few minutes, the girl began swimming back toward shore. Her strokes were slower, more leisurely. Then suddenly, she began swimming erratically. Ned could see that although she stroked and kicked for all she was worth, she wasn't making any headway. *An undertow!* he realized. Jumping to his feet, he cupped his hands around his mouth, yelling, "Swim parallel to the shore! Don't fight against it!" But she didn't hear him. She continued to struggle futilely against the current.

Ned ran to the water's edge. In the distance, he could see that the girl's efforts to resist the undertow were growing weaker. She was tiring, maybe even cramping up. There wasn't a moment to lose! Plunging into the ocean, he began swimming, pulling with all his might against the cold, resistant water, and kicking powerfully. Each time he took a breath, he checked the girl's position. He had almost reached her when he saw a wave close over her head. She didn't resurface. *No!* Ned thought, swimming faster.

Ned reached the spot where he thought she'd gone under. Treading water, he stared down into the salty depths. Would he be able to find her? He saw a glimmer of blond hair, sinking, sinking. . . . He dove.

His own lungs bursting, Ned fought his way back to the surface with one arm; the other was wrapped tightly around the limp body of the girl. She was alive but unconscious. Floating her on her back, he hooked his elbow under her chin to keep her head above water, then kicked back to the beach.

He carried her out of the water and laid her gently on the sand. He was about to begin mouth-to-mouth resuscitation when her eyelids flickered and opened. She stared up at him, uncomprehending. "Shh. Don't try to move yet," he told her, brushing a tendril of wet hair from her forehead. "You have to rest."

For a moment, they gazed into each other's eyes. Ned had an unaccountable sensation as he studied the delicate lines of her lovely face. He was certain he'd never met her, but nevertheless there was something strangely familiar about her tentative smile, her beautiful blue-green eyes.

Suddenly, they were surrounded by a crowd from the beach party. "Alice! Good heavens!" a male voice called in alarm. "Alice, are you all right?"

Ned turned to see Hank Patman pushing his way to the girl's side. Ned stepped back and watched as Hank fell to his knees beside her. *There's something between them,* Ned guessed, surprised and disappointed.

Alice sat up and put a hand to her forehead. "I almost drowned out there," she told Hank, "but this boy saved me."

For the first time, Hank looked at Ned. It had been a long time since the two boys had stood face to face—not since high school, Ned thought. Ned held out his hand. "Ned Wakefield," he said, not because he didn't think Hank would remember him, but because he wanted Alice to know his name.

Hank gave Ned's hand a brisk shake. "I'm Hank Patman. I owe you my deepest thanks."

Ned narrowed his eyes. Hank's words were gracious, but just like in the old days, Ned felt his motives were less than pure. *He's treating me like a stranger just so he can brush me aside.* "You don't owe me a thing," Ned said, his voice flat.

Then he turned back to Alice. And when he looked again into her wide, gentle eyes, he forgot all about Hank Patman and the other onlookers. He and Alice might as well have been the only two people on the beach—the only two people in the world.

"How are you feeling?" he asked her, surprised by the tenderness he felt, his desire to put his arms around her once more, as he had when he carried her from the sea.

"All right," Alice said, her voice still a little shaky. "By the way, I'm Alice Robertson, and I . . . I've never had anyone save my life before."

Ned laughed. "I've never saved anyone's life before. I'm just incredibly glad that I was coming down the beach at the right time."

Ned could have remained like that forever, bending close to Alice, gazing into her eyes. But the moment, the magic, was soon broken by Hank. Hank put his arm possessively around Alice and helped her to her feet. As the couple exchanged a few words in lowered voices, Ned felt shut out. He got the message Hank was sending him: *It's my turn now. Get lost!*

An arm still firmly around Alice's waist, Hank started to steer her back to the party. But Alice hung back. "Bye," she said softly. "And thank you. Thank you a million times."

"You're welcome a million times," Ned said with a smile. And he meant it. It was crazy, but he almost wished he'd have a million more opportunities to save Alice Robertson's life.

Ned hefted the surfboard onto his shoulder and walked over the dune to the parking lot. What could a girl like Alice see in a guy like Hank? Was it his money? No, Ned felt instinctively that Alice wasn't that type. The most logical explanation was that there wasn't any kind of serious relationship between the two. Ned was happy with this conclusion. He couldn't help hoping that Alice Robertson's heart was free.

Ned spotted the familiar sun-gold head bending over a book on the other side of the library reading room. And there was an empty chair right next to her. Ned hurried across the room. "Alice, hi."

"Oh, hi, Ned." She closed her book and looked up at him with a smile. "Sorry I couldn't talk at lunch today. But I was on my way to the art studio."

"You're an art major, eh?"

"Yep." She tapped the cover of the book. "And I have an art history exam tomorrow."

"You probably have a lot of studying to do." Ned knew he should leave her alone. But he couldn't tear himself away. He looked for her wherever he went, and it always seemed that just as he found her she was gathering up her books to go someplace else.

"It shouldn't be too bad," she said. "It's my music appreciation test in a couple of days that I'm really worried about. No matter how many hours I spend in the music lab listening to operas and symphonies, I always have 'Blowin' in the Wind' on my mind."

"I love Dylan," Ned said.

"He's my favorite." For a long moment, they just looked into each other's eyes. Then Alice laughed awkwardly. "Well, I'd better go. There's a SPAN meeting . . . I said I'd meet Hank."

Ned nodded. He'd spotted Alice at a number of political meetings and rallies recently, and Hank was almost always with her. Apparently Hank was quite the liberal activist these days. Everyone on campus knew about his having hired a helicopter to drop food to students at the recent campus sit-in,

322

which had gotten Professor Yarovitch, a civil rights activist, reinstated on the faculty. Maybe Hank wasn't as shallow and self-centered as he used to be —Ned figured he owed it to Hank, or rather Alice, at least to consider that possibility. But it seemed much more likely that Hank was just dabbling in politics, having some college fun.

"Hey, I'm going to the meeting, too," Ned said. "I'll walk you over there."

"Thanks, but actually I'm stopping at Hank's dorm first. I'll see you later, OK?"

"OK."

Alice gathered up her books and stood up. Again, she and Ned just looked at each other for a moment. *Now's the time,* Ned urged himself. *Ask her out.* But he didn't—he couldn't. Hank's name seemed to come up just a little too often.

Alice was blushing. "Bye, Ned," she said quickly. Then she hurried from the reading room.

Ned watched her go. It took a while for his heartbeat to return to its normal rhythm. He hadn't planned to go to the SPAN meeting, but now he wouldn't miss it for the world. As brief as his encounters with Alice Robertson usually were, they had become the center of his existence.

"Alice Robertson. Doesn't she date Hank Patman?" Rachel asked.

It was a school night, and the cousins had met at the coffeehouse for a study break. They'd nabbed a small table at the front of the smoky, crowded room, near the stage where a girl was playing the guitar and singing. "They hang out a lot," Ned had to acknowledge. "But it doesn't matter. I can't get her off my mind."

Rachel's eyes widened. "Ned, I can't believe I'm hearing this from you."

He grinned sheepishly. "She's all I think about. I talk to her every chance I get—I know where she studies in the library, which table she sits at in South Hall for lunch. I know it sounds crazy, Rachel. I hardly know her. But there's something about her. That day at the beach, when I saved her life . . ." Ned's eyes grew hazy, remembering. "It was like we looked right into each other's soul. I saw right then and there what kind of person she was. She's not a fake, like Rainbow. She's for real."

Rachel bit into one of the giant homemade cookies for which the coffeehouse was famous. "This is far out. Is she giving you *any* encouragement?"

Ned shrugged. "She's always friendly, always sweet. But she's also always in a hurry. We usually talk for about two minutes and then she has to rush off somewhere. Usually to meet Hank," he added glumly.

"Hmm. Well, I've only spoken to Alice once, at a Women for Peace meeting. But she seemed very nice. Too nice for Hank!"

"So you don't think I should give up?"

"Definitely not." In Rachel's opinion, it was high

time that her wonderful cousin had some luck in the love department. And what rational woman would prefer Hank Patman over Ned Wakefield? "I'm sure if Alice knew you were interested—look, Ned!"

Ned followed his cousin's gaze toward the back of the coffeehouse. Alice had just sat down at a table with her friend, Jenny Jenkins. "It's her," he said eagerly.

Alice had spotted him as well. Ned lifted his hand in a wave; Alice waved back. "She's going to the counter for some coffee," observed Rachel. "Here's your chance to tell her how you feel. Ask her out! What have you got to lose?"

Ned took a deep breath and pushed back his chair. "You're right!"

He stood up and made his way to the back of the coffeehouse. Rachel sipped her coffee. As she hummed along to the music, she resisted the urge to turn around and see how the conversation was going between Ned and Alice. She took another bite of her cookie. He'd been gone for a few minutes. That was a good sign.

But when Ned returned to the table, it took only one glance for Rachel to see that things had not gone as he'd hoped. "Did you ask her for a date?" Rachel asked.

"In a roundabout way," Ned said, slumping in his chair.

"And she said no," Rachel surmised, disappointed on her cousin's behalf. "I guess she really *is* going steady with Hank. There's no other reason she'd turn down a guy like you! But hey." She made an effort to cheer Ned up. "Maybe things won't last between those two. One of these days, she's sure to figure out that he's a complete jerk, just playing the activist hero for a while, and that all the money in the world can't make up for the fact that he's—"

"They're not going to break up," Ned interrupted her. "They're engaged, Rachel. They're getting married."

"Getting married?" Rachel was so shocked she dropped her cookie into her coffee.

"She's wearing a diamond as big as a golf ball," Ned said bitterly. "I guess there's nothing Patman money can't buy."

"No. It can't be like that between them," said Rachel. "She must really love him." But that didn't make sense to Rachel, either. "Maybe he's not as bad as he was back in high school," she went on, without much conviction. "Maybe he's really changed. Or maybe . . ."

Ned pressed her. "Maybe what?"

"Maybe . . . nothing." Ned was hurting enough. Rachel didn't want to make him feel worse by revealing her doubts about Hank. *Maybe Hank is manipulating Alice the way Becky Foster tried to manipulate Ned freshman year.*

But Rachel could see by Ned's morose

326

expression that a similar idea had occurred to him. The two sat in silence. There was really nothing else to say, Rachel realized sadly. Ned had to face the facts. Not only was the girl of his dreams out of his reach, but she was throwing herself away on a man who might someday make her miserable.

Thirty-four

"I remember when I was young I used to play tennis with my father," Robert Wakefield recalled. "Sometimes for a change of pace we'd go for a run in Central Park, or shoot a few baskets. I guess after a day of bending his brain as a journalist and scholar, Dad needed to let off some steam. We had some of our best talks when we were both pretty sweaty and out of breath."

Ned had driven from C.S.C. to his parents' house for dinner. After washing the dishes, he and his father had headed outside to play one-on-one in the driveway.

Ned tossed the basketball to his father, laughing. "I guess it shows that I have something on my mind."

"It shows," Robert confirmed with a grin. He

pushed the graying hair back from his forehead, then took a shot.

Ned caught the rebound. Dribbling the ball, he considered how best to express his thoughts. It was hard because they were fuzzy. "It's not any one thing that's bugging me," he began. "I just don't feel the way I expected to feel a week before I graduate from college."

"How did you expect to feel?"

"On top of the world." Ned went in for a lay-up. "I was always so excited about the future, you know? So certain that the world couldn't wait for me to get out there and solve all its problems."

"The idealism of youth. It's a wonderful thing," his father said, laughing.

"Well, I don't feel it anymore. I used to think I knew what I wanted to do with my life. I believed in my goals. But now . . ."

Robert mopped his forehead with a towel. Then he waved the towel at the redwood picnic table in the side yard. "Let's sit down."

They took seats facing each other. "Ned, you know your mom and I have always been supportive of your ambition to be a lawyer. We've put money aside for you so that nothing should stand in your way. But if you don't want to go to law school next fall, or ever, that's OK with us, too. We're behind you, whatever you decide."

"I knew you would be, Dad. Thanks. I'm not ruling law school out altogether yet. I guess I just need to figure some things out first." Ned raked his fingers through his shaggy brown hair. "I need to find a way to get rid of this . . . lost feeling. I don't know when it started. Maybe it has something to do with how shaken up our country's been lately. I know a lot of kids feel like they don't know where to go next."

"This crazy decade has unsettled everybody, even old folks like your mom and me," Robert assured his son. "But I get the impression there's more to it for you than just that."

Ned nodded. "There is. There was a girl. . . ." He gave his father a brief account of his friendship with Alice Robertson. "When I saw her and talked to her, everything made sense somehow. Just looking at her, I felt like the ground was a little more solid under my feet. I could see a little more clearly." He laughed. "I bet you think I'm a nut, huh? Falling like that for a girl I hardly know."

"I was as much of a nut about your mother," his father confessed. "I decided I wanted to marry her before I even laid eyes on her!"

"That's because you and Mom were made for each other. But Alice and Patman . . ." Ned frowned. "When I heard she was going to marry him, everything stopped making sense. It was like all the pieces of the puzzle I'd started putting together were scattered all over the floor again. I don't know, Dad. I don't know what to do next," he exclaimed in frustration.

"No one ever said growing up was easy, son. And it certainly hasn't been easy for us Wakefields. There have been plenty of broken hearts in this family."

"Really?" Ned was curious.

"Take my father," Robert said. "He was devoted to my mother while she was alive, and since her death he's remained faithful to her memory. He never remarried. But there was another girl before he met her—the sister of a college roommate, I believe. I don't know all the details, but I do know that she disappointed him so deeply that he dropped out of school and took off for the West Coast on some kind of crazy journey of self-discovery."

"Wow." Ned couldn't imagine his grandfather, a tweedy college-professor type, doing anything so cool.

"Now that I think of it, there's sort of a pattern," his father continued. "Wakefields have always done a lot of journeying—we've really zigzagged across this country. Of course, it all started with Theodore Wakefield, my great-grandfather."

"Wasn't he the one who came over from England?"

"That's right. He gave up a family fortune and title in order to gain his independence. The legend is that he met a girl on the ship over, but lost her when they reached the shores of America. He wandered for years trying to find her before he settled down with Dancing Wind."

"So everybody found something—someone— even if it wasn't what they started out looking for," Ned reflected.

"I think that's the way life works most of the time. It has to do with destiny. Come on inside, Ned. There's something I'd like to give you."

Ned followed his father into the house and down the hall to the study. Robert opened the top drawer of his desk, removing his checkbook and a small black jewelry box. From the box, he took a gold ring. "This belonged to Theodore Wakefield," Robert explained, handing it to Ned. "It's been passed down for generations. I think it's seen Wakefields through a lot of adventures, through good times and bad. I hope it brings you luck."

While Ned examined the family crest engraved on the ring, his father wrote out a check and handed it to Ned. Ned whistled when he saw the amount. "This is a lot of money, Dad. I can't take this from you."

"It's a graduation gift from your mother and me," his father insisted. "You can use it for law school tuition or you can spend it on travel. Whatever you want."

Ned slipped the ring on his finger. "Thanks, Dad," he said. He felt a lot better knowing that he wasn't the only Wakefield to experience doubts and disappointments. His father had also showed him that his uncertainty about the future was really a valuable freedom. He was standing at a crossroads. His life had never held so much possibility, and probably never would again. Like generations of Wakefields before him, he was about to embark on his own personal journey of self-discovery.

Ned crossed his bedroom on the top floor of the rambling white house he'd shared for two years with a few other C.S.C students. Lifting the arm of the record player, he set it back to the beginning of the album. *I'm lucky the other guys aren't around,* Ned thought wryly. It was about the tenth time he'd played "Blowin' in the Wind." Ned, however, couldn't hear the song too many times. It reminded him of Alice—it was one of her favorites, too. Alice, whom he would never see again. Alice, who was marrying another man that very day. In fact, she was probably already married. By this time, Alice Robertson had probably become Mrs. Henry Patman.

Dusk settled over the house, but Ned didn't bother switching on a light. Since he was taking only his backpack on the trip and it was already crammed full, he supposed he was done packing.

He sank down in an ancient armchair that leaked stuffing and looked around the room. His cap, gown, and diploma lay in a heap on his desk, a reminder of the previous day's commencement ceremony. On the bed was a pile of things he still had to stuff in his backpack: plane ticket, passport, traveler's checks, maps. Thinking about the trip he was about to take, Ned felt a flicker of excitement. First he would fly to London, then travel north to Yorkshire to visit the village of Wakefield, the ancestral home of his great-great-grandfather Theodore. From there, he intended to see as much of Europe and Asia as he could before his money ran out. To make the cash last, he'd travel cheap—hitchhiking, taking trains, and staying in youth hostels.

From the front of the house, Ned heard the doorbell ring. *Someone looking for the girls in the front apartment,* he guessed. The sound reminded Ned of the phone call he'd made earlier that day. The phone had rung and rung . . . and finally Alice had picked it up. He was probably the last person she wanted to hear from on her wedding day, but he had had to tell her one last time that he would never forget her, that he would always be there if she needed him. And something in her gentle voice as she said goodbye had told him that she believed his vow, and appreciated it.

His elbows propped on his knees, Ned dropped his head in his hands. *Stop thinking about her!* he commanded himself. *It's not going to get you anywhere. She's Hank's now, forever and ever and ever.* But the fact that Alice loved another man couldn't alter Ned's devotion. Since the day he had saved her life, he'd felt connected to her in a fundamental way. He knew he could travel to the ends of the earth and that wouldn't change. Alice Robertson was a part of his heart.

It took a moment for the voice to penetrate through the music to his consciousness. Someone was calling his name from the yard. He ran to the window. A figure stood on the lawn below—a girl in a long white wedding dress, her feet bare, her loose blond hair shimmering in the moonlight. It was Alice! Alice, dressed as a bride. But she wasn't standing at the altar with Hank. She wasn't dancing in Hank's arms. Instead, she had somehow found her way to his house.

Ned bounded down the stairs and burst through the back door. If there had been any question in his mind about why Alice was there, it disappeared when he saw the love and hope in her angelic blue-green eyes. In three strides, he was at her side, sweeping her up in his arms. Through the thin cotton of his T-shirt, he could feel her heart beating fast against his. And when she lifted a hand to touch his face, he saw that she was no longer wearing Hank's ring.

Ned's joy was too intense for words. With gentle fingers, he traced the curve of her cheek, her forehead, her lips. Then he put his mouth on hers. They kissed, and kissed again. Finally, they fell onto the grass, dizzy and laughing from the intensity of their feelings.

"No shoes," Ned observed, reaching to tickle Alice's foot.

"I left them behind when I left Hank," Alice explained.

"And you came here." The thought of it filled Ned with awe and love and gratitude.

"You said you'd be there if I ever needed you. And I did, and you were."

Ned pulled her close for another kiss. "I want you to need me for the rest of your life, Alice Robertson. I know *I'll* never stop needing you."

Thirty-five

A few years later. Sweet Valley.

Ned stood with his broad shoulders held stiffly and his hands clasped in front of him. He resisted the urge to adjust the knot in his tie or run a hand over his hair. He hadn't been this nervous since the first time he had gotten up the nerve to ask Alice for a date. On that occasion, her answer had been no. But today it would be different.

He looked out at the rows of faces, also eagerly waiting for the bride to appear. All the people he and Alice most loved in the world were seated in the Robertsons' backyard.

The processional began. First came the brides-maids, dressed in cornflower-blue with daisies woven in their hair. Alice's best friend, Jenny Jenkins, walked down the grassy aisle, followed by Rachel. Then came Alice's sisters, Laura and Nancy. The bridesmaids took up their positions opposite the groomsmen, Ned's friends from college and law school. A hush fell over the gathering. Ned's heart pounded as he heard the chords of the wedding march. A moment later, Alice appeared on the arm of her father, Charles.

There was a collective sigh of appreciation at the sight of the bride. Her long white dress was simple. Instead of a veil she wore a wreath of white flowers on her hair, and for a bouquet she carried an armful of lilies of the valley. The simplicity was an ideal foil for her perfect beauty. She had never looked more exquisite.

Ned's eyes misted as Alice walked slowly down the aisle toward him. On her smiling face, he saw his own emotions mirrored. Alice was as profoundly happy as he.

She reached the first row of chairs. She kissed her father on the cheek and then released his arm in order to take the hand Ned extended to her. Side by side, they faced the judge, an old family friend of Alice's father. As the judge spoke, reflecting on the meaning of marriage, Ned and Alice looked at each other out of the corners of their eyes. He squeezed her hand. She returned the pressure.

Finally, the moment came. It was time to exchange vows. For a while, Ned and Alice had considered composing their own wedding vows, but in the end they had decided that no words could be more beautiful and appropriate than those traditionally spoken. "Besides," Alice had said to Ned, "they're the words our parents spoke when they got married, and their parents before them. That makes them especially meaningful."

Alice and Ned turned to face each other. Ned took both her hands in his.

"Do you, Alice Robertson, take Edward Wakefield to be your husband, to love and to cherish till death do you part?" the judge asked.

Alice's blue-green eyes shone with love. "I do," she said softly.

"And Ned, do you take Alice to be your wife, to love and to cherish till death do you part?"

"I do," he said in a firm voice.

"Alice and Ned, I'm happy to pronounce you husband and wife!"

The judge gave Ned an encouraging nod. "Go ahead!"

Everyone waited breathlessly for Ned to kiss his bride. But Ned didn't want to hurry through this moment, because it was the happiest moment of his life. He and Alice were finally married!

He squeezed her hands tightly. She smiled up at him, her eyes damp with tears of joy. "We did it!" she whispered.

Gently, Ned drew her to him. She lifted her face to his. They kissed tenderly.

Ned gripped Alice's arm, holding her close to his side. He could feel her body against his, but as they walked up the aisle together he didn't feel the ground beneath his feet. He could have sworn he was walking on air.

"It was a beautiful wedding, wasn't it?" Alice said dreamily.

After changing from their wedding clothes into more casual travel outfits, she and Ned had met in the upstairs hallway of her parents' house. Downstairs, the guests were waiting to see the bride and groom off on their honeymoon trip.

Putting down his suitcase, Ned wrapped his arms around his new wife. "It was," he agreed. Suddenly, he remembered something. Not too many years before, Alice had nearly gone through with another wedding to another man. "Alice, have you ever regretted . . . ?"

Alice looked up at Ned. "Not for a single minute," she said, her voice soft but sure. "I started on a brand-new path when I turned my back on Hank Patman. And it led me straight to you." She stood on tiptoe so their lips could meet in a light kiss. "Come on, let's head down. They're not going to leave, no matter how long we hide out up here. We're still going to get nailed with rice!"

Alice took Ned's hand. She rubbed her thumb across the backs of his fingers, then lifted up the hand to inspect it. "What's this ring?" she asked curiously.

On Ned's left hand was his new gold wedding band. But on his right, the one Alice was examining, he wore an old family ring. "My father gave it to me a few years ago. It's been passed down since the days of Theodore Wakefield, my great-great-grandfather from England. That's the Wakefield family crest. Today seemed like an appropriate day to wear it."

"It's beautiful, and unusual." Alice peered at the intricate design. "Actually, now that I think about it, it looks a lot like . . ." She bent to unzip the smaller of her two travel cases.

"Like what?"

"This." Alice handed something to Ned.

It was a delicate life-sized rose, carved from some kind of smooth, white wood. Ned had to admit that, with its tight cluster of petals, it did resemble a larger version of the rose on his ring. "This wooden rose has been handed down from generation to generation in *my* family," Alice told Ned. "According to my mom, it belonged first to my great-great-grandmother, Alice Larson. A man she met on the boat from Europe gave it to her as a token of his love."

Ned shook his head. "This rose is almost an exact copy of the one on my ring. What a coincidence!"

"Maybe it's not a coincidence," Alice speculated. "Maybe—"

At that moment, Alice's younger sister, Laura, appeared at the top of the stairs. "You guys had better hurry up. You're going to miss your flight!"

Ned put an arm around Alice's slim waist. Together, they walked down the stairs and outside to the waiting car decorated with streamers and Just Married banners. As they were showered with handfuls of rice and good-luck wishes, Ned turned to Alice. "Are you ready?"

She smiled up at him and nodded. She was ready. They were both ready to start the greatest adventure of their lives.

Epilogue

"Guess what?" Ned asked Alice as he dropped his briefcase on the living room floor in their Sweet Valley home. He lifted his toddler son high into the air.

Alice smiled at little Steven's giggles. "What?"

"I've been named a partner at the firm!"

"Oh, Ned!" Ned set Steven back on his feet. Alice gave her husband a big hug. "I'm so proud of you. That must make you the youngest partner."

He nodded. "It's a big honor. I never expected it to happen this soon."

"Well, you deserve it." She stood on tiptoe to kiss him. "No one works harder than you do."

"How about you? How was your day?"

Alice worked part-time as a graphic designer for a company in Sweet Valley. "Actually, I didn't go

343

into the office today," she told her husband. "I had a doctor's appointment."

"A doctor's appointment?" Ned's brow furrowed. "Honey, is anything wrong?"

Alice attempted to keep a straight face. She had thought she'd try to drag out the suspense. But she couldn't help it. Her lips curved in a smile as bright as the sun. "Nothing's wrong. I think it's absolutely *right* that Steven should have a little brother or sister."

"A little . . . ?" The meaning of Alice's words registered on Ned. Now it was his turn to grab her and hug her tightly. "Oh, Alice. Another baby! Nothing in the world could make me happier. Nothing."

He sat down on the couch and pulled her onto his lap. Bending, Alice picked up Steven and settled him on *her* lap. "What a family!" Ned groaned, pretending to be crushed.

Alice laughed. "Are you really sure you can handle another child?"

"Sure. I could handle two!"

"I suppose you'd like another son," Alice speculated.

Ned smoothed a hand over Steven's dark, baby-fine hair. "I have one perfectly wonderful son. I wouldn't mind a little girl this time around."

"Imagine a baby girl." Alice's eyes grew dreamy. "I wonder what she'd be like."

"She'd have blond hair and blue-green eyes," Ned predicted. "Just like you."

"That's right. The blond hair and blue eyes go all the way back to my Swedish great-great-grandmother. I wonder if she'll be a brave pioneer, like Alice Larson. Or a spunky tomboy, like my great-grandmother Jessamyn, who was a bareback rider in a circus and then ran a hotel in turn-of-the-century San Francisco. Maybe she'll love poetry, like Great-Aunt Amanda. Or maybe—"

"Wait a minute!" Ned exclaimed. "We've had some pretty great women in my family, too. Starting with my mother, Hannah, and going all the way back to my great-great-grandmother, Dancing Wind."

"I suppose it's OK if our daughter takes after them," Alice teased. "Or looks like them."

Ned wrapped his arms around his wife and son. "Actually," he said to Alice, "I'd be happiest of all if she—or he—takes after you."

Alice nuzzled her husband's nose with her own. "I guess we'll just have to wait and see." She knew that, boy or girl, this new baby would make their little family complete. The future looked golden for the Wakefields of Sweet Valley.

The most exciting stories ever in Sweet Valley history...

FRANCINE PASCAL'S

SWEET VALLEY Saga

☐ **THE WAKEFIELDS OF SWEET VALLEY**
Sweet Valley Saga #1
$3.99/$4.99 in Canada   29278-1
Following the lives, loves and adventures of five generations of young women who were Elizabeth and Jessica's ancestors, The Wakefields of Sweet Valley begins in 1860 when Alice Larson, a 16-year-old Swedish girl, sails to America.

☐ **THE WAKEFIELD LEGACY: The Untold Story**
Sweet Valley Saga #2
$3.99/$4.99 In Canada   29794-5
Chronicling the lives of Jessica and Elizabeth's father's ancestors, The Wakefield Legacy begins with Lord Theodore who crosses the Atlantic and falls in love with Alice Larson.